The Image, the Icon, and the Covenant

I^{The}mage, the Icon, and the Covenant

Sahar Khalifeh

Translated by
Aida Bamia

INTERLINK BOOKS
An imprint of Interlink Publishing Group, Inc.
www.interlinkbooks.com

First American edition published in 2008 by

INTERLINK BOOKS
An imprint of Interlink Publishing Group, Inc.
46 Crosby Street, Northampton, MA 01060
www.interlinkbooks.com

Copyright © Sahar Khalifeh, 2002, 2008
Translation copyright © 2008 by Aida Bamia
Published by arrangement with The American University in Cairo Press
First published in Arabic in 2002 as *Sura wa ayquna wa 'ahdun qadim*

Library of Congress Cataloging-in-Publication Data
Khalifah, Sahar.
[Surah wa-ayqunah wa-'ahd qadim. English]
The image, the icon, and the covenant / by Sahar Khalifeh ; translated
by Aida Bamia.
    p. cm.
Novel.
ISBN 978-1-56656-699-5 (pbk.)
I. Bamia, Aida A. (Aida Adib) II. Title.
PJ7842.H2938S9413 2007
892'.736--dc22
                                        2007025641

Printed and bound in the United States of America

To request our complete 40-page full-color catalog, please call us toll
free at 1-800-238-LINK, visit our website at www.interlinkbooks.com,
or write to Interlink Publishing
46 Crosby Street, Northampton, MA 01060
e-mail: info@interlinkbooks.com

The Image

Mariam was a wonderful memory, the most treasured time, and the most beautiful image. Every time I remembered her during the years I spent away from the homeland, I felt my soul pull me toward Jerusalem and its environs; it was as if necklaces of carnations surrounded my neck, changing me into a twenty-year-old lover. Time was then my friend; I was in love. I was like a sparrow with golden eyes and wings, and a magical mirror that could probe the world around me and see Jerusalem's domes.

Jerusalem is a different city now, a city that belongs to history. But Jerusalem to me was Mariam. It was my memory, my first love, and a part of history. Today I am a man without a present, without Mariam, and without history. I surrendered my existence, scattered my first love, and splintered my soul. I searched long for love, for memories, and for a future, but I only stumbled upon the past, an old photo, and the echo of muffled bells in the courtyard of a convent. Was Jerusalem there? Were my love, my memories, and my nostalgic soul there? The soul hangs by a thread, like a kite floating on the horizon, neither reaching high nor falling to the ground. The story of my love is like a paper kite, and my soul and my memory hang at the tip of the thread.

The story began when I ran away from an arranged marriage. I took a job in a forgotten village on the outskirts of Jerusalem. My conscience and my yearning for my uncle, the artist, filled me with a feeling of guilt, and I blamed myself for his sorrow and disappointment. He used to tell me, sadly, "You should have been my son; you're an artist," whenever I eagerly watched him paint or play the 'oud.

My uncle, whose children were not very bright, wanted me to marry his blue-eyed daughter. She was beautiful like a doll, with eyes like pieces of glass in a plate of milk. I ran away from my uncle and his daughter and all the dolls, leaving my mother and my sister, Sarah, alone in Jerusalem. I rented a miserly room in the village, and visited my family only during school vacations and holidays.

It was a very large room of the sort they used to build in the old days, with large stones mortared with natural products, mainly animal dung, long before cement was discovered. The ceiling was shaped like a dome, resembling that of a mosque. It had small windows that barely allowed light through, forcing me to keep the lights on to find my way around. I covered the platforms and basins with wooden boards and cushions; in the past they had contained the animals' water and feed. I used them as seats, shelves, and cupboards.

I lived a spare life in this chicken coop, hardly going out, and paying little attention to my surroundings until spring. The weather warmed up and the world around me became green with an explosion of flower buds, inducing me to roam the village to discover its hills and valleys. I went up to the top of its mountain and scrutinized the horizon, which stretched over the beaches of Natanya, Jaffa, and Tel Aviv. I dreamed of writing a long novel telling the story of the land and its long history. I would think of my uncle's joy to see me involved in a literary activity to which he had been the first to introduce me, but as I recalled his gloomy face when I refused to marry his stupid daughter, I would return to my room and hide for days until I got over my depression. Spring and the scent of the blooming gardens persuaded me to go out and roam the village roads in the company of my dreams and the singing of birds.

One day I ventured all the way to the southern corner of the village. I discovered a cemetery I hadn't noticed before. Its tombs were low and flat, covered with crosses and unusual names such as Michael, Anthony, Antoinette, and Simone. I noticed that the ringing of the church bells was followed by the disappearance of half the village inhabitants. The shops were closed on Sunday as well. I even found out that there was another school that belonged neither to the government nor to UNRWA, but was the property of the church. A priest who had a long, thick beard like that of an artist ran it. He spoke Arabic without an accent, and even preached in it, using a language that almost surpassed mine in purity. He expressed pride in the history of the Arabs and Jahili poetry, and taught his students patriotic songs that I later taught to my own students. I gradually became acquainted with a community within my society that had its particular characteristics and traditions. They were refined and affable, and I wished I could plant my roots in this community.

I got into the habit of sitting every Sunday on the hill that overlooked the courtyard of the church and the cemetery. I spent my time watching young men and women going to pray in beautiful new clothes, laughing joyfully, followed at a distance by older people in black attire and lace veils, swinging left and right like a band of ducks with full craws. I would then hear the collective chanting of male and female voices, creating a melody that could be heard beyond the church, floating over the olive and pine trees, and all the way to the horizon. It lifted up my soul and carried me like a bird above the clouds.

I can't recall how and when I fell in love with Mariam. The church atmosphere, its mystery and its charm, might have attracted me. Mariam might have fired my imagination herself by the strange stories surrounding her life. I fell in love suddenly; I woke up one day and found myself enamored and unable to think of anything else. My thinking was scattered and troubled; I was overcome with nostalgia and sadness for no obvious reason. For many months I never saw her up close; nor did I talk to her or hear her speak. She wasn't even aware of my presence. I hold the spring months, the flowers, the songs, the church chanting, and the organ responsible for my condition. I might have been affected as well by the charm of the sunset I saw from the top of the hill, the color of the sky, and the redness at the horizon.

Mariam was always dressed in black and appeared like a vision in the shadow of the dying twilight that covers the world and the tombs of bygone years. The cemetery was like a dot in history, difficult to date; it was full of crosses, the remains of Roman columns, and an old olive tree that dated to the time of Christ. It was even said that Nur al-Din al-Zanki sat in its shade while fighting to liberate Jerusalem. I wonder how all those things got mixed up, making the place seem like a paradise, a temple of secrets, and she a dream in the midst of my poetry, my tales, and the fictional stories of the fifties.

The story began on a Sunday. I sat, as usual on the hill, watching the rituals of the worshipers on their way to church. They walked through the village roads and met in the churchyard, then entered the church to pray, listening to the organ, to the priest's sermon, and to the chanting, surrounded by the scents of spring and the pine trees. As they left at sunset, I noticed a form leave the group and walk alone in the direction of the cemetery, then stand in front of one of the tombs. It looked like a black dot to me, moving in total silence. All the other worshipers had disappeared; the voices had stopped while the form stayed behind, a black spot moving against the red horizon.

I immediately felt a strange confusion, as if I were on the edge of a precipice. Was it the mystery, the charm of the surroundings, the melancholy of the isolation, and the passions of youth, or was it my imagination? She was not crying; she was reading from a small book, and a rosary was dangling from her wrist. Then I saw the cross, a small cross the size of a butterfly; her head was covered with a black lace veil. She must have gone to a nuns' school, or perhaps she was a novice nun. I felt like crossing her path, jumping from the hill to console her and tell her that she was an icon, a poem, an angel, and a love story worth living for. I wanted to say, "Let's elope," but I didn't know where to. I wondered who she was and what her story was, what she was doing in life and who she was mourning? Was her name Salma, Fadwa, Najwa?

I later found out that she was called Mariam; she had lost her younger brother and lived practically alone. Her brothers were all in Brazil, while she lived in the village with her blind mother. She was watched closely by her brothers and was surrounded by relatives and a large tribe. The family owned property that spread all the way to the mountain vineyards, and included groves of olive, fig, pomegranate, and quince. She lived in a new house at the edge of the mountain, built with emigration money. It had the traditional village décor, a thick trellis, a thicket of pomegranates and pine trees. There were also a cow, chickens, a granary, and an idle oil press. Her father had emigrated long ago, after he was married to his maternal cousin. They had many sons and only one daughter. When the father died, the boys took over the business, and when the girl reached puberty they decided to send her back home with her mother and her younger brother, while they stayed in Sao Paolo.

I got all this information from the grocer and a long list of volunteers from all over the village. All I had to do was sit in front of the grocer's shop, sip coffee, smoke a water pipe, chat, and open my ears to people's gossip. They announced deaths and marriages, those who had taken a second wife, and those who had divorced their wives because they had given them nothing but girls! They talked about girls who had strayed and how they would have handled them had they been, God forbid, a daughter or a sister: they would have strangled them with their own bare hands. It was, in their minds, the right thing to do, and the tradition in the village.

Then there was Mariam. Strange stories began to emerge about her. Some said she had returned to marry a relative from the village; others maintained that she had returned to become a nun; and a third group swore that she was sent back home because she was leading a wild life there and needed to be controlled. It was also alleged that she had returned to look after her mother who had lost her sight, and if life in exile was difficult for the seeing, one could only imagine the difficulties encountered by a blind woman.

Mariam's name and image accompanied me everywhere I went. I continued to watch her every move, sitting on the hill and looking at the church and the cemetery. I was in love with her for no reason other than my vivid imagination; it drew a beautiful and grandiose image of a love story that had the potential to become legendary. The more I learned about her, the more I felt I knew her. Little did I know then that other people had imaginations almost as fertile as mine. Each one saw her from a personal angle, and their stories differed from and contradicted each other. But my youthful imagination, my idleness, the limitations of the village, and my way of life convinced me that the contradictions in people's words were a reflection of her rich personality, of its dramatic and complex nature. Her mourning clothes, her black veil, her goat, and the sound of the church organ persuaded me that my love story was meant to be and was planned by a higher power that watched over us and controlled our destiny.

I went back to the novels I had read and delved avidly into their events until I identified with their subject matter and their characters, with what their authors experienced and what they dreamed of experiencing in real life. I was twenty years old then, and I ignored the fact that the novels were fictional. I believed that all the stories were those of their own authors or of people they had known. In this environment, with those feelings and dreams, I became even more enamored of Mariam. I had never seen her up close or even heard her voice; to me, she wasn't human—she was a vision, an image.

One day I met her, heard her voice, and saw her up close. I was a few yards away from her during a dinner party organized by the priest for a saint's feast. There were three or four guests, and she was there. The priest sat at the head of the table and his wife, Yvonne, sat at the other end. She invited us to begin when it was obvious that the other guests would not come; her husband, obviously a patient man, asked her to wait a few more minutes, but she didn't give in, and we began to eat. The priest served wine but was hesitant to offer me any; I encouraged him, saying, "Why not?" He replied, apologetically, "A little wine cheers one up."

I nodded in agreement and proceeded to drink a large amount of alcohol.

One of the guests said, "In the past, in the desert, people used to drink palm wine. It was very strong; it knocked people down from the first glass, especially with the heat . . . oh, man!"

Everyone laughed. I did too, and drank some more. I was feeling dizzy, though the wine was not made of date palm and the weather wasn't hot like in the desert. Everything around me was spinning; I had never even tasted wine before. I had seen wine only in movies where Farid Shawqi would drink with another loafer as a belly dancer danced close by. Those were the films of the fifties, and I was the child of my time. My parents were conservative, and our family was bound by the traditions of the neighborhoods surrounding the Aqsa Mosque. Alcohol never entered our house, and we never learned how to respect it. We feared it instead, in the way we feared adultery, gambling, and political activities. In other words, our life was "decent." Then came my parent's divorce and my father's remarriage, and we were told that he drank heavily. We heard it but we didn't believe it or, rather, we had doubts. What could we know of his life after his remarriage? A person changes with a new situation. Can we claim to know people forever? Don't they change? Do we know them as a whole or partially? To make a long story short, my father did not drink, and I saw alcohol only in the movies when Stephan Rustom used to say, "Hey Christo, give me more."

The doorbell rang, and someone opened the outside door. The priest said, "It might be her."

Yvonne whispered, "Oh! The knafeh!" We resumed eating. Suddenly Yvonne stood up in front of the door and said, "Welcome, you're late. There's nothing wrong, I hope?"

I turned around and saw her standing only a few feet away from me. The blood rushed to my head, and I felt I was about to die. It was quite a shock, and I felt that my heart had stopped beating for a few seconds. My blood rushed back in a strong jolt that made me see everything around me red. I felt that the ground was shaking, and I couldn't see or hear anything for a short moment. When I regained control of my senses, she had already settled in front of me and spread her napkin on her lap. She was sitting before me, very close, only four feet away at most; only the width of the table separated us. Was this possible?

She was my age or slightly younger, with a fair-skinned, milky complexion; she wore a black suit and her long wavy hair reached her shoulders. Her face was oval, and because of its thinness it seemed long. Her bone structure was perfect; her lips were turned a little upward and seemed thick due to some protrusion in the teeth. Her eyes were amazing; thick, long lashes revealed profound whiteness and mysterious blackness. When she looked up I felt my heart jump and I almost fainted. It might have been the effect of the wine as well as the shock of the first encounter.

The priest said, jokingly, "Mariam wants to enter the convent. Who could believe it?"

His wife reprimanded him, "Didn't we agree not to bring up this subject?"

He apologized, then turned to me and asked, "What about you, Ibrahim, what do you want to do?"

The question surprised me, and I didn't understand its meaning. I replied, stupidly, "To do what?"

He repeated the question, clarifying, "I mean with your life. What do you want to do with it? What are your future plans in life?"

I replied, looking around me and specifically at her, "Nothing much. I'll continue to teach."

I looked at the priest and saw him smiling encouragingly, waiting for details, something more than what I had just said. I explained, timidly, "I correspond with a university in London."

"And you write poetry as well," the priest added.

Embarrassed, I explained, "It's not poetry, but stories and people's secrets."

Yvonne said, "You hunt people's news to write about them?"

I felt my ears turn red, and said, confused, "No, of course not. I write about the secrets of the soul in order to better understand it. I only want to understand, that's all."

Someone said teasingly, "No one but God knows the secrets of the soul. Isn't that so, Father?"

The priest marked a moment of reflection and then acquiesced. He was silent for a moment, then said, whispering, as if talking to himself rather than his guests, "There are also writers who understand, some writers only."

I was a little drunk and in a contentious mood. I yelled as if to attract the attention of the beautiful girl, "Writers? Which writers? What about astrologists, astronomers, Sheikha Fatmeh, and the priest of Ram? It's all false, it's all charlatanry. No one knows the soul but the Creator."

The priest smiled. He was a great admirer of Russian literature and an avid reader. He asked gently, "Have you read Dostoevsky and Chekhov? Have you read *War and Peace* and *The Brothers Karamazov?*"

He went on talking about Dostoevsky's greatness and his excellent analysis of the soul and its secrets. I was transported to this world, a world of darkness and sadness, a charged environment, full of life, characters, and action. I moved in the world of Ivan, Demetrius, and Eloisa. I was with Mariam in that environment. I wasn't at the dinner anymore; I was there, one of them.

I looked at her inquisitively, and my soul whispered, "You are the heroine, you are the story, and you are the personification of my dreams." Then I emptied my glass.

Here was Mariam a few inches away from me, listening quietly, not uttering a word, just listening. Her eyes wandered far, then returned to grasp the words with a smile. Her smile and the shake of her head did not resemble everybody else's. She observed the speaker, then lowered her gaze, before drifting as if in a state of unconsciousness. I only heard her whisper. Her silence added a new dimension to her mysterious nature and the halo that I had drawn around her, on top of the atmosphere of the cemetery, the mourning clothes, and the redness of the sunset. I went back to my role of observer and spy. I marked every movement, every smile, and every blinking of her eyelashes, interpreting each in a different way. I became even more deeply involved with her emotionally. I was a prisoner of my imagination and my dreams, of their interpretations. The priest asked, "Have you read that book?"

The question pulled me out of my stupor. I asked, "Which book?"

They all laughed, and I did too. She only smiled, revealing shining teeth and causing my world to shake. Yvonne invited me to visit her in the library the following day to get the book.

Their school had a library situated behind the church, in a hut with a tiled roof surrounded by pine and cypress trees. Yvonne was in charge of the library and the organization of the books. Whenever the priest recommended a book for me to read, he would turn to his wife and ask her to have it ready for me. She would usually reply enthusiastically, "Tomorrow morning." I used to sneak out of my school in the morning to fetch the book that would be waiting for me on the counter. It became a habit for him to recommend a book and for me to go to the library between classes and return before the bell rang.

One day, much as I had imagined or planned, I saw her in front of me, returning a book she had finished reading. As she moved to the stalls, I rushed to borrow the book and returned hurriedly to my school, then to my house. I immediately plunged into it and its world, imagining it to be her own world, Mariam's world.

It was a book by Françoise Sagan, the writer who had exploded onto the literary scene when she was barely twenty. The book offered a jumble of ideas, emotions, and desires. It was torn—clearly many readers had borrowed it. Some comments had been written in and erased; others, more difficult to erase, were still legible. I knew that the priest had brought those books from the American University of Beirut, and in all probability the comments were those of the students. But my enamored heart and investigative mind made me interpret every comment as I wished, considering them an aspect of her complex personality. A highlighted paragraph describing emotions was certainly hers, as I believed that those dreamy eyes and wandering looks could only be those of a girl with an extra-sensitive nature. If I happened to fall on a paragraph discussing the freedom of the individual soul, I concluded that it was hers, since she shunned society, spent time in the cemetery, and wanted to join the convent. To me, Mariam became the protagonist of the story. I no longer knew who I was in love with. I had become so entangled with her image through the books I read that it didn't occur to me at all that the problem was me and not Mariam. It took me years, twenty, thirty years, to understand this aspect of my personality. This tendency colored my relationship with people in general because I interacted with characters I made up and from my readings. I interpreted their personalities according to my taste, explaining their behavior and attitudes as I pleased or according to the ideas and dreams that filled my mind. I experienced ups and downs as a result of aspects of their personalities and unfounded expectations. I usually suffered dis-appointments, and I was shocked by people's attitudes. I spent days and even weeks, especially in the case of women, suffering and heartbroken because my dreams had dissolved like salt. I went back to my condition before the story, or the encounter, feeling lonely and dejected, immersing myself in books and patching my broken dreams.

One day, Yvonne, as she saw me watching Mariam from behind the bookshelf, asked, "Are you an admirer?"

"What?" I said, and looked out the window to escape her gaze.

She whispered, "Be careful, and stay away."

I looked back at her and saw her busy cataloging a book, but she was smiling kindly. She had noticed my pursuits, my intentional arrival at the library when the young woman happened to be there. First the matter had seemed a coincidence, but when it was repeated, she had become suspicious. She was now alluding to it, rather critically, and warning me gently, "Be careful and stay away." She added, "Mariam has enough troubles with her seven brothers watching over her like guards. She is all alone, and if it weren't for the priest, she would be in a convent by now."

I said, totally surprised, "The convent and the priest, I don't understand."

She smiled gently, adding, "Of course not, but Mariam and I mean the Catholic convent. . . . Anyway, here is your book."

I took the book and rushed out in a state of total shock because the forbidden had become more attractive; it had now become madness. I considered myself the victim, and her, the victimizer.

Save your skin. You're but a dreamer.

Who is Mariam to you? No one. Mariam is a dream you created. What do you know about her, about her character? Are you even sure that she wants to be with you or any other man, for that matter? She wants to join a convent—what does that mean? Even if she chooses you, there is still the issue of religion and your financial situation—you are poor, you have nothing, not one red cent to your name. Then, there are your mother and your sister, other family members, and people living in the neighborhood of the Aqsa Mosque. Think the matter over and wake up from your dreams. This is what I told myself one morning after a sleepless night filled with anxiety and pain.

On the first weekend I took my small suitcase and ran off to my mother. When I arrived home she was cooking in the dark kitchen of the house, an old family house that my father had bought from a family who had immigrated to America with the beginning of the Israeli invasion and the establishment of the State. The house is, or rather was, an elegant building with expensive furniture that my father bought from the best shops in Jaffa, the object of his pride. He bought an old piano from an immigrant Jew who taught him do, re, mi, and the art of listening to Beethoven. But my father got nowhere with the lessons and preferred to listen to Umm Kalthum. He loved music and singing, he loved the cinema and the theater, he loved life! When he had an opportunity to live in a livelier and more exciting environment, he abandoned us and married a woman who played the *'oud,* twenty years younger.

My mother was beautiful, the most beautiful girl in an aristocratic, old family. Her father was a judge in Turkey, and when my uncles returned to the old country, they were broke and full of their importance, having inherited nothing but conceit. My mother, on the other hand, continued to dream of the old glory and boast in the family name. When my father proposed to her, he was turned down twice, despite his wealth, because he did not belong to the same class. He swore, standing in front of the Aqsa Mosque and hundreds of people, that Wedad, daughter of the Mufti, would be his or he would kill himself. He threatened all her suitors and scared them away until he was the only one left, an "errand boy, son of a stonecutter," as my grandfather used to refer to him in moments of anger. My maternal grandfather was a high judge with a big turban, whereas my paternal grandfather was a stonemason and wore a *serwal* as big as a parachute.

My grandfather bought a saw from Jaffa and became a stonemason, removing rocks from mountains. He became wealthy, whereas my maternal grandfather, a high judge from the Astana, cultured and quite knowledgeable in matters regarding the Israelis, died poor. He said, to whomever would listen, that my other grandfather sold the land to the Israelis. The rocks extracted from the mountain were used to build houses in a Jewish quarter in West Jerusalem. Be that as it may, my father ended up marrying my mother in a funny deal he has never ceased to boast about. My father gave my uncles a hundred gold pounds, *majidiyyeh*, which they divided among themselves, leaving only five pounds for my mother. She made it into a necklace and wore it as a statement of her beauty and worth. My uncles were worthless, and only the one with beautiful handwriting had anything to boast about.

Whenever I look at my mother I see only a woman who used to be beautiful. Her hair is gray and neglected, she is heavy and flabby, and her neck is thick with layers of waxy-looking fat as if deprived of blood.

My beautiful, lively, and contented mother has changed into a fat old woman. Time and worries have contributed to her present condition, but afflictions stripped her of her pride and reduced her to a heavy woman who can hardly move. As soon as she saw me she exclaimed, "Ibrahim, you're late!"

When she hugged me I felt her shaky body and her brittle bones through her embrace. She wiped her tears, pulled me aside, and asked anxiously, "Tell me, how are things with you? Tell me everything."

I sat down with her and told her about my work, my teaching, my room, my eating and drinking habits, washing my clothes, and my correspondence with the university. I explained that in a few years I would receive a degree that would qualify me for a school principal's position. When she asked me eagerly if I would return to Jerusalem then, I felt an unexplainable pain and my heart sank.

My sister, Sarah, returned home before sunset; she was busy preparing her trousseau. She whispered that my father had done something but I didn't hear the whole sentence because my mother asked, angrily, "Why the whispering? Let's hear what you have to say."

My sister stopped talking, and then she said, hesitantly, "Can't I ask a question? Well, Ibrahim, tell us about the village, have you gotten used to life there?"

My mother whispered, "May God forgive you, Muhammad." She was referring to my uncle, the calligrapher who was the cause of my departure.

Sarah said, "His stupid daughter is engaged now. Why don't you come back?"

My mother added in a commanding tone, "You have to come back. Is it conceivable that I should stay alone? Your cousin is engaged, and your uncle is extremely happy. There is no reason for you to stay away. The house is so empty, and soon your sister will get married and move away, leaving me alone here. You must come back."

I felt extremely sad as I heard her speak because her words didn't carry the power they used to have when she was young and beautiful. My mother had been the master in the house. Whenever she spoke she shook the household. We would run and hide anywhere we could, under the beds, behind the cupboards, or in the bathroom. She did not shout or beat us: a look was sufficient for us to freeze; a look as piercing as that of an eagle would stop our activity and scare us. Despite our young age we were sad for my mother's sake. She was in a permanent state of mourning, having tragically lost a beloved young son. One day he ran away from school and joined al-Hussaini's liberation army. A few years later he died at the outskirts of Jerusalem. She replaced him with me, but after my brother's death she suffered from a hemorrhage and a strange illness that caused her to miscarry all her pregnancies. So we were reduced to being a small family, too small for an Arab man who wanted a good stock and many heirs. This was his excuse for remarrying. He used to say, "I want a woman who gives birth to men."

What about me? I wondered. Am I not a man? I probably was not because I was a young boy, tiny and pale, delicate and anemic. My father used to look at me with doubt in his eyes, possibly wondering if I would live to bear his name. He repeated constantly, "I need a male descendant to carry my name. Is it conceivable that Ismail dies without descendants?"

"What about me?" I said. He was caught by surprise, as I was hiding behind the furniture. Embarrassed in front of his guest, he looked at me, repeating, "You, you!" He shook his head, perplexed and apologetic. The guest mumbled, "There is no power and no strength except God's."

My sister had nothing to say because she was not a man or close to one. She would listen and look away, shake her shoulders, and whisper sarcastically, "Here we go again!" Both my mother and my sister are my problem. If my mother were not alive, I would have gone to live with my father. I would have accepted him, as he was, and tolerated his new wife and his 'oud. He might have sent me to the American University in Beirut like all the upper-class children; he might have shared his fortune with me, which would have spared me the hardships of a life of misery in an ugly shepherd's room and even a cattle barn. But being the way I am—hotheaded, and the product of my education, my books, and my brother's example—I stood by my mother and disavowed him. With time, I forgot him and he forgot me; we became like strangers. My mother said, "Your sister wants you to talk to him. He promised her a huge sum of money and a bedroom set." She fell silent and did not continue. When she looked at me I looked at the horizon and said nothing. She resumed angrily, "A bedroom set! Only a bedroom set! A wealthy man like him, owning real estate and warehouses, should have given her something worthwhile, but your father, shame on him!"

She mumbled and rumbled, and Sarah whispered her usual phrase, "Well, here we go again!" My mother heard her; she stared at her and went to the kitchen carrying a pot.

I turned to Sarah and asked her, "What do you think?"

She asked coldly, without looking at me, "My opinion?"

I said to remind her, "The bedroom set."

"The bedroom set? Which bedroom set?" she inquired.

When Sarah acts stupid, in situations like this, I lose my temper and start screaming. I shouted, "Which bedroom set? Don't you know which bedroom set? Didn't you hear your mother? Weren't you here when she spoke?" She stared at me for a couple of minutes, shook her shoulders, then mumbled, "Well, here we go again!"

This time I was embarrassed because I had been absent for many weeks. Mariam had occupied my thinking and was watching me. I stayed away because Sarah was getting married and my mother would be alone. I would not return to the neighborhoods of Jerusalem because my soul was there, my life was there, and culture was there, as well. The village had become a magical heaven where I went to hide from the world and my problems, my father's problems, my mother's problems, Sarah's dullness, my uncle's anger, and the family complexes.

I said calmly, changing the subject, "Would you like to visit him?"

"Visit whom?" she asked.

I smiled patiently and replied, "My father."

She was silent for a few seconds as if examining a complex and important topic, then said, "If you like."

For a very brief moment I thought that had she been my wife I would have divorced her on the spot. How would her future husband put up with her? They didn't know each other except from the photos and their phone conversations. My father planned the whole thing in his own way. He met the man on one of his trips, had lunch with him and learned through intensive questioning that he had three children and no wife. He was either a widower or divorced, I couldn't remember. My father offered to find him a wife, and the man asked if my father had someone in mind. He described the woman he intended for him in these words: "She is a good girl, a little old, she is thirty-five years old, but mature. She would be ideal to raise three children and take care of you. She has everything and comes from a good family, a respectable family. She is an accomplished housewife; she sews and cooks very well."

The man wondered if she would be willing to marry him because his children were "devils."

My father reassured him, "She is a devil herself," causing the man to exclaim, surprised, "What!" But my father saved the situation by enumerating her qualities,

"She is intelligent, capable, and artistic. Trust me, you will be happy with her."

Everything was arranged through the photo: the engagement and the marriage. The bridegroom gave a friend his proxy and the wedding was concluded on the phone. When she objected, her father told her, "You're getting older, do you have an alternative?"

Sarah did not comment but later whispered, "A husband with three children!"

My father explained that he was a company director, he was successful in his work, and he came from a reputable family!

She was still apprehensive and said, "I'll be exiled to the desert."

My father was quick to explain while still on the phone, "What desert? It's a sea of oil and a river of dollars. The heat is bearable. I am ready to pay for your trousseau, from head to toe. What do you think?"

He convinced her gradually, but she bargained some more and asked for a bedroom set. My father smiled on the phone and said, "Why not? A bedroom set it will be. But how would you take it there? Let me tell you, take the money and do with it what you want, buy a bedroom or a dining room set, do as you please. What do you say?"

She accepted, and the marriage was concluded on the phone.

I looked at her and felt sad, worrying about her future. What if things don't turn out to be the way she expects? What if the man turns out to be like my father! What would she do if he divorces her? Would he like her? How would she deal with his children if they turned out to truly be devils? She doesn't know him. What are the chances for a successful phone marriage? All she saw of this man was his picture.

I took her hand and said sadly, "Are you sure, Sarah?"

When she looked at me and realized that I was truly sorry for her, she melted and said, "What's the alternative?"

I said, spontaneously, "Do you want to live your life based on a photo?"

She whispered, as if revealing a secret, "Who among us is living his life?"

She then pulled her hand from mine and said, pensive and passive, "A photo in exchange for another photo!"

Her words hit me in the middle of the night and I couldn't go back to sleep. A photo in exchange for another photo—what kind of reality does this make? My mother, my father, Sarah, my uncle, my cousin were just a photo. I, too, like all of them, would live and die for a photo. I was in love, I suffered and withered away because of an image, but who was Mariam? She didn't know me and I didn't know her, but I was madly in love with a woman named Mariam. As soon as I heard the name, I began singing; my heart felt as free as a summer butterfly and was immaculately pure, flying away in the morning breeze and the scent of the roses. When I woke up I said her name, "Mariam, Mariam," and I imagined her in my arms. I showered her with my love, while rolling, sighing, sobbing, and moaning. I kissed her avidly on the lips; I hugged her and held her tight. This was love for a young man like me, and that was the way to live for young men and women such as Sarah and myself. Like Sarah, we don't live a realistic life, and we replace it with the image of life, thus exchanging a photo for a photo.

I returned to the village on Saturday, and on Sunday I went to the hill to watch her. On Monday, as I saw her enter the library, I went in to return a book. I greeted her, then I greeted Yvonne and gave her the book. She told me that the priest was looking for me. He needed to go to Beirut and was wondering whether I could teach his classes. I was hesitant and asked if there were no substitute teachers. She explained that those were Arabic language classes and she could not teach them. She turned to Mariam and said, jokingly, "Maybe you can teach them!"

Mariam smiled and looked at Yvonne, then at me and said, "Not I, it would be impossible."

She had a strange accent and her voice was heavy and crushed, slightly husky. I lost my mind when I heard it; it was music to my ears. She turned to me and asked, "Can you give me lessons?"

They were clear, simple words, but the strange accent gave them an extra charm and a certain mystery.

Yvonne tried to interfere to prevent the matter, staring at me meaningfully, and I, in turn, tried to avoid the situation, keeping my answer vague. I said, "Maybe, it might be possible. Let me see what I can do."

She insisted, asking, "When would it be possible?"

My heart was pounding, and I replied, hesitant, "Maybe later. Let me see."

The following Sunday I was watching her from the top of the hill, when she raised her head and looked at me intently as if she were telling me, "I see you, you exist, I feel your presence." I was confused and embarrassed, like someone caught spying on people's secrets. That cemetery was her world, the place of a deep grief that she alone experienced. It held her brother's grave or someone else's—what does it matter to me? Why did I spy on her?

That night I couldn't sleep from embarrassment at being caught in the act. I saw myself through her eyes, a sneaky thief, a shameless intruder on her life. I made a firm resolution that I would not see her or pursue her and that I'd stop going to the hill to watch the church and the cemetery. But what about the Arabic lessons and the priest's recommendations? Were they excuses I made up to justify breaking my promise and intentionally walking through the cemetery? But I used to go through the cemetery on other days, as if I were passing through the ruins of Layla's abode, reliving a love story buried in time, while its echoes still resounded in my aching heart.

One day other than Sunday, as I was walking down the church path, I saw her near the tomb under the clinging pinyon tree. It was dusk, when the sky turns red. She was dressed in black, a scarf covered her hair, and she was crying. Her heart-wrenching sobs expressed deep grief. I stood there watching her, motionless and baffled. I was surprised and moved by the beauty of the scene. There were tombs, pinyon trees, crosses, flowers, and cactus plants with elongated leaves, fragrant white flowers, the smell of the evening, a flight of doves, and total silence. Only her sobbing, the singing of birds, the sound of falling leaves, and the flapping of wings could be heard.

I stood there for a few minutes and then got closer to her. She felt my presence and turned in my direction. When I saw her tears, I lowered my gaze and waited for her to say something, but she stood before me, her face uncovered. I felt as if she were naked and vulnerable. I got closer to her, but she didn't move, I took a few steps forward, then I saw her sit down on the edge of a grave, bend over, and resume crying. I stood before her for a few moments, not knowing what to do or what to say. Finally I sat down on a grave close by. Time passed, and the sobbing stopped. Night fell, and silence covered the place while she held her face in her hands. I gathered my courage and offered her my hand; she gave me hers, and I helped her to stand. We walked in total silence, our fingers intertwined, until we reached a crossroads, where she stopped and squeezed my hand. I stopped to find out what she wanted to do. She didn't say a word but signaled with a light movement of her head that we would part at this spot. She would go her way and I mine. She left, and I remained standing, watching her until she was far away; then I turned back and walked in the opposite direction.

At night I was unable to sleep; I was lost in a state of merciless passion. I imagined scenes and conversations, kisses and emotions pouring violently forth. She explained to me the secret of her tragedy, and I shared my secret love with her. She told me about the convent, the story of her escape, and her brother's death. She described her life in a foreign country, talked about her brothers, about Brazil, and a strange world I did not know but dreamed about. She described the green tropical forests, the coffee trees, and the banana plantations, cardamom, monkeys climbing on trees, naked and semi-naked people, dancing, music, and love on the sidewalks, in the streets, and in the forests. Where was she in all this? How did she live? Has she loved? Why does she want to join the convent? With every question and every mystery, my passion increased.

In the morning, with the crow of the rooster and the ringing of the school bell I became aware of my strange condition. I rushed, but when I reached my class the director was there, bringing some order to the chaos. He saw me arrive late, disheveled, pale, and unshaven. He asked if I were sick or had a fever and advised me to take a vacation. I shook my head, annoyed, and said, "No, no need for a vacation," and I proceeded to teach my class.

The following day I walked through the passage behind the church and found her waiting for me, or so I thought at that time. Encouraged, I got closer and sat down on the same grave, in the same spot as yesterday. And like the preceding day, we were surrounded by the same silence, the same quiet, the pinyon trees, a peaceful atmosphere, the shadows of the evening, and the approaching darkness.

She whispered to me, "I am responsible for my brother's death."

I lifted my eyes and met hers. I noticed that she was avoiding my gaze and twisted her hands and neck as if I were judging her.

She said sadly, "I did not mean for it to happen. My mother knows the truth, but people say frightening things about me. Haven't you heard?"

As I didn't reply, she went on, saying, "You must have heard, I'm sure, I'm sure you have. I know that you must have heard."

Confused, I said, "I haven't heard."

Then I looked at her and said, firmly, "I'm here to listen to you. What counts is you, what you feel."

She placed her hands over her chest and said, confused and shaken, "I don't know. Sometimes I feel responsible for the events, and sometimes I feel that I'm dead like him. I'm dead, and he is too. I'm above the ground, and he's under the ground—there's not much difference. He was sick and weak and he would have died anyhow. That's what doctors told my mother and me. My mother knows, my brothers know too, and I know, but I wonder why I feel guilty." She looked at me expecting a reply, but I remained silent. She said angrily, "I am not responsible for his death, he was sick. I don't know why I should feel guilty."

I said, to appease her, "You're not responsible. Since he was sick, as you say, and in danger of dying, as others said, then you're naturally innocent."

She smiled sarcastically, and said, "Me, innocent!"

When she stared at me, her look was strange. Her eyes had something unusual about them; they expressed a certain defiance that was far from innocence and kindness. Oh! Her eyes! Her eyes were so uniquely beautiful. They were black: her eyebrows were raised, and the iris was hidden under long eyelashes. They were very strange. I felt something inexplicable happen to me, a certain fascination. Something mysterious overwhelmed me and fired up my curiosity and my passion.

She said, suspiciously, as she was examining me, trying hard to know me, "You're a writer, aren't you?"

I smiled and said sadly, "Me, a writer? I'm a teacher. I do nothing but teach, and I don't pretend to be anything else."

She stared at me guardedly, saying, "No, no, don't deny it. You're a writer. The priest told me and so did Yvonne."

I was somewhat relieved and rather flattered to learn that I was known among the village inhabitants to be a writer. I wanted to appear important to her, a great man with a strong personality, quite capable despite teaching in a rundown public school. There was nothing there to get excited about—the windows were broken, the ceiling leaked, the bathrooms were abominable, and the courtyard was filled with mud. There was also my room, a shepherd's room. Despite all that I was a writer! What a great thing, let me dream on.

She asked with a naive interest, "How do you write?"

I didn't know how to answer her question. I don't know how I write. I take hold of the pen and I write things I know and feel, things I observe. I describe people, trees, the pinyon, and the singing of the birds. I describe this grave and this cross, and you at this place. I hear your voice and I see things through you. I draw you, I draw what I see, I draw you in me, and I draw myself.

She said reproachfully, "How do you write? Don't you want to tell me? I read books in three or four languages."

I looked at her in amazement and said, "Four languages?"

She must have wanted to impress me, to measure herself up to me, a woman who understands and appreciates learning. I am a writer, and she is a reader, handling books in three or four languages.

"Three and a half," she said. She counted them on her fingers, saying, "Arabic, English, Spanish, and Portuguese."

I smiled and asked, "Which one is the half?"

She stared at me, smiled, and then asked, "Are you making fun of me?"

I shook my head and said, "I didn't mean it that way. I truly envy you. You're lucky."

"I'm lucky?" she wondered.

"Of course you are . . . ," I said, and looked at her. She understood the look and said, "Mary, I mean Mariam. There, my name is Mary, and here it is naturally Mariam. My name is Mariam."

I smiled and said, "You're lucky, Mariam"

She gave me a suspicious look and said, "I'm lucky? Why?"

I looked at her intently and began counting on my fingers as she had done, saying, "Arabic, English, Spanish, and Portuguese. You have two names, Mary and Mariam, and two countries, here and there, and two eyes, and this face. You're beautiful."

She looked at me with that same inquisitive, surprised look and said, "Are you making fun of me?"

I shook my head and said enthusiastically, as my sleepiness was becoming obvious, "Making fun of you? I would never do that."

She said, uncertain, "You are a writer and some writers make fun of people, and this upsets me."

"But I'm not an established writer; I'm only an amateur writer," I explained.

She objected, saying, "Don't deny it, you're a writer. The priest said so, and I believe him. This priest is a knowledgeable man."

"A knowledgeable man?"

She twisted her hands and rolled her eyes, trying to find the right description, "I mean, this means that he is wonderful, he is excellent, he understands people and life, and also death. He says beautiful things. A knowledgeable man is someone who knows, do you understand what I mean?"

I shook my head in approval, saying, "Of course I understand what you mean, he is excellent."

"Do you believe him?" she asked.

"Of course I do."

"Why then do you deny what he says? He says that you are a writer and that you write beautiful things, great things."

"Great things, what a designation."

I was elated and filled with self-importance, but I feigned modesty in front of this woman, this young woman.

She said, with conviction, "That's what he says, and I believe him. He says that one day you will become a famous writer. That's very serious, don't you think so?"

She sounded naive and young, and her halo slowly faded away, but her beauty increased as she talked with an accent. She became more excited as she tried to convey her point. She asked me insistently, "How do you write?" I smiled once more and did not answer, but she went on passionately, "If I knew my people's language I would have written great stories, but unfortunately, I do not."

I said eagerly, "I have a solution. You tell me your story, and I'll write it. What do you think?" She stared at me with that same suspicious look but didn't reply. I insisted, explaining my idea, "I won't tell anyone; I'll just write what you say, without names or locations. No one would know who I was writing about."

She went on smiling, and her smile grew so wide that it almost became laughter. We had forgotten where we were, what we were saying, and how it all started.

We began with sad events and death stories, people's gossip and accusations, and we ended exchanging smiles and talking endlessly. How can such moments end? If only time could stop, if only the world could come to a standstill! Here she was standing before me in a moment in time, and that was the only thing that mattered.

I began to see her everywhere, in the library, at the priest's house, at the grocery shop, everywhere I went. Was she intentionally appearing in my way? I was, but was she? Did she mean to see me? I never knew, and I never will. I ended up knowing her whereabouts, the people she liked to see and those she avoided. I felt that she too knew a great deal about me, more than anyone else.

I began to see her through the school window, at the grocer's where I spent the evening hours. I saw her at the library and, naturally, at the cemetery, while she saw me on the hill, pretending to read. We became lovers from a distance, or so things seemed to me. One day as I was walking toward the Jerusalem taxi stand I found her there. We exchanged smiles. She explained that she was going to Jerusalem to shop. She wanted to buy a peasant dress to wear at a friend's wedding. Then she begged me to go with her, and I agreed. We sat side by side in the taxi; having her so close to me drove me mad. As the car sped up, her silky hair flew and hit my face. It felt like a swallow, a summer butterfly, and smelled of wheat, pine trees, and the morning breeze. She was there, close to me, her shoulder next to mine, her hip and her thigh next to mine. What a euphoric feeling—I almost died of joy.

I don't remember, despite the years of love stories I've experienced, that any woman has had such a powerful effect on me. Was it desire, deprivation, the appeal of forbidden fruit, or was it due to my innocence? Deep in my heart I wasn't innocent, because I trampled everything sacred in my imagination, seeing her in every imaginable position. But in reality, I was nothing more than a repressed person, an adolescent in my twenties. I had only my dreams, my books, my teaching in a village, and my life in a miserable neighborhood in the old city, near the Aqsa. As for her, things were different. She spoke four languages, had seven brothers, traveled the world, lived in a new villa built with emigration money, and had lots of money at her disposal.

We arrived at the market and entered through Bab al-Amoud. As soon as she went through the gate, Mariam became a different person: she became Mary, acting like a crazy tourist, excited and amazed at what she saw, calling me to examine the merchandise, saying, "Ibrahim, Ibrahim, look how beautiful it is, have you ever seen anything like it? Come inside, come see." I was extremely embarrassed when I saw people turn to look at us and the vendors greet us, repeating, "Welcome, welcome." A colleague of mine saw me and smiled and winked at me, saying, "That's quite a catch you've got there!" I frowned and didn't reply, but went inside the shop and hid behind the clothes, the leather merchandise, and the glass of Hebron. She was holding a burgundy dress embroidered in fire red, and she turned toward me and asked, "Look, Ibrahim, does this look good on me?"

The vendor shook his head in amazement and said enthusiastically, "By God, I have never seen a dress flatter anybody the way it flatters you, and I never will!"

She stood in one corner of the shop looking in the mirror, holding the dress and swaying right and left, bending her head to one side and then the other. She was examining her face, raising her eyebrows and her chin like someone walking in a procession of princesses and beauty queens. She was stunned by her reflection in the mirror and the dress as well. Mesmerized, the vendor could not help but say, "Like the picture!" He pointed to a photo hanging on the wall, showing a woman wearing an embroidered peasant dress, her hair covered with a *ghutra* and Ottoman coins. She laughed flirtatiously, revealing her perfect teeth and asked, playfully, "Do I look like the photo?" Then she turned to me, and asked, "Well, Ibrahim, do I look like the photo?"

I didn't reply. I was busy comparing what was happening before my eyes with all the things I had heard and seen, wondering which image showed the true Mariam: was it her in tears before the grave? Her distant attitude at the priest's dinner? Her mixed-up image known to the people? The way she looked now with this dress, or the image I had built up in my imagination?

She entered the dressing room to try the dress on and came out looking like a queen. She had black hair, fair skin, a neck like a gazelle, and a small, thin waist. Meanwhile the stupid vendor was shouting, "Like the picture!" I smiled and whispered, despite my timidity, in amazement, "Truly a picture." I almost fell to my knees.

After that I lost all reserve and became her obedient servant, doing everything she asked me to do. Whenever she said, "Let's eat," I would reply, "Let's eat," and if she said, "Let's drink," I would repeat, "Let's drink." If she told me "Let's go there and see what they have," I would follow her inside the shop without objection. We entered countless shops, and she bought myriad things: wooden crosses, mother-of-pearl crosses, rosaries, and silver jewelry. Sometimes we would stop at exchange counters to exchange dollars to dinars and sometimes she would pay in dollars. At first I tried to pay for her shopping, at least I pretended to, but I soon stopped as it became obvious to me that money meant nothing to her.

She insisted on buying things, saying, defiant and vindictive, "It doesn't matter, let them pay. Who wants to save?" At first I didn't understand what her words meant, but then I asked her, curious about the identity of those she referred to as "them." She stood in the middle of the alley, in the old city, and laughing sarcastically, asked me, "Don't you know them? They are the seven giants and Snow White. Don't you know them, don't you know her?"

I said, confused, "Do you mean the seven dwarves?"

She smiled maliciously and said, "That's true, so true, the seven dwarfs."

"And you are Snow White?" I asked.

She looked at me, seductive and defiant, and said, "Me Snow White? You decide."

I didn't know what to say and remained silent, wondering if she were Snow White or Jabineh.

I said, "The equivalent of Snow White in the Arab stories is Jabineh."

She replied, diligently, "And Mary in Arabic is Mariam."

I stared at her, wanting to eat her up, and asked, "Tell me who you are, Snow White or Jabineh?"

"Guess," she replied.

I gave up, and in my confusion I told her that I didn't know. My bewilderment grew, however, when I lost her in the Church of the Holy Sepulcher. We had entered with a group of tourists and got lost in the crowds that flooded the place. There were candles, incense, many columns, narrow, winding stairs, darkness, and high ceilings for domes where birds and pigeons had made their nests. A priest directed a group of tourists to the Golgotha; they moved ahead and I followed her, or so it seemed to me. As I saw her follow the group I walked slowly in the back, observing this and watching that, and listening to the mixed languages and strange talk. I heard Spanish, Greek, American, and a group of pilgrims from Ethiopia and another one from Egypt; there was a whole world in this cave! We walked through caves, subterranean vaults, domes, and marble columns. Is it possible that this whole world existed in my country without my knowing anything about it? All my life I had passed before this temple without thinking that I had the right to visit it. It was probably because I thought that the church was not for us, that it was for them. We had the Aqsa Mosque and they had this. I had entered the Aqsa hundreds of times; I knew every single corner of it, and as for this place, I hadn't visited it until today!

I walked slowly with the floods of people, feeling as if I were entering a strange world, the world of stories. I recalled the labyrinths of history and the story of Mariam and her crucified son on Golgotha, nailed to the wooden cross. I whispered Mariam's name, but she was neither in the group of Greek visitors nor in that of the Copts or the Ethiopians. I kept calling, "Mariam, Mariam!" going up stairs and through queues of candle burners. I saw a priest telling a group of other priests the story of the crucifixion, the way of the cross, Christ's mother following him to Golgotha, crying and wailing, and hiding from the Roman soldiers. I kept calling, "Mariam, Mariam," in every passage and through every cellar, before every altar. There were many altars for different groups, each one with its altar, peoples of all nations and every denomination. There were priests with strange habits and shaven heads, nuns with head covers like the wings of pigeons, Orthodox priests with beards and hair combed in a bun. What a strange world. I felt like a stranger lost in a magical world, searching my way, not knowing how to arrive at my destination.

I kept calling, "Mariam, Mariam!" and then I saw her in a corner before a statue of the Virgin. She was sitting on a wooden bench, facing the Virgin, praying, her fingers intertwined. I tiptoed forward and sat at a few feet from her. The corner was completely empty, wrapped in an impressive silence. It was lit by a weak ray that filtered through the colored glass of the ceiling and dim candles flickering in the draft. I heard Mariam cry, repeating, "Mother of Christ, Mother of Christ," but the Virgin remained silent and motionless, smiling aimlessly. Mariam continued to weep and moan. I became concerned, sat near her, and put my arm behind her. Suddenly I felt her close to my chest, shaking, wailing, and whispering incoherent words. I encircled her with my arms, and we remained in this position until we heard the bells and the chanting above, shaking the whole temple. We left in silence, with her still as close to me as if she were a part of me. We climbed stairs and walked through alleys and neighborhoods and then entered an Armenian convent. In a corner there, we hugged so hard that our bones cracked. That was my first hug with a woman other than my mother, but was I the first man she had hugged? I didn't know what to do. Should I treat her as the protagonist of a novel or like a human being? At that time, I was still discovering her world and was willing to fall for her with every fiber in my body. I was willing to live the experience to death.

We entered the convent, then went into a strange alley, one of the many alleys occupied by minorities from all over the world—Armenians, Greeks, Russians, and Germans. We went through many convents, while she walked close to me. I discovered magical worlds hidden under the ground and others on mountaintops, in the midst of olive trees, while Jerusalem stretched before our eyes like an open palm. She told me her story, the story of her exile. She was a stranger in her homeland, a stranger in the other land, an only girl among seven brothers, lonely amid strangers. She felt at ease only in Jerusalem, in a dark convent where she hid from the world and her family's supervision. She loved dancing and she loved God, she fancied beautiful clothes, and she liked to look at her reflection in the mirror. She had fallen in love with a priest in that country and had almost caused him to leave the priesthood.

"He was handsome," she said quietly, as if relating a story that she had read years ago. "He was the most handsome man I had ever seen and the most beautiful creature in the world. He felt things deeply and was touched by them to the point of tears. I would see tears in his eyes and wonder whether he was a man, a woman, or an angel in the image of a man. I became obsessed with him. He became my nightmare and my obsession. He had become a dream and the substitute priest of the convent. I used to enter the convent and watch him from behind the glass as he played the piano or the organ. I would get carried away by his tunes. I felt as if I had entered a magical world and that I couldn't live without him. I followed him everywhere, on his way to prayer and during the tourists' visits. I would go to his classes without his permission. He would see me among his students and ignore me. I joined the church choir for his sake. He listened to my voice in awe, as if I were an angel in the wind, ethereal. When I was with him I felt that I was nothing. He ignored me, and whenever we met face to face he would talk to me quietly, in a soft and touching voice, like a lamb. He drove me crazy. While everybody else tried to please me and get my attention, he ignored me. Whenever I heard him play the piano, I would leave my class and spy on him from behind the glass door. Once, he saw me listening to him play and asked me if I liked Bach. I hated Bach after that. It was obvious that the priest didn't understand what I was going through. I sent him a message that I placed in his music book, but he didn't notice it. I rewrote it, changed the date, and put it on the piano chair, but he pushed it aside without reading it. He put it on top of the piano, over the books. I placed the message in a book I offered him, but he returned the message, and said kindly, 'Don't forget your message.'

"I hated and worshiped him. He had become a saint, and I was Thaïs. I read the story of Thaïs and got even more excited, trying to act like her. I sent him a letter by mail, but he hid in the convent and avoided me for days. No one saw him; they said he was ill, I went to the hospital to inquire about him, but he wasn't there. Then came the flower festival, and he headed the flower arrangement competition. I entered the competition and surprised him with the most beautiful arrangement. He said that it was the most beautiful he had ever seen, with the most gorgeous flowers, but it was removed from the competition because the flowers had come from another country. He saw people gather around me to cheer me up and admire my arrangement despite the fact that it didn't win. He waited until they had all left to explain his position, 'It is truly beautiful; it is even the most beautiful arrangement, but the flowers are foreign.' Then he held his cross, kissed it, and disappeared in the crowds.

"Shortly before dinner, as he was reading in his office and the courtyard was empty of students and priests, I knocked at his door and confronted him, saying that Christ had Mary and I was Mary. He was surprised by my presence and what I said to him. He stared at me, trying to grasp the meaning of my words. I repeated what I had said, 'Mary Magdalene was his.' I do not know how I had the courage to talk that way. I was tense from head to toe. I felt as if my head was filled with cotton. I kneeled at his feet and told him, 'You are my only love.' The surprise shocked him, making him lose any remnant of resistance. He became docile like a piece of batter; I held his head in my hands and kissed him on the eyes, on the cheeks, and on the lips. He took me in his arms and kissed me. It was more biting than kissing, as if he wanted to hate me and hurl me into hell, but I was in his arms. He melted like a candle and fell to pieces like a broken necklace. He started crying like a baby and was shaking like a bird. I loved him with all my heart, and I vowed to remain faithful to him. I was willing to join the convent and become a nun for his sake. He smiled sadly, and said, 'You a nun, Mary!'

But I said insistently, 'I am Mary Magdalene.'

"The rest is history. Someone saw us kiss in the dark, and he was transferred to a convent in the far south, near the Indians and the army barracks. I was expelled from that convent and locked up in the house attic. A few months later they placed me in another convent run by very strict nuns. I tried to run away to join him, but I couldn't find any trace of him. I lost any desire to live, and I came here against my will. They said that I was growing up and that the home country was better for me. I would marry like other girls, have children, and forget him. I came here against my will; my heart, my mind, and my feelings are over there. I think about him day and night."

I asked, saddened by her story, "Do you still love him?"

I felt that when she hugged me she was hugging another man, a transparent man, an ethereal vision I could neither see nor defeat.

She said, sorrowfully, "I will become a nun for his sake."

I watched her and remembered her raised eyebrows in front of the mirror, moving right and left with that dress, standing under the photo. I said, teasingly, "You, a nun, Mary?"

She looked through the olive trees and at Jerusalem that stretched before us like an open palm, then whispered, "I'm Mary Magdalene, I'm Mariam!"

Mariam was not mine after all. The dreams, the illusions, and the obsession were nothing but the baggage of the deprived. I was moved by her sad story. It was like a live drama for a writer. But the man in me was awakened, and I became mad with jealousy. I tried to distance myself but failed because I saw her everywhere I went. I doubted my eyes and ears and what I heard from her. She confessed to me that she was still thinking of him, but she was thinking of me as well! Could this be possible? Was she really thinking of me? How else should I interpret her passing before my window daily? How should I interpret her arrivals at the library seconds after me? How to interpret her inquiries about me to the grocer? She asked if he had seen me and left a message with him informing me that she was waiting for the lessons. What lessons, I wondered? She must mean the Arabic language lessons. I would not teach her, I was in deep enough water already.

I began avoiding her to save myself from drowning and obsession. We met one day at a wedding in the church. In the celebration that followed the religious ceremony there were *dabkeh* dancing, a parade, and music. Mariam changed dresses and wore the burgundy peasant dress she had bought in Jerusalem. She greeted me, asking reproachfully, "Why did you disappear? I asked about you everywhere."

"What for?" I asked.

She explained, "After all you're my friend. Aren't you my friend?"

She stared at me with a meaningful look that silenced me. She asked innocently as she drew closer to me, "Did I do something wrong? What is it?" Seeing my surprised look, she whispered, "Because I trusted you with my secrets," then left.

My thoughts began to trouble me. I told myself that I was nervous, crazy, and stupid. That priest was in her past, while I was here, in her present. He was a man of the past, and I a man of the present. But the woman had a past, a teenager's past spent in exile, lonely, sensitive, and full of life. She loved his music and his saintliness. She loved the forbidden in him. But you, what are you? A repressed adolescent, an eastern man, a hypocrite. You want her to be like Jabineh, like Snow White? You want her to be like your mother and like Sarah? You're looking for your mother and for Sarah in her.

We exchanged smiles and looks across the parade and over people's shoulders, and my heart was beating again. On Thursday when I was going to Jerusalem I found her at the taxi stop. We sat as we did the first time, and we went to the market like the first time. We ate and drank wine and laughed and walked around. She took me with her to the Armenian convent to visit her friends. In the convent there was a celebration of some kind, with food and dance and music. A dark man danced, jumped, and tapped the ground with his feet like a Spanish dancer. He danced with all the girls and then with her, before my eyes. She was swaying like a scarf in the wind, her body twisting like a snake and her face turned up to the moon, as if waiting to be kissed. The Armenian man was like the wolf waiting to attack his victim, ensnaring her before seizing her. The singer said words I did not understand but that contained hints that made the people around him cheer and clap. Mariam danced close to me and straightened herself up, revealing her chest muscles, while her stomach pulled inward, making her look like a lioness about to attack.

Oh my God, what beauty, what seduction, what provocation! The priest paid the price and was exiled to a convent in the south near the Indians and the army barracks, while I was in this convent, between the Aqsa and the Church of the Holy Sepulcher, her seven brothers in exile, the gossip of the people in the village, and Yvonne's warning. What could I do? What could we do? What did she want us to do? I was now at her mercy, a slave to all her wishes; she only had to ask and I would do all she requested.

She suggested that we spend the night in Jerusalem. I agreed. I would stay at my mother's, but what about her? She looked at me and smiled mockingly, then took my hand and led me through a hall, a street under the arcades, on twisting stairs, stony tiles, platforms, and an iron gate of another convent. Concerned, I asked if she wanted us to sleep in the convent, but she smiled and said that it was a hostel.

We entered the hostel in the early morning, as we heard the call to prayer from the Aqsa, inviting people to wake up and perform the dawn prayer. The milkman was pulling his donkey and calling, "Milk"; the assistant to the baker was opening the oven for a new day. We stood in the upper hall and saw Jerusalem covered with the morning mist. The jasmine tree reached high up, climbing on the China tree and the bougainvillea trees. Its scent spread and perfumed the air around us, transporting us over the domes and the bell towers. In the darkness I had discovered light and the shadows of paradise through a woman made of fire. That woman had become mine, yet I couldn't help feeling that I was the other—in other words, that she was using me to replace the other, the faraway person, the exiled one, the preferred one, the executioner. She cried and I cried and we remained enlaced, she consoling me and I comforting her, trying to mend what was broken in our hearts. We fell asleep at the sound of the bell for the mass.

After breakfast I told her that I would leave her for an hour or so to visit my mother. I couldn't be in Jerusalem without seeing my mother. My real intention was to visit my father and ask him for a few dollars to pay for lodging at the hostel. I was told that the rent had to be paid in dollars, and I had nothing but a few dinars. I left her and walked in the crowded alleys filled with people, tourists, priests, peasants, pilgrims, and merchants from everywhere. There were displays of all kinds of products on carts pushed by vendors: bananas, dates, figs, apples, quinces, corn, and sweets. Other merchants displayed halva, sugarcoated almonds, eggs, falafel, and candy. Jerusalem felt different this time as I was still bewildered by last night's experience. A deep sadness tore my heart though. I felt that I might lose Mariam and that it would destroy me; she would certainly go back to Brazil or enter a convent. In either case, I would lose her and lose myself. I felt a lump in my throat, my tears froze, and I could see only shadows. A human wave pushed me into a narrow alley, and I would have fallen if I hadn't leaned on a peach cart!

The human wave and the tourists pushed me farther, and I found myself in the oil district, in front of the western side of the Aqsa. I collapsed, feeling that a higher hand, God's hand, had pushed me there to make me face my actions. I sat on the lowest step and held my head in my hands. An old man jumped over me as if I were a dog or a cat. A beggar passed by and flooded me with his good wishes. I took out a few coins and gave them to him, seeking redemption in the gesture rather than bestowing charity. I felt guilty, having committed an abominable act for which I deserved to be punished. I was an adulterer, an apostate, and a betrayer. And now I was going to visit my father to complete my sins, to lie to him to get a few dollars, and for what? For a night of sin and debauchery! I was a sinner, a criminal, and a betrayer because I had betrayed a helpless man, the priest exiled among the soldiers in the far south. What did I know about the feelings of that poor man, his suffering, his endurance and his regrets? Was he remorseful? If an ordinary man like myself was remorseful, what about him, a priest? His regrets and his embarrassment must be overwhelming.

I wanted to enter the Aqsa in search of a pious shaykh to confess my sins, to tell him that I had sinned and committed adultery, that I had soiled myself and a woman who was not mine. That woman was not of my religion or my origin; she was different from me in everything. She was Christian and I was Muslim, she was rich and I was poor, she knew the world and had traveled the world over, boarded a ship and a plane and been to America, Europe, and Brazil, while I had never even seen Beirut. She knew four languages and the Armenian people; she had visited churches and mosques in every corner of the world, from the Vatican to Istanbul. I, on the other hand, didn't even know the Church of the Holy Sepulcher in my own country. We were two different beings. She didn't love me, but loved him; she loved a man in exile and used me as a decoy. I loved her to death, and I desired her to death. She was all I had, or rather all I did not have. What could I do? Should I marry somebody else's woman, a woman of a different faith? Between her and me there were continents and distances, four languages, seven brothers, and the resurrection. What would the shaykh say?

I entered the Aqsa for seconds only, and then I left. I later saw an old man sitting in the shade of the mosque's wall in the courtyard, surrounded by a group of men wearing different types of headgear; some wore hattas, others turbans, and there were even a few fezzes. Some didn't cover their heads and protected themselves from the sun with a newspaper. They were all listening to the shaykh who kept his eyes half-closed against the bright sunlight. He sat on a platform, while the men sat on the ground, under the sun.

He was saying that there was no help and no recourse but in God, that the human being was weak, very weak, and that his strength and power came only from God. We were born of water and mud, and God gives life and takes it, and no soul knows where it will die. God is the omniscient, the omnipotent, and the eternal. Nothing happens without His knowledge. Say amen. All the men repeated, "Amen, amen," with a great deal of submission. The shaykh rumbled and repeated, "From water and mud, amen, amen, fire and light, amen, amen, nothing escapes his knowledge, amen, amen."

A man nudged me in the back and told me to sit and listen. He was poor and weak, wearing torn clothes and a worn fez wet from the water of the ablutions. I had the feeling that I was standing in a strange place, among people I didn't know and with whom I had no connection and whom I could not understand. So the human being is weak, he has no control over his life and death, not knowing where he will end his days. He doesn't know where good and bad come from. God is omniscient, omnipotent, He is destiny and predestination. Thus everything is assigned to us and we have nothing to do but execute. If He didn't want something to happen He wouldn't have chosen it. Why then? How and why? Why me? And why them? I looked at the men sitting under the sun and could not find anything in common with them. I couldn't understand and wouldn't understand. What would I say to the shaykh and what would he say to me?

The poor man asked me whether I wanted to sit; he wanted me to make room for him. He was pulling his *kumbaz* from the right and the left, revealing a very dirty serwal under it. I made room for him and moved backward. I heard the word "amen" but I didn't respond.

I walked into the street feeling lost; was it the lack of faith or money? Would I have felt so weak had I been rich and strong? What would I do if my father refused to see me on the pretext that I remembered him only when I needed something. How would I explain my need for the money? I would have to lie, of course. Would he give me the money if he believed me? What would I do if he didn't?

I went to him shaken, my dignity crushed. He received me in his pyjamas. He invited me to sit down and asked after my news. Before I opened my mouth to talk he said, "No, wait, before you start talking let me get dressed for the Friday prayer."

He left me in the sitting room waiting for him to shower and get dressed for the noon prayer. I was surprised to learn that he prayed; I had never known him to pray. We used to hear rumors about him and his wife, drunk at night in the streets of Jerusalem. We had heard that our father had bought his wife an *'oud* studded with rubies. We had heard that our father was teaching his wife how to drive at night, that he would sit her on his lap and she would drive, while he kissed her as she continued to drive. One day she ran over a man who works for the *Jerusalem Newspaper*. How did we know? All Jerusalem knew, and we found out when it was published in the *Jerusalem Newspaper*.

I looked around me at the house of "Mr. Bridegroom," one of many nicknames my mother used to refer to my father in her moments of frustration. She would say "the bridegroom," "the Jew," or "the effendi," and we immediately knew that she meant our father. Whenever she was fed up with him and poverty had gotten the best of us, she would ask me to go to the serwal for some money. The serwal symbolized wealth from illicit sources, ill-gotten gains from the mountains of Jerusalem ripped open, and the quarries.

My father returned looking clean, with his hair shining, and wearing a suit, a necktie, and carrying a rosary from Kareb. He sat down and observed me with great interest, all the while playing with his rosary. He said, suddenly, "Why don't you leave your school and come work with me in the quarries?"

I was confused, as always happens when I'm surprised by an unexpected or unusual question. I mumbled, stupidly, "The quarries?"

He said hurriedly, "Yes, the quarries, what's wrong with the quarries, professor?"

He stretched out the word "professor" to ridicule the teaching profession and me. He believed that teaching didn't pay enough to let one survive and put food on the table. No one, according to him, becomes rich from teaching. He considered it a stupid activity, a symbol of poverty, a source of humiliation and an activity that destroyed one's eyesight. Teaching for him meant a cheap book, poverty, and even cheaper sweat. It was true that teaching was synonymous with poverty and deprivation, but it also represented education and culture, two things my father lacked and wished to have. He was a stonecutter, the son of a stonecutter, despite his costume, despite the piano and the *'oud* studded with rubies. His fingers were too hard to play a musical instrument; instead he bought a woman to play for him. This proved that he loved and enjoyed music and education. He enrolled in a language center and graduated a few months later having learned nothing but the sentences, "I love you" and "thank you very much." He used this language with the tourists until the day he married and he bought an 'oud, but the piano was never opened.

I looked at the piano, then at my father, repeating, confused and stunned, "Stones, and quarries and more stones?"

He shouted with his strong voice, "What's wrong with the quarries, professor? You don't like them?"

I looked aside, trying to hide my profound annoyance and despair. I was still sad, and my heart was broken after I had heard Mariam's story. There was also the feeling of loss I experienced at the mosque, the lack of money, my weak faith, and the wounds of the heart. At this specific moment, with all the worries of the world piling upon my head, I could do without a new worry. I tried to please my father, saying, "No. Father, I didn't mean it that way."

It was the first time I called him "Father" in many years. I kept silent after I said it, ashamed to have used the word for the sake of the money. I felt that I was nice to him only because I needed money, that I was breaking down because of money.

He said slowly, deliberately, as if talking to a stupid boy, "Look, my son, I know how you live, your miserable room that no father would wish for his only son. You are my only son. You do remember that, Ibrahim?"

I took a quick look at him, then I lowered my gaze, fearful of him or rather fearing my own anger, lest I explode in his face and tell him, "Now I'm your son, your only child? Here you are now, as in the past, in need of a boy to carry your name."

My father carried on, "Look, Ibrahim, neither the school nor the books will help you. Can you really live on a few dinars from teaching? Don't say anything, don't reply and don't tell me. I know, I know very well that all your life, since your childhood, your only concern was books. You spent all your pocket money on books. We accepted the books, but writing, I don't understand that. To make a long story short, I am planning to start a project with your sister's husband." I looked at him inquisitively, but he replied before I asked my question, saying, "I understand, I understand, I mean her future husband, you know. It is an import–export company; we would export stones from the West Bank for buildings in the desert. I have the permit already—who would have imagined! Well, what do you think?"

"What do I think?"

My father explained, "Yes, you would go with Sarah, be there for her marriage, then open the branch of the company and run it. I would send you the merchandise, and you would market it. Dollars would flow through your hands like rivers. Well, what do you think?"

This man can't be satisfied! He has a saw in Nablus, one in Ramallah, and another in Jerusalem and Hebron, and now he's moving in to the desert. Won't he ever be satisfied? I said, rigidly, "All right, it's possible. Let me think about it."

"Think about what?" he said. "Be wise, my son, and go ahead, in God's name. Please, don't leave me in limbo and tell me about the school or the books. I am sixty years old, Ibrahim, and I want to see you married with children like everybody else. I would like to see you with a son bearing my name. I was planning to talk to you long ago, but you are far away and you are stubborn. You live in a damned village and avoid Jerusalem. And the room you live in, what a dump!" He stared at me as if he were about to announce an important piece of news, "Did you know that your room used to be a stable? It was a stable and a sheep barn. What kind of a life is that? Ibrahim, don't you live in this world?"

My concern grew. My painful story with Mariam was proof that I was a dreamer, weak and ignorant. I didn't know the world, I hadn't visited the countries of the world, I hadn't struggled to earn a living, I didn't understand worldly language, I knew nothing but teaching.

It was almost midday, and the receptionist at the hostel had said to pay around noon, and Mariam was waiting for me there. I must have those dollars. When we heard the *muezzin* call for the noon prayer, my father said, "Let's go, today is Friday and the Haram mosque will be full. Did you do your ablutions?"

I shook my head and did not reply. He said hastily, "You can do your ablutions there, let's go, let's go."

He stood before me while I remained seated. He looked tall and handsome, but he didn't feel like my father. He was my biological father, not really my father; I didn't care for him.

"Why are you sitting? Is there something you want to say?" he asked.

I said hastily, without thinking, as if to get rid of a burden that had weighed on me for hours, "I need dollars."

He was pensive for a while, and, smiling his yellow smile, he said, "What's the problem? The usual? But why dollars this time?"

I wanted to say "the fees for the university in London," or something of that kind, but my feeling of loss, the voice of the muezzin, and the call to prayer frightened me. Who was he to make me lie? He is worse than I am; why should I beat around the bush and pretend, adding to my concerns and sins? I decided to tell the truth and said hurriedly, "I slept in the hostel, and they want dollars."

He was pensive for a moment then laughed loudly and took a deep breath. Without further ado, and without any comment, he ran out of the living room and left me alone, waiting. When he returned he was carrying a stack of dollars. He gave them to me, smiling cheerfully, and said, "How are things? All right, I hope? You're not doing too badly! I thought you understood nothing but books! Here you are, let me see what you are capable of. Be smart. We'll soon get you married and start the biggest project for you." He laughed again and said, maliciously, "And here I was, trying to get you to pray with me! Go, take a bath and join me. Don't forget the new project to build in the desert. Come, join me there."

When I returned to the hostel, Mariam had left. I was extremely angry. She had settled her account and left without leaving a sign.

I asked the receptionist if he knew where she had gone. He shook his head without looking at me and continued to examine his papers. He then answered the phone and ignored me. I was very embarrassed and left the place surreptitiously, as if I were a thief or a criminal. I felt that he knew things about me that I didn't want him to know. He probably also knew that a woman had paid for me and left me without a word. I felt increasingly like a victim. I felt guilty and weak, while she was strong. I felt I had no capital I could count on except my father. It was a capital that neither pleased nor satisfied me, but I was pushed in its direction because I was stuck. If this situation continued I would lose myself and would be humiliated and without dignity. Here was a woman who paid my hostel bill and a father who did not acknowledge me and whom I denied until the moment I needed him. He was now making demands I didn't like. Abu Ismail had a new project, a new saw to build in the desert with stones from the mountains of Jerusalem. What a price to pay and for what—a woman I didn't own but who owned me, a woman in love with another man.

I was overcome with resentment and a powerful desire to take revenge. I immediately returned to the village, in a state of anger. Strangely, I never for a moment thought that she might be angry. I was concerned only about my feelings and the pressure and doubts I had experienced; as for her and her feelings, what she thought and what she endured, none of that concerned me; I didn't give it a thought. I returned to the village only to settle accounts and discover where I stood with her. I wanted to know what I was for her, a mere replacement for another man? At this moment I hated her from the bottom of my heart, believing that nothing was left of a love story that had ended. I did not believe and I did not know that love was multifaceted, the first side being suspicion. I was too young to know that a thin thread separates love from hatred, and when in love we oscillate over this thread, on one side or the other, until we settle on one of the two, but we never really settle. Young and inexperienced, I was comparing the pure love I had lived in my imagination with the pulling and pushing in our relationship as it entered the tangible stage. Little did I know that relationships, in reality, are a mixture of the two.

On my way to the taxi stop I saw Jerusalem in a different light. All the things, shapes, and places had become dull and gloomy. Where were the colors in the squares, those of the streets and the arches, that I had seen when I was with her? All was lost and appeared desolate, grayish, threatening me with the dryness of death. By God, was this the same world I had seen when Mariam was a mere vision, transparent and ethereal, still untouched? I had not asked then whether she loved me and was faithful to me because I loved her no matter who she was and regardless of how she felt or acted. Now that she had descended to earth with her body, I began to wonder where I was in relation to her and what she was feeling. Strangely, knowing her body did not constitute an achievement of any significance. Why do they say that the body is a gate and that storming the gate is in itself a sign of success? I had not reached my destination. How could I make that happen?

Riding the bus with the wind blowing in my face and the mountains of Jerusalem before my eyes, I slowly regained control of myself and started recalling the events of the previous night—her dancing, running, jumping the stairs of the alley, and her crying in my arms, and my crying. Unexpectedly, tears filled my eyes and melted away my anger, erasing all my doubts, the memory of my father, my humiliation before him, and my cowering before the Haram mosque and the crowds. I don't like crowds; they suffocate me. I feel that they limit me and demand more than I can give. I can't face the crowds of Jerusalem, and those of the Haram. I am not comfortable in large crowds; I feel helpless, scared, and lost. The environment of the village saves me from myself and the large crowds of the cities. There I feel anonymous, like a closed book, a blank book. In the village I feel reborn and I delve into open worlds where there are the priest, Beirut, Mariam, Brazil, and stories and tales about the world in which people live beyond my borders. I live life from the outside, because if I entered it I would become dizzy and collapse. What I felt was, therefore, a reaction to the crowds, but when I left them I became myself and returned to my dreams and the spheres of love.

When I reached the village I looked for her everywhere, at Yvonne's, with the priest, at the cemetery and the church. I asked the grocer about her, then I waited for her after the tourists' visit on the hill. I watched the cemetery until darkness, but she didn't come. I roamed the streets like a madman, wondering how to find her. Finally, I decided to do something adventurous that only a crazy man or a lover would do. I went to her house to inquire about her, having prepared an answer for every possible question. If I were asked, I would say that Mariam had asked me to give her Arabic lessons. It was quite a convincing answer, supported by the books, papers, and pencils I carried with me.

I put on my best clothes and perfumed myself. I had forgotten all my suspicions at that moment; my only concern was seeing her, embracing her, and spending a few moments alone with her—oh! To be alone with her! I recalled all the details of the previous night, the sounds, the smells, the scent of the dawn, the church bell, and the milk vendor. Even her crying kindled my fire, and the taste of tears increased my passion for her. It made me fumble about, seeing only Mariam before me and behind the trees, on the roads, across the vineyards, and under the trellis covering the long passage leading to the entrance of the house. There were apricot trees, berries, quinces, and pears on each side, then the stable and the oil press. I saw Mariam everywhere, in every corner of the farm; I saw her in every imaginable position. It didn't matter anymore that she loved the priest or the Cardinal or even the Pope; what mattered now was finding her.

I chose to knock at the door instead of ringing the bell. I soon heard the sound of wood being moved and the heels of shoes, or rather slippers, the steps were small and slow. My heart was pounding. A voice behind the door asked who it was and then said to wait. The door opened revealing an old woman, covered in black, with thin gray hair pulled to the back in a bun. Her bones were thin and visible, and she wore very thick glasses, and their concave lenses made her eyes seem very far away, behind circles like rings of water. She asked, while curiously examining me from behind her glasses, "Who are you?"

I told her I was a professor and that I had come upon Miss Mariam's request.

"Miss Mariam?" she interjected, with an artificial smile, repeating sarcastically, "Miss Mariam? Miss Mariam went out for an errand with her goat. Come on in, make yourself at home."

I asked politely if it would be all right to enter, and she repeated her invitation, saying, "Please do, please come in."

She walked before me with difficulty, feeling her way with a hand stretched in front of her. I remembered then what was said about her, that she was almost blind.

It was a two-story house with inner stairs, a large parlor with thick glass that revealed the vineyards and the distant mountains of Jerusalem. Despite the wealth visible in furniture, the house had some rural touches. There was the picture of the Virgin Mary carrying the child Jesus, and a cross made of olive wood. The truly beautiful things in the house were the plants, which filled the living room and the parlor and looked like green falls. There were all kinds of plants, with small leaves, large leaves, waxy leaves, a climbing plant, and branches with leaves that intertwined throughout the ceiling, forming a beautiful second ceiling. I had never seen anything so beautiful. I stood looking at them, amazed. I said, "How wonderful," despite myself. The woman smiled and asked me if I liked plants. I replied, enthusiastically, "Very much."

She offered to give me cuttings but I turned down her generous offer, explaining that I had no veranda or garden. "It doesn't matter," she said, "plants grow anywhere!" I agreed with her and listened as she carried on enthusiastically, "You should see the greenery in other countries; they have even planted the desert. We, on the other hand, do nothing—it's such a shame! Do you see that spot over there? There used to be a walnut tree there that was planted during my grandmother's life; it was replaced by bricks and stones!"

I commented on the beauty of the house and its unique location, offering a great view of Jerusalem. She invited me to sit down and carried on commenting on the old house, which was demolished to make room for the new one. She wanted to know where I live.

I gave her a detailed description of my room with a great deal of sarcasm to convince her that old does not always mean beautiful. She objected with a movement of her hand and said, "Nonsense, I know your old house well, and I've visited it a thousand times. The Abu Saada family neighbored ours, wall against wall. The old man stayed in the house until he died. All his children are overseas, and his eldest son built a new house and turned his back on the family properties. Well, my own children are no better; they left their livelihood here and turned their backs on it. I put up with the absence of the father, but the children too! Their father lived for forty years in exile, maybe more, while I stayed home. He would be gone for two years and return for two months to visit. Every year he would say it was the last year until he died. Then the children left and took me with them. I didn't move with my husband, but my children somehow twisted my arm. How strange it is that our children are more important than our country, don't you agree?"

The idea moved me; I reflected on it but said nothing. She insisted, saying, "Isn't it true?"

I said, confused, "It might be true."

She waved her hands and said, "The day you have children you'll understand. You'll find out that a child is dearer than life. Life is precious, but our children are dearer to us than our lives; you'll find out. We discover their value only when we lose them. When any of your children die you feel as if you'd lost your life with them. You then remember and regret and wish you could go back and wish you had done this or that; you wish you had died in their place. You wonder why God didn't choose you in their place. May Christ forgive me, but sometimes, when one has suffered so much, one says strange things. Christ died on the cross and he didn't complain and didn't say, 'Mother,' though his poor mother cried over him until her tears dried up. He did not call for his mother but said, 'Abba, Father!'

"I too had a son who looked like the image of Christ. He was fair and tall, with long hair. He was very quiet and even during his agony he never said, 'Mother!' He went to hospital three times, and every time they used to say it was the end. Medicine is more advanced there, and America is close, only two hours to Dallas. But we came back, it's our luck! There is also Mariam, Miss Mariam! What can we do!"

I asked, apprehensive, "Your daughter Mariam?"

She shook her hands and said indifferently, "Forget about it. It was his fate. Had we stayed there Micho might not have died, but Mariam, Miss Mariam . . . . Well, it was his fate." She looked into the distance and then turned to me, asking, "What about you, sir, does your mother live with you or in Jerusalem? Take care of your mother, protect her like you would your heart and eyes. A mother is not a joke, my son. No one can protect you like a mother would."

I remembered my mother in all her circumstances, her continuous mourning and her tragedies. I remembered her standing at the sink, exhausted and withering away. Strangely enough, I didn't feel a connection, a closeness to her and part of her world. Maybe because before her divorce she was not warm and intimate with me. I didn't feel that she was with me but rather that she was close to my brother, Waddah. His photo was in the central spot in the house. There were his things and my sister's problems, my mother's miscarriages and then my father listening to Umm Kalthum while she stayed far away, in the kitchen or the bathroom or the bedroom with my sister. She would stay in bed for days, her head tied up with a scarf, windows closed to block out the sunlight. When my father came home, Sarah would prepare his meals, and he would eat alone, then sit in his chair listening to the news and to Umm Kalthum. My mother, on the other hand, liked Nasser; she found his voice to be as melodious as Umm Kalthum's. She enjoyed listening to him and forgot my sister, she recalled my grandfather's words, the judge in Turkey, and agreed with Nasser's words. Is this the reason she supported Waddah?

"Take care of your mother; don't neglect her. Let me tell you, the mother gathers the family and would bless you no matter what you do. I tell my children the same thing, but no one listens. Their father sometimes listened and sometimes did not; my life was so hard with him. I suffered during his lifetime and after his death, but at least when he was alive I had dignity. He sent gold and sent money and told me to spend it as I wished. I did spend, bought and sold a lot; I raised my children and brought them up as I wanted. My word was as sharp as the edge of a sword. When he died they took my income and I was pushed aside. It is amazing how time changes; one moves from a position of power to being pushed aside. That's life. Frankly, with the death of the father I lost my place in the family, and the loss of my son broke me completely."

I asked quickly, without thinking, "Which is more difficult?"

She turned to me, surprised to find me there, as if her weak vision had made her forget my presence. It is also possible that her isolation in that house, in the middle of the vineyards, far from the village, neighbors, and family, made her eager for a listening ear and she then forgot her listener's presence. It might be age and incapacity and some mental deterioration, neglect, and disinterest in basic issues that lose their importance with time. The heart opens like a weak muscle, the tongue becomes like a faucet, and the mind loses its valve. Things that are essential in youth lose their appeal in old age. My mother too was strong, better even, she was an unbreakable valve. She did not shout or warn, one of her eagle-like looks would rivet us in our place. She isn't scary anymore; she only talks and prays, protests and complains. A valve suddenly became loose; it became either loose or damaged, leading her to talk about everything, what can and cannot be said. She talks about things that once were deeply buried, revealing secrets and casually using vulgar language. During her youth she was revolted by words that reminded her of the people because she felt superior to them. She felt superior to all the people in her circle and when she was broken, she fell hard. It is clear that with time people lose their prudence and acquire a sense of humor and become talkative.

She was still thinking. My question had taken her by surprise, and she repeated it aloud, indifferent to my presence. "Which is more difficult? Both are difficult. When my husband died and I became marginal, that was hard, and when my son died, it broke my heart, and that was hard. A person dies once, but we die many times when our loved ones pass away."

So, my mother was broken. She had died many times and had become marginal. She had died once with Waddah's death and another time when my father left her, and she had died a final death when she became marginal, like a photograph on a shelf. My mother was reduced to a photo! I was overcome by a feeling of oppression. I stood up and said, fearful, "I must go to see my mother." She looked at me, surprised, but quickly I explained, "My mother lives in Jerusalem. I haven't seen her or inquired about her, at least by phone, in a long time."

Shocked, she stared at me from behind her thick glasses, saying, "You haven't inquired about her!"

I turned toward the wall and saw a cross, and the image of Mariam and the child Jesus. On the other side I saw Jerusalem and the Ram Mountains. My feelings of oppression grew and I was overcome with a strange sadness and the fear of the unknown. Here I was neither with my mother nor with Mariam.

I excused myself, saying, "I must leave before the evening."

She asked, surprised, "And Mariam?"

I replied rather abruptly, without meaning to, "Mariam? Later."

I shook her outstretched hand, then hurried out, crossing the hallway breathless, trying to make it before sunset. But the night surprised me, and Mariam came. When I saw her, I forgot myself, my mother, and Jerusalem.

Mariam came out of the shade and my heart shook, riveting me in place. I stood motionless, watching her with the goat, hearing the sound of a ringing in the silence. The sunset darkened her image and reduced her features to those of a shapeless shadow. I could recognize her walk even in the dark, in the midst of a crowd. Whenever she was absorbed in her thinking she took slow steps, her head bent to the right. She looked at the ground without blinking, while her arms moved like two rhythmic pendulums.

She felt my presence but ignored me and continued to move at the same pace. When I caught up with her she stood before me, her head bent down and to the right. She asked me, indifferent, "Why did you come?"

Her tone surprised me, but I thought that she might be angry because I had left her at the hostel until noon. Was it possible that such an insignificant matter would upset her to that extent, making her avoid me all this time? Or was this an excuse to leave me and return to him?

As I remained silent, she raised her eyes and said softly, "Listen to me, Ibrahim, you're my friend; let's keep it at that."

I said, dumbfounded, "And what happened yesterday?"

She said, coldly, "It was a mistake."

She broke my heart. I thought that she was rejecting me to return to him, to her past life, while I was simply a mistake. If she went back where would I go? To my world, which now seemed arid and barren? I was overcome with a deep feeling of self-pity, bemoaning my lost youth and my desperate position. The village, which was my refuge from the hubbub of the people and the world, a hiding place for my timidity and shyness, had become a very dark cave. Where would I go if she were to leave? I wouldn't stay in this cave. I wouldn't stay here; I wouldn't be able to take it. I would run away and seek refuge with him. My father is my harbor after the village, my refuge from this love.

She asked softly if I had heard what she'd said. I didn't reply. I stood shocked and tried to digest everything that had occurred in these few days, when the world was turned to turmoil. She said sincerely, "You're my friend; I'll never forget you, but our relationship has no future; it's a dead end."

Saddened, I repeated what she had said, controlling my anger, "It was a mistake."

She shouted in a weak, suppressed voice, lest someone hear her, "Oh! You see, you're angry with me, and you're trying to get back at me, to punish me."

I didn't reply, and she stood there for a few minutes waiting. When I did not respond, she said insistently, "You're my friend, I'll never forget you."

I turned my face away from her, but she insisted, saying, "Listen to me, it's a dead end, a doomed relation from the start. There are the issues of religion, people's opinion, my family, and myself. A million things stand in the way. Besides, you're weak and I'm weaker than you."

Attacked, I defended myself, "I am not weak, Miss."

I then put my hand in my pocket to produce the dollars and prove to her that I was not, what? Weak? That I was rich? That I was presumptuous, speaking the language of materialistic people, the tradesmen who place no value on feelings and emotions, the elevation of the soul, the beauty of the soul, cheerfulness, and the truthfulness of the heart? I'm not strong, but rather weak, very weak. The worst aspect of this feeling is the fact that I inherited it from my uncle with the beautiful handwriting.

She held my hand, pulled it to her, and said, "Come with me, you won't leave my house in this condition. You're my friend, I wouldn't hurt a gentle person like you. You're very gentle."

"I'm rather weak," I replied, bitterly.

She said again, "You see, now you're angry with me. Why would you be angry with me? I didn't hurt you, did I? What do you think of me? Do you find me strange? Do you find me scary, an indomitable mare without a bridle?"

I didn't reply but I kept listening to her, motionless, my head bent down.

She asked, somewhat fearfully, "What are you thinking about? You think that I'm strange."

"Why would I think that?" I asked.

She replied, hesitant, "I don't know, but I feel that people sometimes do not understand my behavior."

I asked, despondent, "What have you done?"

She remained silent for a while, observing me to assess the significance of my words, wondering whether I was sarcastic or angry, and whether I understood or hated her.

Uncertain, she changed her tactics, instead of attacking and controlling the course of events, she was on the defensive, "I told you everything. I told you that I was sad, very sad, and that my sadness for Micho is still deep in my heart."

I looked at her sideways, measuring the extent of her lies and her malice. She was a liar; she was cruel and selfish. She blamed everything on the priest, then on me, then on her brother and me. I wondered who had killed her sick brother?

She was collapsing, slowly. "I am sad, very sad," she said. "My sorrow for my brother is still very strong."

I shook my head incredulously and mumbled maliciously, "Of course, of course."

She was stung by this and yelled, "Don't you believe me? Why don't you? Is it because I danced and drank and wore the fiery dress? Tell me, tell me!"

I didn't reply, and my silence angered her. She yelled again, "Say what you want to say! Go ahead."

I replied, stressing every word, as if I meant what I said, "What do you want me to say? What do you want me to do? I do what you require of me."

She shouted angrily, "Stop, stop! Do you mean to say that you did what you did only because I . . . ." She stopped and looked away, then stared at me. She drove me crazy, and I lost my temper. I overcame my timidity and said what I had concealed until then, "Of course, of course, if you hadn't encouraged me I wouldn't have dared. You were a dream for me, an image. I never thought it possible, but you, you . . . ."

She was staring in disbelief at what she was hearing. Here I was objecting and confronting her, not the weak being she had believed me to be. She said, baffled, "I had thought you were an angel."

I confronted her with the courage of a desperate man, "Which of us is the angel, Mariam? I'm not an angel and neither are you, but there is something in both of us, something I do not know how to describe, but you, you . . . ."

She whispered, perplexed, "Me, me, what do you mean?"

I stared at her as she was staring at me, and I saw the white of her eyes shine in the darkness and her pupils became wider and froze. I heard her fast breathing.

"What about me? Go ahead, say it," she said.

What could I say, what was the use? She knew very well what she wanted, and I didn't. She wanted to have fun and forget the absent beloved. She wanted me to be that one. When I was with her, at the height of love, she had whispered incomprehensible words. What did they mean, which language was she speaking, to whom were they addressed? Did she intend them for the absent beloved, the one I so clearly represented? Isn't that what made her cry and made me cry when I realized that I was the replacement? I recalled yesterday's encounter as she melted in my arms and planted her fingers in my hair and my back, pronouncing those words, those words in that language. I was so unhappy.

I controlled myself and returned to my repressed anger, and said, "You want me to forget? I will. You say that our relationship is doomed? All right, I understand. You talk about your brother, and your other brothers, the difference in our religion and background, I understand. This is what I say, nothing else. I won't say anything I might regret. As far as I'm concerned you are an image that I won't destroy no matter what you say. I'll leave this place, I'll forget you. I'll do what you want, I promise. But I truly love you, Mariam, and if you had reciprocated my love I wouldn't have hesitated to do anything for your sake. But now, and from this minute on, I will forget you."

I quickly walked away across the hallway, and I didn't look back. All I was thinking about at that time was a way to take my revenge on my life and my weakness. I wanted to forget what she had said about my weakness, I wanted to become another person than myself because I wasn't good for her, for anything, or even for myself.

I walked fast in the growing obscurity of the place, and she walked with her goat, and the bell shook.
Things returned to normal a few days later, and the village began telling the story of my love. I was young then and very much in love, filled with my readings

and a huge ambition to prove my manhood, my capacity as a writer, a lover and a pungent *fida'i*, a believer who would never break a promise or betray a sermon until death. Mariam was more than my beloved, she was part of me. I believed that when a person makes a choice, all obstacles disappear. I found strength in a verse someone wrote, which read as follows:

"My will is a fate, days and destinies
Are shattered at its gate."

I did not know then that, deep down, a person is not free. He is confronted with love and war, illness and old age, accidents and coincidences. There was also death. All those are things we deny when we are young and unabashed. Later on we realize that events destroy us while they remain intact.

I thought I was strong, but in reality I was weak. My imagination was filled with a huge story about an eternal love that feeds on contradictions in the heart of death. I began dreaming of a university degree that would save me from this environment. I believed that with a degree from London I would move to Jerusalem and become famous and wealthy, with all the money I need, glory, and the best position. If I were to receive a university degree from London, I would be the only one among thousands of my peers who never came even close to a university education, and who had no access to a university in their own cities. When we were part of Jordan, we used to hear about universities in Beirut, Cairo, and Damascus. From the West Bank we used to correspond with Beirut, Damascus, or London.

For me and my like, London represented a distinguished place, of high standards and irrefutable distinction. If I were asked about my degree, I would say it was from London; this would be sufficient. But in reality it was not sufficient for my father, who considered a degree from London a losing bet on an insignificant position that would not spare me from hunger.

Mariam's brothers, on the other hand, were concerned with one kind of profession, the profession of faith declaring that there was no god but the one God and that Muhammad is his Prophet. As far as they were concerned, Islam was simply a joke, a deviation in history, a desert, a camel, a date palm, and Arab tribes. The Westerners in London and Rome considered it a place in history and a civilization. London's control extended over continents, where it imposed its will and determined peoples' destinies. Rulers the world over bent their heads before it. Rome cheers at Christmas, and the bells ring in celebration all over the world, especially in the Church of the Nativity and the Holy Sepulcher. London was the center of government, and Rome was the house of the Lord, but I, naturally had no family ties and no favors connecting me to the center of government and the house of the Lord.

I was described as an apostate and an ignorant man because I didn't leave my country and kept the religion of the Bedouin. I heard people mention Mariam's brothers Victor, Tony, and Michel, but I was not intimidated. I remained faithful to what I loved, concerned with no one but Mariam and dreaming of a diploma that would help transfer me to Jerusalem.

Mariam continued to visit me, or rather I visited her. The mother's weak eyesight worked to our advantage; whenever she surprised us in daring positions we stayed put, not stirring or breathing until she moved away. But people didn't leave us in peace, they told the mother that Mariam was in love with a Muslim, and the Muslims felt vindicated because Christian girls were loose like Mariam. Yvonne saw me at the grocery store one day and didn't respond to my morning greeting. The priest told Mariam that men are brothers, but the village and its traditions, her brothers, and people's conditions in this country and at this time required that a person be considerate and think of the others before oneself. He reminded her of her mother, her brothers, and her reputation as well as the reputation of the daughters of the community vis-à-vis the Muslims. What would they say, what would they repeat? What, what? But Mariam didn't listen; she had had enough of this kind of talk, of advice, and of having her heart broken. Her story with that priest, her brother's death, and her guilty feeling about both made her defy any warning and face it harshly. People cursed and ostracized her—the Christians because she loved a Muslim, and the Muslims because she was a sinner who deserved to be stoned.

Mariam stopped showing up in the village, going to the grocery store, or visiting Yvonne and the house of the priest. I became her world, and whenever she felt trapped she went to Jerusalem and we met at the Armenian hostel. But the trip to Jerusalem was hard on the wallet and the nerves. She was not in control of the house expenses anymore, the money was in her mother's hands. She was strict with her and threatened to have her brothers Eissa and Tony deal with her in the coming summer. She began dreaming of running away through the Mandelbaum Gate to Nazareth. Her aunt, a nun in Nazareth, used to visit them every Christmas through that gate. She said that Nazareth was a paradise and the house of Christ. Mariam explained, using a strange logic that somewhat surprised me, "Life there is a paradise, life in Israel is a paradise. We can enter from the Mandelbaum Gate, hide there for a while, and then marry."

I stared at her, shocked, "What are you saying? That we hide there, in Israel?"

She said very simply, as if she were not one of us, unaware that we were at war, "There we would be free and get married. Life there is like life in America."

I said angrily, "Don't you know what is Israel to us? Don't you know what Mandelbaum is! My brother Waddah, and al-Hussaini, the walls and the thousands of martyrs and those who died trying to enter Jerusalem, don't you know all that? We are at war, don't you know that!"

"I know that, I do," she replied. "But what's more important?"

I remembered then what her mother had said about children and the homeland and which one is more important. She had talked about Brazil, the priest, the convent, and Mariam growing up in that environment. She had no affiliation to this country, this reality, and the national cause, she was like a tourist! I, however, was born in this reality. I was Waddah's brother. There were others in my life: my mother, my father, and Sarah, my job and my diploma and, above all, a dream to become my own master. The circumstances required that I be patient, advance one step at a time, and persevere. Rushing would not pay, it would be better to show patience while building for the future.

We were surprised by Mariam's pregnancy. All the pills to end the pregnancy failed, leaving us only one choice—abortion. But abortion required money that we didn't have. I had no choice but to seek my father's help. He insisted on meeting the "Christian" woman who spoke with an accent he had heard about from jewelers and silver merchants. They had told him that his son was in love with a Christian woman, and had advised him to intervene, but he didn't, and here I was asking for his help. He bargained with me to get involved in his projects, which had multiplied. He said casually, "What if she is Christian? Let me meet her. The merchants said that she is beautiful."

Mariam refused categorically to see him, saying disgustedly, "I didn't disobey my family to fall under your father's control."

Frustrated by my helplessness, I replied, "At least his name is Ishmael and not Tony."

My words angered her, but two days later she returned to reconcile with me, saying, "Let's think about a solution; my belly is growing quickly."

My father advised me to work for him in the desert, earn good money, and take Mariam with me.

He advised that I be smart and kill many birds with one stone.

The birds soon became cages, which imprisoned me and threatened my well-being. I was sad, fearful, and diffident. I felt lost, my dream of becoming a famous writer with an advanced degree was waning. My ambition to publish was fading, with my stories awaiting revisions, correction, and concentration. I wasn't writing anymore; I had stopped reading and studying. I had stopped building my future, and I was losing my ambitions and myself. Mariam became my only preoccupation. I was looking for a solution, and I gradually lost control of my life and the trust of the priest. I became a slave of my circumstances. I had no wings to fly, no self-respect. The priest came looking for me, but I ran away to Jerusalem. My sister Sarah tried to understand the reason that I refused to accompany her to see my father and finish the preparations for the wedding. My mother was resentful because I was neglecting her and was not making any preparations to move back to Jerusalem. I was lost in the middle of all those concerns and harassed by everybody—my mother, my father, Sarah, and the priest. There were Mariam's brothers, people's gossip, and an abortion, which did not take place. There was Mariam's son: he as well had become my enemy, my rival. He turned my life upside down and changed my convictions. I used to believe that a human being decides the course of his life, but Mariam's son proved me wrong.

I had refused to join the common people, thinking that I was superior to them, stronger than those who seemed to me like paper boats tossed helplessly by the waves. I found them totally weak, scared, helpless, lacking reasoning and the capacity to plan, while I was an artist, a writer, a future degree-holder from London, and a publisher of stories. In a few words, I was better and superior, and if Waddah and al-Hussaini took up arms and fought untiringly, I would fight with the pen, if it weren't for Mariam and her son. Why wasn't he aborted? Here I was the prisoner of a woman I loved, a woman who did not know Waddah, al-Hussaini, Israel, and the Mandelbaum Gate, a woman who lived like a tourist, a woman who was brought up in exile, in Brazil, in a convent, a woman who spoke broken Arabic and destroyed her ancestors' language, a woman who could not read what I wrote or understand what I said, a woman who considered Micho, like Waddah, a martyr. She was a woman with a narrow vision despite the distances she traveled, a woman so different from me, a woman who turned my life upside down. Then there was Mariam's son—was he really my son? Was he my flesh and blood? What proof did I have that he was mine and not the son of the priest? What proof did I have that I was the father?

Summer came while I was still feeling lost, searching for a solution. Mariam's belly was growing and she could no longer hide her pregnancy. She stayed home and became very nervous and emotional. Her mother discovered her pregnancy despite her weak vision and became stricter with her. Mariam was not guilty of only Micho's death but that of the whole family.

Tension increased with the general excitement about a possible war. Nasser was making declarations about Sharm al-Sheikh that created a tense situation. Broadcasts around the world were incensed, and victory songs filled the airwaves and The Voice of the Arabs radio station. The streets were filled with young men, and the cafés broadcast programs through loudspeakers so all their customers could hear Nasser's voice and the revolutionary and liberation songs. Streets in Jerusalem were filled with victory arches, pictures of Nasser, and stories about the liberation of Jaffa and its shores. People wondered about the fate of Jewish families who had occupied Arab homes and driven away their Palestinian owners, reducing them to a life of homelessness. They wondered about the beaches once they recovered them.

Excitement filled the streets, and young men drove in cars waving their shirts and shouting, "Palestine, we are coming." Famous singers chanted victory and liberation songs, while others sang about Arab unity being born in the heart of Jerusalem. Women formed small groups for military training and first aid. They met in schools and began training a few days before the war started. When Sarah tried to join them, my mother took her away and brought her to the village to protect her and to protect me. When they arrived that morning I was at school, listening to the news of the activities in Sharm al-Sheikh and the king's decision to join the war. The front grew wider and included all the countries surrounding Israel except Lebanon. When the school guardian announced their arrival, I rushed them to my room in total disbelief.

I was in a state of total disarray as a result of my circumstances, the war, my mother and Sarah staying in my miserable room, and Mariam harassing me. How to handle all this pressure? I was moved by lingering enthusiasm and Waddah's memory, Haifa and Jaffa, a poem and emotions I had not experienced before this summer. I fell victim to my feelings, reacted strongly to the news on the radio, and roamed the streets, driven by the enthusiasm and chaos. Mariam visited me with her goat to remind me of our situation; I felt disgust and aversion toward her. She tapped on the door and on my window. Sarah answered her knock and asked what she wanted. "I want Ibrahim," replied Mariam. Sarah said loudly, to make sure that I could hear her, "Ibrahim isn't here, he's in Jerusalem. What do you want from him?"

She examined Mariam from head to toe, then asked maliciously, "Are you Mariam?"

Mariam did not reply, acting as if she hadn't heard her. She thanked her and left while I was still hiding behind the window.

"Tell me frankly," my mother asked, "who is Mariam? Is what I heard about you and her true?"

I did not reply and reacted by putting my ear closer to the radio, asking her to listen instead to Nasser talking.

Sarah commented on the situation, "Love is for deranged people; are you deranged?"

My mother asked again, "Is it true then? Tell me frankly!"

I did not reply. She put the paring knife down and said, "As if we don't have enough trouble. When your sister marries you must go with her to Saudi Arabia and I'll accompany you. You're her brother; you're in charge. Your loud-mouthed father is not up to the responsibility. You are all we have; you are our support and all that's left for me in this world. You are my life."

She then looked at me in a way that wrenched my heart from its roots. Our relationship had never been emotional. She was not in the habit of addressing me with such sweet words, or maybe she did, but Waddah and his shadow blurred the situation for me. My father used to repeat, while looking at me,

"This boy feeds on mud, God have mercy on us."

I grew up with this feeling, believing that I was a rotten fruit that would fall from the tree before it ripened. I was pale and weak, while Waddah was tall like a palm tree. One day the tree fell and disintegrated, leaving only Sarah and the replacement child, "the lamb that replaced the palm tree." I had heard that expression very often and repeated it in my subconscious. It hurt me very deeply; on the other hand, perhaps I didn't hear it but simply imagined it. Who knows how memory and remembrance work? Do we truly remember what we see or rather what we feel and hide in our subconscious? It didn't matter; the result was conclusive since I felt that I was a boy who fed on mud, while Waddah was a palm tree. My mother was disheartened and she broke my heart when she said, "If anything should happen to you, I would kill myself. Once I lost Waddah and your father left, I had no one but you. You are my eyes, you are my life."

She then looked at me with her sad eyes and said pleadingly, "Don't you dare leave me like your father."

I reassured her, "Is this possible, Mother? You are our treasure, you are dear to us and the queen of all mothers."

When she lowered her head, I saw her thin gray hair and the skin under it. It broke my heart, and I thought that she didn't deserve all that had happened to her. She was left without a husband, without a son to take care of her and no brothers to lean on, and here we were, a war threatening us.

I whispered to her, "If you were given the choice between me and Jerusalem, which one would you choose?"

She was shaken by my question. She stared at me, her hand holding the knife stiffened, then she asked, scared, "What question is this?"

I said delicately, "It is for information's sake only; which of the two would you choose?"

She did not reply and went back to peeling the vegetables, but I insisted, "Let's suppose they take Jerusalem."

She raised her head and stared at me with the same look that scared me as a child. I felt as if I had returned to my childhood while she stayed old-looking. I saw her eyes fill with tears of helplessness. Defeated, she bent her head and didn't say a word. I was sorry and regretted my question when I saw her shrinking head and the skin of her skull under the thinning gray hair. I apologized to her and turned my attention to the radio. Nasser was delivering an important speech that determined the fate of the Arab nation and presaged a war. When my mother heard him she said, spontaneously, "May God protect this voice," and went back to peeling her vegetables. She pricked up her ears listening to the radio.

She loved Nasser and believed that, had Waddah lived during his rule, he would have been like him. Jealous, I used to ask her, "And me?" She used to reply, "Be diligent and study, eat well, and you will grow up to become a man like Waddah." Here I was, a grown man, I ate well and studied well, but I did not become like Waddah. Oh, Mariam, where is the way?

In the morning I accompanied my mother and my sister to Bab al-Amoud after I had made conflicting promises, one to my frightened mother, another to Nasser and his dreams, and a third to Jerusalem, though Nasser's promise was my promise to Jerusalem.

Mariam's brothers arrived seconds before the war started. They rushed to the village seeking a resolution for the scandal. They had left their work in Brazil, and, despite the state of emergency declared in many ports and airports, they had come to save face and their dignity in a village waiting to see bloodshed. Honor killing is part of tradition, and only blood washes away the shame brought about by a girl. Mariam ran away and hid in the church, then came to warn me despite my dodging her earlier. She knocked at my door, then the window under the fig tree, and whispered, "Run,

run, Eissa and Tony's bullets are near." A few minutes later I heard a man call my name, "Ya Ibrahim," followed by a hail of bullets.

I hid in a cave under the fig tree, then I sneaked out through the vineyards on a muddy, tortuous road until I reached the outskirts of Jerusalem. I saw young men wearing khaki fatigues, running and training to fight, followed by a military car. I joined them and continued to run with them until we reached Bab al-Amoud. I left them and entered the shopping area and made it to my house with the call for the dawn prayer. My mother, who was awake, opened the door and burst into tears when she saw me. My extreme fatigue and the dust of the road on my face reminded her of Waddah.

In the morning I saw young men in the alley standing in line, training to disassemble and clean their weapons. An officer used his revolver to teach them, then showed them how to throw a grenade. The equipment was old, but the young men were singing with the radio that broadcast news of victory and the liberation of West Jerusalem, Haifa, and Jaffa. I was watching them from the window, and I felt embarrassed that while people were celebrating the liberation of Jerusalem, I was hiding from Mariam and her brothers. If only it hadn't been for Mariam and her son!

In this flux and excitement Mariam was lost, I placed her on the back burner. I began to mix with people and got involved with the political situation. It took a few days for me to be drawn into a flood of events and the excitement of my father, who was trying to visualize the situation after the liberation. He believed that Jerusalem would become a different city, a new Jerusalem, or rather the old one but without divisions and barriers. The wall would collapse, and the masses would rush to the coast, to the port of Haifa, to boats and to trade with a vaster world, a wider horizon, and cut across barriers and history. We had become a nation that had awakened and was taking control of its future. The whole atmosphere reminded me of my dreams and of Waddah, while Mariam had receded to the back of my memory, an old story tossed by the wind. It was an insignificant story not worthy of being part of history. History had come alive in my documents, and I had become the backbone of history. I was writing historical stories, and in the midst of heroic stories, the individual stories shrank. That is how Mariam was reduced to a pale memory, soon forgotten, a past memory of a lost love.

Mariam and her memory were lost; so was I, and so was Jerusalem. We had become two individuals on separate shores divided by a river and an occupation army. I had become a member of a revolutionary group that became part of a cell active across the Jordan River. We had become the symbol of exile.

The Icon

Years passed while I moved between capitals, organizations, and companies. I joined an American oil company that transferred me from Kuwait to London, to Rome, and then to New York. There I married an American activist in the anti-Vietnam War movement. The marriage lasted two years and produced no children, but my wife gave me a green card. I moved to Austria and married an Austrian woman, but we divorced a year later. Then there were Eva, Evelyn, and Suzy; then I married an Arab woman and moved to Saudi Arabia. There I got in touch with my sister, Sarah, and I found out how successful the stone project had become. My brother-in-law took me around the country and showed me all the buildings constructed with stones from the West Bank. Those stones were very much in demand in the Gulf countries: Dubai, Sharja, Abu Dhabi, and Umm al-Qiwayn. The market was very active, and oil flowed in abundance. We swam in petrodollars. I entered the market full steam ahead, importing stones and laborers from the West Bank. My father's project was successful, and to prove myself I built houses and factories and sold apartments. I became an entrepreneur during the Gulf War and provided the American army with stone saws and tractors to dig trenches and open roads. I became very rich, I was a millionaire. I formed a charitable organization bearing my name to help Palestinian widows and orphans. I had become an economic icon and a generous contributor to the needy, a protector of the arts and culture though I had published no more than a few political essays and short stories.

I became a respected and well-known financial advisor. I returned to the homeland with other returnees, and I stepped on Jerusalem's soil after a long absence that felt like a million years. My mother died a few months after my return, and my father had died a few years earlier, having left us some circulars. I took care of the circulars, and bought a house in Ramallah, where I lived served by a Filipina maid and an excellent Moroccan cook, but without a wife, children, or friends. I lost touch with my companions; some had died and found peace, and others were lost like me. I was left without solace, without feelings, and without a hobby. My interest in literature was gone, and gone was the nostalgia of the soul. The only thing I had was a new red passport that allowed me to cross the bridge with special privileges. I had become an important person.

One day, as I was visiting my charitable organization, al-Nour, I received a strange phone call that brought back the memories of the past and forgotten dreams. It was a call from the priest, who had become an important archbishop. We had a friendly conversation;

he reminded me of the village days, of our friendship, of our hobbies and our literary dreams. I told him that literature had forsaken me; he laughed at the joke and said that a man is the result of his actions and I was a man of action. I took his meaning and expressed my willingness to donate any amount he needed for projects. He was happy with my response, which confirmed our friendship, our long-lasting relationship and his trust in me.

I had an uneasy feeling following his response. It reminded me of a past I had denied. I tried to probe his intentions by mentioning the village and the past, hoping he would say what he truly felt. He replied politely and subtly that times had changed, that it was another period with different events and different people. He explained gently that had the past happened in the present, the story would have been different. I understood from his words that he did not resent my behavior, or condemn me for what I had done, and he invited me to visit his office in Jerusalem. He told me about his confrontations with the forces of occupation, and his strong political stand that had become the talk of the town and the subject of newspaper articles.

Things had truly changed, and times now were different; even peoples' features had changed. We had grown older and needed help to walk. I was using a cane for my evening walks, though I was still strong and as straight as a palm tree. My hair was thinning and gray, and my hands were covered with liver spots; I had indigestion and other ailments of old age. I suffered from high blood pressure, diabetes, and heart arrhythmia.

My arteries were chronically blocked, and I had them cleaned regularly in London. I still loved women, and I remembered Mariam; I loved culture, knowledge, and I believed in money as a motivating factor. I trusted human capacity and the technology of information. It was a world different from the one my generation had known in the sixties, the seventies, and the nineties. We were in the year 2000 and we had become an Authority; I was a monetary authority, and with money I was able to reach the authorities in power and the events that took place behind the scenes. We were called Palestine instead of the West Bank, and we now turned to the USA instead of the Soviet Union for help and support. The Soviet Union had disappeared, and the world had moved toward a market economy. We had been privatized: we had become private Palestine and divided Palestine, and we had changed. We had become followers instead of revolutionaries. We were nothing but shrapnel. I, too, had changed. I was a different Ibrahim, and Jerusalem was a different city. I dreamed of worries, loneliness, emptiness, Alzheimer's, and the loss of Jerusalem.

I walked with the archbishop in the marketplace as the day wound down and people were leaving. They hid in their houses to escape the soldiers' boots. The covered streets and the narrow alleys were empty except for the lights of the municipality, the street sweepers, and small trucks that zipped gracefully through the alleys like children's toys and picked up cardboard boxes and garbage bags. Jerusalem had become very dirty; it was neglected and looked like the face of an old woman. Gone were the old days, the days of our youth and our hearts! We walked past the Armenian convent, which reminded me of Mariam, jasmine, bougainvilleas, the China tree, and our nights spent at the hostel. I had been handsome then, and the world had been very beautiful, filled with hopes and dreams. I had had white wings like the Jerusalem doves and the house sparrows that flew over the domes and bell towers. I had felt I could soar with the souls throughout time; I had felt ethereal.

Jerusalem was full of souls, full of visions and history. People's houses in the alleys were arch-shaped and built with old stones that had witnessed our ancestors' sorrows and Christ's fears. Those same stones had seen various religions, the rule of the Romans, the Bedouin tribes, and cities buried under the ruins and layers of earth. Here we were, the two of us, walking on the ruins of the past the way the next generation will walk on our generation. It will be a different generation, though, one that will have doubts about its predecessors. Have we made mistakes? But who has not? Nevertheless, collective mistakes do not absolve individual sins.

I turned toward the archbishop as he walked, absorbed in his thoughts and I wished he would open up and tell me what he had so far not said. In a way, I knew what he was going to say. He would repeat what has been said in churches since time immemorial and in Christ's sermons. He would talk about remorse, love and purgation, tolerance and charity. This has been said in every prayer, in all sermons and in every language, but what did he hide in his heart, what?

With the innocence of a young child trying to find my way to a deeper conversation, I said, "Tell me, my friend, do you believe in the soul?"

He smiled gently as he continued to walk, looking straight ahead, examining the piles of garbage, the shops and the faces of the sad salesmen in the darkness of the road. He said kindly, "Of course, I do," and added slowly, as he continued to stare at the garbage and people's faces, "And I believe in the flesh and peoples' sorrows."

He then turned to me and asked, gently, "But tell me, do you believe in the soul?"

If I believed in the soul? I did, and also in the flesh. There has never been any doubt about that in my mind. I am not sure anymore if I believe in people. There is something else I had my doubts about; I did not know if we were the soul, and if not, who was the soul? Is Jerusalem a city without a soul in this real world?

I said, confused and disturbed, as I was becoming more and more aware of the state of being we had reached and the looming loss of Jerusalem, "If Jerusalem has a soul, why does it accept injustice?"

He did not reply, so I continued, "I don't understand the importance of the soul if injustice is its end product."

He didn't utter a word and listened to me without comment. I fell silent, lost in my thoughts, imagining what I would say and where I would begin and how he would react. Finally, I stood in the middle of the street, too fed up to beat around the bush, and said very quickly, "By God, tell me, do you know anything about Mariam?"

The archbishop gave me a long stare, then said slowly, "Do you truly want to know where Mariam is?"

With hands at my side, I searched inside myself for an answer. I found doubts, fear, anxiety, and desolation. I felt like running away from the situation, but I took hold of myself and opened a new subject to wrap matters up. I said, "You see, my friend, where this has gotten us?"

We had reached the edge of Bab al-Khalil, where the cement, the floodlights, and a bridge that stood above a thousand roads could be found. The cement was surrounded by a fence that resembled prison bars. West Jerusalem was staring at us and reminding us of a face we had forgotten since the Nakba and the partition of the city in two, when the body was separated from the soul. Who would be able to unite us? How could I find my soul lost over a thousand roads? This was not my way. I was a train that lost its whistle and its direction, that was derailed. My soul was like a spaceship forced to land and unable to take off again. I went around looking for her, then like a coward pretended not to understand. I had forgotten my sorrows, but deep inside, in the deepest corners of my soul, I was still that writer with the soul of an artist who did not dare tell the truth.

The archbishop asked me once more, "Do you really want to know?"

I took him by the hand and we stood before a beautiful European woman, an unknown face that did not remind me of anyone, a face that would deny me and one that I would deny. I was presently, under a holy sky, filled with a nostalgia for a certain kiss and the road ahead. I wanted to know what I had denied, how much I changed, and how to go back.

I looked at him but did not reply. What could I say? Would he understand me? Did I understand myself? I have returned a changed man, and I wanted to know, but fear stopped me. I wanted to know where I stood, what I wanted and what I was doing. Part of me was that writer with the soul of an artist pinned down by fear, while the other part of me was insatiable, limitless, and unable to find a harbor. Who was I now, at this moment? Looking around me, I saw a jungle filled with wolves. How would I be able to go back to what I was? Who could pull me back? Nothing could bring back the innocence of the past except what belonged to the past; where was Mariam?

The archbishop turned to me and asked, insisting, "Do you truly want to know?"

"Of course I want to know."

"Listen to me, then. There is a man who knows about her, or rather a man who would reveal things to you."

"What do you mean?" I asked.

He explained, "Listen to me carefully, and think about it. There is a man who is like a priest, with special gifts. He reads a person's thoughts, predicts the future, and knows things we don't know, such as hypnosis, reincarnation, and telepathy and similar matters, you know."

"No, I don't know," I said. "Do you mean things dealing with spirits?"

He continued, "I truly don't know, but Yvonne says strange things about him. People say that the priest-like man uncovers hidden matters, sees the future, and miraculously finds lost things."

"You mean a fortuneteller or a charlatan!"

"I don't know," he said, "but Yvonne says credible things about him."

"Do you believe them?" I asked.

He explained his position, "I do not know, but, to be honest, I have read books about such a science or rather that art and I have begun to have doubts. What if there are things we don't know? What if there were a world we haven't reached yet?"

I stood in the middle of the street, stared at him in disbelief and said, "Of all people, you're the last one I would have expected to say such things."

"I'm puzzled by what I read, and I would like to know." He then added, "People say things about this man, this priest, things I don't understand."

I asked him, "What do you mean, in a nutshell? Do you want me to go to that priest to find out where Mariam is? Is this possible?"

He raised his hand in a sign of impatience and smiled patiently saying, "Listen to me, listen. I'm not pushing you to do it; all I am saying is try. What would you lose if you tried?"

"Is this possible, Archbishop? Do you want me to go to a charlatan to look for her? Is this possible?"

"He is not a charlatan, at least I don't think so. He is truly unusual and he piqued my curiosity. I followed his activities, and I discovered unusual things about him. He was raised in a convent, and there he mastered the art of decorating icons and carving saints' statues. He took up photography, then music, and finally studied theology. Have you heard about Reike?"

"No, I have not."

"Would you like to know something about it?"

"The only one whose whereabouts I want to know is Mariam. How can I find her?"

He didn't reply and continued to walk, tapping the ground with his cane, but I felt he was tapping inside my head. I pulled his arm and pleaded with him, saying, "You're hiding things from me. What do you know? Where did she go? What happened to her? Did she give birth to a son or daughter? Tell me, please!"

He stared long at me as we stood under a street light that shined on his head. His hair resembled a white halo spread over the skin of his skull. I thought about time passing and how old the archbishop had grown, and me too. Time had taken so much away from us. What was left for us to do in this life? I was holding on to him to find out what I still needed to know and said impatiently, "Tell me, please. I have nothing more to hold on to and I have no one left in this world, neither a daughter nor a son; I have no descendants. The only thing I have left is the past. Let me know, tell me about her, give me a sign, tell me please, I miss her."

He mumbled, "Despite all the money!"

"Money doesn't mean a thing, believe me; it doesn't mean a thing. At this age, as you know, all the money in the world is useless."

He shook his head, saying, "Now you know."

I replied, angrily, "You're punishing me for the past! You're enjoying seeing me suffer. This isn't a Christian attitude; I'm so surprised."

He stopped and protested saying, "I told you all I know; I gave you the beginning of the thread. What could you lose if you try?"

Hurting, I yelled at him, "Do you mean to say that I would find her with the help of a charlatan?! Is that the beginning of the thread? Is that the best you can do?"

"That is all I can do. I can do something else, as well, I can send you to the priest in the bus of the Association, tomorrow."

I asked, "Why are you so insistent, why? What is the secret? I don't understand."

"He is the beginning of the thread," he replied, adding, "Try, you won't lose anything if you try. If you find anything out let me know, I'm curious; I want to know what you know."

The following day Aziz, the driver of the Association, came and told me that he would take me to the priest. I boarded his small bus that was filled with books and a basket of fruit that Yvonne was sending to the priest.

Aziz was a man in his fifties, of medium height, with a big belly and thin hair. His breathing sounded like an air pump. He had a lisp and pronounced the 'r' like an 'e'; he stuttered often and continuously cleared his throat. He was annoying, and I wished he would stop talking for a few minutes at least, but Aziz didn't stop talking and addressed me as *ustadh*, teacher. I wished I could throw him from the bus window to have some peace. He told me strange stories that defied belief and puzzled the mind. He told me stories about the priest being like Christ, resurrecting the dead, curing the sick, and helping the blind see. He performed unbelievable things.

I looked at him and smiled, furious, wondering if this man was my messenger to knowledge. He was half-stupid, half-crazy, and he stuttered—quite a combination.

I looked out the window at the road to see where we were. But the road that curved and twisted across the hills and the Jerusalem mountains was misleading. There were olive trees, grapevines, fig trees, and almond trees everywhere. The earth was the color of henna and the rocks were milky white. The land was divided by barriers and chains and groups of peasants; men and women were going to their farms, some of which were high up as if to protect them from an imminent invasion, or maybe to put them closer to heaven!

The driver said, breathing heavily, "Do you know something, ustadh, there's a dervish in the ruins who befriended the jinn. He wears shabby clothes and cuts his beard every two to three years. He sleeps in the mosque or in the cemetery between the tombs, and if you meet him on the road he neither hears nor sees you.

He survives on charitable donations. He picks up food from fruit stands and bread from bakeries and no one objects. Do you know why? Because he is blessed."

"You mean crazy," I said.

"Ask God's forgiveness, ustadh, he is rather blessed. Be careful sir, ya ustadh, dealing with spirits is a serious matter. If they heard you, they would be very upset."

"Really?" I replied.

"Really," he responded.

I smiled and thought that this was the beginning of the thread mentioned by the archbishop. Aziz went on talking enthusiastically, "Do you know what he said the day the earthquake struck? Do you remember that earthquake, when the ground opened, houses and shops collapsed, and people moved about like butterflies and ants pushing with their shoulders to make way and escape God's wrath? The dervish had warned them. Do you believe it, ustadh? I swear to God he did a few days before it happened. He had a seizure and began to crawl like a baby, put his ears to the ground and shouted these words to the people: 'To the mountains, creatures of God! To the mountains, to the mountains!' Are you listening to me ustadh?"

"Of course I am," I replied.

"I thought you had dozed off."

"I didn't doze off," I said, "I am listening to you attentively, and I wonder what happened next. Did they go to the mountains?"

"I wish they had gone! They made fun of him and felt sorry for him. They were convinced that the jinn had inhabited his body," he explained.

"And then?" I asked.

"Nothing, ya ustadh, the earth moved and the ground opened, swallowing the people, the racks, and the shops."

"And then?"

"The country was covered with a thick layer of dust and people were buried under the ruins."

"And the dervish?" I asked

He explained, "He went up to the dome and continued to shout, 'People of God, to the mountains, to the mountains.' They all ran away while he stayed on top of the dome as the ground swallowed everything except the dome. He didn't move from his place and neither did the dome, can you believe it?"

I shook my head and mumbled angrily.

He turned to me and said, "You don't believe me? He is a blessed man, he predicts the future, people's fate, and sees the invisible, like the priest. Don't you believe it?"

I ground my teeth and grumbled, thinking to myself that this was the beginning of the thread. I told Aziz to hurry up and take me to the priest.

"At your service, ya ustadh," he said.

He seemed pleased with himself because he was showing me the path to goodness.

We finally reached the desolate ground and crossed the town, or the place referred to as a town. It consisted of a mere asphalt street, which gradually filled with holes and crevasses, and a mixture of sand and asphalt. The bus was having difficulty moving on that road. I closed the windows to avoid the sand and the dust of the road and the curious eyes that were examining me. I was a stranger, and they were at the end of the earth, on top of a mountain that reached the sky but not the limits of the municipality. But there was a TV antenna, and a single telephone line that connected the mayor to the police and the suburbs of Jerusalem. The municipality had not arrived there, and there was no electricity, no sewage, no running water, and the only TV antenna at the guesthouse worked thanks to Aziz's frequent trips and a battery. He would take the empty battery and bring a new one in the bus of the Association, an organization that had branches in distant areas, in villages, and in the suburbs of Jerusalem. The priest Michael moved back and forth in the bus, visiting the various offices of the Association and the clinics. What was he doing? Was he reviving the dead, curing the blind, or providing this wasteland with electricity, sewage, and water from Jerusalem?

The bus stopped in front of the clinic of the Association. It was in part of an old building originally owned by a family. Half of its members had left; the men had gone to the city, and some had gone to the Israeli settlements. Only Umm Muhammad, her daughters-in-law, and a horde of children stayed behind.

Umm Muhammad peered through the entrance of the house adjacent to the clinic and asked Aziz if he had brought the medicine. He shouted back that he had. She then asked about the *mahaleb* and the cigarettes, which he had brought. This earned him an invitation to tea together with his guest.

Aziz turned to me, winked, and whispered happily, "The radar is already at work. They noticed you and now you'll experience the generosity of the wasteland and Umm Muhammad. There will be pies, mahaleb, figs, cheese, and village bread. God sent you!"

He patted his belly and smiled at me encouragingly, as if I were responsible for the invitation, for the curiosity of the mother-in-law, her daughters-in-law, and their army of children. I saw a child get into the bus and hide between the boxes while the others stood behind the windows pressing him on with cries, "Hurry up Tawfiq, hurry up." Aziz scolded them, chasing the boy out of the bus. The mother-in-law shouted from behind the door, "Sakineh, mind the children! Tawfiq, Sakineh!"

Sakineh arrived, preceded by her big belly, her large hips, and a plastic slipper visible from under her dress. She went on slapping one, pinching another, and twisting a third's arm, while they ran around like a flock of chickens being attacked by a ferocious cat as she shouted and threatened them. She later talked to me cheerfully, as if she were not the same person who seconds earlier had been shouting, swearing, and promising all sorts of punishment. She said, "Welcome, welcome, tea and village bread are coming. Do come in, please, consider this your house."

I smiled and tried to be gentle, but the children's attitude and the racket they created, coupled with Umm Muhammad's spying, reminded me of my past days in the village, of Mariam and our story. Weren't these the people responsible for escalating matters, for our scandal, for turning Mariam's mother against her daughter, and the arrival of the brothers to wash away the dishonor and pursue me? Had it not been for the war I wouldn't be alive today, or I would be living in this cave, with the people of the cave. Many efforts have been made to change them; I have tried so hard to change them, but in vain. Now I am told about this priest who cures the sick and revives the dead!

I hurried to the clinic to examine the place; there was an examination room with a modest bed, a white curtain, a medicine cabinet, and a waiting room for the patients. Where then does he cure the sick and raise the dead? How does he fool them? I could not see electric connections, loudspeakers, and listening devices, or even a crystal ball! The receptionist saw me and inquired about the reason for my presence. I pretended to be looking for the bathroom. There I washed my face so that I would be alert to the priest and his maneuvers. As I was getting ready to leave the clinic Aziz arrived, stammering with a mischievous smile on his face, and announced, "There is village bread, figs, cheese waiting under the fig tree—nothing can beat that."

I found myself sitting among those people, eating, drinking, and burping, listening to Umm Muhammad's stories and jinn stories. I heard some unforgettable stories that made me despair of ever changing this people. What could be done to change a people who lived with the mentality of prehistoric times, feeding on stories, illusions, and superstitions!

Aziz brought me back to reality as he nudged me, saying, "Take a fig from the blessed hand of the *hajjeh*—go ahead, taste it."

He took the fig from her hand, cut it, and gave me half. I tried to peel it, but it slipped and fell on the ground. This amused the group, and women roared with laughter, attracting the attention of the bands of children. They whispered among themselves, then broke into an appropriate song for the occasion, saying, "Shake the fig tree, fig collector, shake the fig tree." The women's laughter increased as they heard the song, forcing Umm Muhammad to intervene, "Enough you all, behave. Go get the tea. And you children, you devils, go away. Tawfiq, go away! Leave us in peace to talk and entertain ourselves."

She then turned to me and inquired about the purpose of my visit to the clinic, whether I was complaining of an illness, God forbid: a stroke or cancer? Or if I had a son in an Israeli prison?

I replied evasively, "Something like that."

Umm Muhammad slapped her hands together and said, clearing her throat, "God Almighty, I knew it. The moment I saw you I said to myself that you must be hurting, and that you have a son who's been thrown in prison. Is he condemned? For how long?"

She didn't wait for my reply but went on to explain that my visit to the clinic would not be in vain because the priest is an enlightened man who can read the future. He cures the sick and prepares talismans to undo magic and release prisoners. She then undertook to tell a strange story that had nothing to do with the priest but that was concerned with his area of expertise, about the prediction of the future and the force of spirits. She said, "Listen to this story, believe it and believe in God. My maternal grandmother was blessed and befriended a spirit. My paternal grandfather had a son in a Turkish prison in Istanbul, during Ottoman times. He had a high position but was later imprisoned. He stayed there for two years, and then it was said that they might hang him. My grandfather was crying and wailing like a woman and became as thin as a thread; he didn't eat or drink and refused to see anyone. His wife went to my grandmother and implored her to do something for the sake of her husband and her imprisoned son. My grandmother went to the tomb of a holy man, a *wali*, where there were two tombs: that of the wali and that of his son. She spent forty days there. One day she pulled her clothes up, mounted the wali and began shouting."

I interrupted her and asked sarcastically, "Mounted the wali?"

Aziz explained, saying, "She means his tomb. Do not make fun of the actions of the spirits. Do not take them lightly. They would be upset with you."

Umm Muhammad scolded him and came to my defense because I was her guest; she said, "Well, let him ask, he won't joke about such matters."

She resumed her story, "My grandmother mounted the tomb and shouted, 'Wali of God, for my ancestors' sake, bring Hassan back.'"

I suddenly became aware of the abrupt silence that had fallen over the people sitting under the fig tree and behind the clinic where the children were playing.

Everybody was listening to the story with wide eyes. They were amazed by the perplexed expressions on the faces of the women, Aziz, and the assistant. Their fear and awe were transmitted to the children, a fear that controlled them and would never relinquish them no matter how old they got and how far away they went. Even I, despite my doubts and my suspicious mind, felt a certain awe that stirred old feelings in my subconscious. I was, after all, the son of this land and the alleys of Jerusalem.

She stared at us and asked, "Do you know what happened?"

We did not reply, overcome by a heavy silence that was disturbed only by Aziz's heavy breathing. She went on, "That night she slept between the two tombs. At midnight she heard some noise inside and a conversation in the tombs. One asked the other why she was sleeping, why she didn't go home. The second night she heard louder and more powerful words wondering why she was still asleep and hadn't gone back home. The third night she heard a noise like an earthquake. The tomb shook, a light filled the place and dispelled the darkness, and then a voice addressed her, ordering her to get up and go back home. She went on sleeping. This continued for forty days. On the last day he called her and told her to go home because Hassan was free. She went on sleeping. The other voice said: 'See how stubborn she is, call Hassan.' Darkness was dispelled, and she saw the full form of Hassan. He told her to tell his father that he would arrive home that same day at the call for the noon prayer. His family waited, and as the muezzin was calling for the noon prayer, Hassan entered the house. Well, what do you think?"

We were unable to utter a single word. A heavy silence fell on the place, interrupted only by Aziz's breathing. A child moved, but everybody hushed him, urging him to stay still while they were trying to imagine the tomb of the wali as the hajjeh was riding it, swearing by her ancestors, imploring the wali for Hassan's safe return.

Umm Muhammad tapped my hand and said, offering comfort, "Your son too will return, God willing. Just meet the priest and implore him to intervene on your behalf."

The waiting room at the clinic was swarming with people coming from all over the wasteland and other villages. They had heard about the priest and his intercession with the spirits. There were people suffering from diabetes, cancer, stomach ulcers, incurable coughs. Infertile women, abandoned women, and old maids had also come looking for a miracle. The priest had begun his work behind closed doors, while the silence of the waiting patients conveyed apprehension and an acceptance of the presence of spirits in the air. No one knew exactly how they moved or to where they flew, but people generally believed that spirits were everywhere. They awoke and showed interest in human beings when a blessed person sought their help.

A woman whispered her question to another, "Well, what did he tell you?"

The woman replied submissively, "He said that cancer has no other cure but faith. If a person believes and is convinced that he will recover, he will, God willing."

"Is your father cured, then?"

The woman tapped her knee lightly and said sorrowfully, "How can he be? I must admit, though that his condition has changed."

"Does he feel better?"

"Much better."

I couldn't help butting in. I asked her, "What about the expenses?"

She looked at me, surprised and disapproving. I explained, apologetic, "I'm sorry, good people, but a person in need is a slave of his circumstances."

They stared at me, examining my clothes and my appearance, as I obviously did not belong to their group. I didn't look like a needy person. I reacted quickly, saying, "My son is imprisoned in Israel."

Their looks changed immediately, and one of them said loudly, "May God help you, I hope he will return safely."

The other woman said compassionately, "May God help you, just have faith, show a good intention, and ask the priest to write you a talisman."

"And the cost?" I asked.

The first woman twisted her hand and said, "Well, I do not know, each according to his means." Then she stared at me and asked me with the same curiosity, "Pray tell me, how much do you intend to pay?"

I thought for a second and then said ambiguously, "As much as he requests."

She said with much confidence, "He doesn't ask. You donate what you want, as much as you want, from one shekel to a hundred. You pay what you can and you leave him, God willing, feeling better and at peace. People say that some leave his office flying."

I expressed my admiration and belief and said, "They left flying?"

She explained, "That is to say they walked as if they were flying. That's what people say."

I was filled with anger. This is the ambiance he created, feeding on people's ignorance, on the peasants' poverty, bleeding the misery of the needy. He was feeding them opium, and if he were asked he would say that they were ready to be exploited, the way we were brought up since our childhood, it was fed to us with milk. We grew up, and our pain and our defeats grew with us. Is this the beginning of the thread?

It was late afternoon when I entered his examination room. He was standing near his desk, a pile of papers and notebooks before him. They did not inspire awe or suggest the use of magic. I wondered what he used to hypnotize his patients. He was not a priest in the traditional sense of the word but looked more like a Buddhist monk with his long brown robe, his long sleeves, the rope tied around his waist, and his sandals. Had his head been shaved in the middle, I would have said he was a Franciscan priest, but his long, thick hair proved otherwise. I estimated his age to be no more than thirty.

He approached me and said in a friendly manner, "My name is Michael. I am the priest. Have a seat. How can I help you?"

I remained standing, not knowing where to begin. Should I tell him that he was a charlatan, the opiate of the people? Should I talk about spirits and legends and tell him that this was a proof of our defeat? Should I ask him about raising the dead, curing the blind, and bringing back the missing? His eyes, his features, and his quiet voice gave me pause. I came in inflated like a balloon, and I soon deflated. Anger had taken hold of me and filled me with doubt, sadness, and bitterness because the question was bigger than I. I could not fathom how we had stooped so low. For years we have been working for the people and the cause, for a revolution and change, and now I return to find this! We have lost so many lives, we have fought so many battles for the sake of revival and the cause, and then comes this impostor and takes people back to the past and to the dark ages. I will not remain silent, I will turn things upside down on his head and that of the Association and its members. But something in his eyes and his strong nerves held me back.

He said quietly, "You seem tense and agitated. Sit down, sit down."

He took me by the arm and seated me on an old bamboo chair in the middle of the room. He looked me straight in the eyes for a few seconds and then whispered with the voice of a magician, "Don't worry, don't worry. I'll find out the cause of your ailment. Sit, relax and don't worry. You'll be all right, you'll be all right."

I asked, concerned, "Will you use hypnotism?"

He replied quietly and frankly, "If we need it, but for now I will use only energy."

Fear made me shrink, and I shouted, "What energy?"

He moved a few steps away from me, watched me, and asked, "You don't have any idea?"

I replied rudely and sarcastically to hide my fear and my emotions, "If you mean doing the work of Christ, reviving the dead and such things, of course I know."

He did not move but said quietly, "I said energy and nothing else."

He then smiled and said, "Oh! I understand. You were listening to people's stories about undoing magic, calling spirits, and such matters."

I asked him rudely if he could deny those stories. He moved away from me, went to his desk, held a book in his hands, then said in English, "This is Meditation and Medication. This is energy, human energy and its power, the hidden force in human beings."

I commented rudely and sarcastically, "Do you mean Christ and His powers?"

He replied quietly and confidently, "There are proofs that Christ used energy to raise the dead, cure the blind, double the bread, and similar actions. We do not know exactly, but all proofs point to energy and charge. Christ was advanced for his time and even our time. He knew the secret of energy and human secrets and human power. He knew what was stored in the depth of the human being. Do you know that a person uses only twenty percent of his capacities and the remaining energy remains stored, unexploited, and unknown? In other words, a human being is a live time bomb whose fuse has not been removed. Who would remove the fuse and let the jinni out of the bottle? Tell me rather who imprisoned the giant in the bottle?"

I said, surprised, "I don't know, do you?"

"Of course I do."

I asked, carefully, while watching him, "May I know who imprisoned him?"

He said, sure of himself, "Religion, sex, and civilization."

I said, amazed, "I don't understand!"

He shook his head, saying, "You won't understand now, not now. At your age and with all the programming and the taming you've gone through, you can't understand. It's not easy. How old are you—sixty? Seventy? Imagine after all those years and the programming you've gone through, it's not easy to comprehend. Do you follow me?"

I shook my head, and he continued with confidence, "What I mean exactly is that you are programmed and you can't get rid of the taming and the customs and beliefs easily. There is also the impact of your knowledge, your experiences, and your readings. It won't be easy to erase all that. It isn't normal to exit from all your files and become, suddenly, a new file; it is impossible to do it. You are now ready, you are perfectly programmed, and the only approach that would work with you is hypnosis."

I yelled, victorious, as if I had awakened from a daze, "Aha! I understand. I knew that you resorted to hypnotism. Through hypnosis you can control their minds and remove them from their reality, isn't that so? You put them to sleep, you remove them from their world, then you use your will to instruct them to do what you like."

"Rather, what they like; and for your information, I don't remove them from their world but I introduce them to the spheres of energy; I remove the fuse and let them free. I do nothing but practice accumulation; I gather the dispersed charges in a crucible that becomes a light bomb. When it explodes, and the light illuminates the world, we become free of all restrictions."

"What restrictions? What do you mean?" I asked.

He explained, "The restrictions of the body and those of the soul, those of religion and nationalism and those of the Jews; even the Jews would not be Jews and would not be occupiers and the chosen people and all this nonsense. We would all be together without restrictions, without differences between religions and nationalities."

I stood up as if I had been bitten because I felt that he either was crazy or I had lost my mind. I said terrified, "What are you saying? I don't understand! Aren't you a priest? Tell me, who are you and what is your religion?"

"Is it so important for you to know who I am and what my religion is? Anyhow, I'm a human being, nothing more."

"And this robe?" I asked.

"It's only a formality."

"What about the convent?" I asked.

"It is a fertile ground that produces what fate allows. I am not one of them; I am not one of them."

"Who do you follow then?" I asked.

"I am for the human being."

"What about God?" I asked.

"God is for the human being."

"How do I find Him and reach Him?" I asked.

"Through energy. Concentrate deeply and you will find Him. Do you want my help? I'm ready. Let's try a simple procedure, and we will reach your depths."

I stood up and moved away from him. I said, "What do you mean? Do you want to make me lose control?"

"All I want is to make the void around you and remove the charges in order to reach your depths. Let me try, you might respond. I would know your pain and illnesses, I would know your secrets and your aspirations. With me you will get to the truth and find peace with yourself and with others."

I said angrily, "I am happy with the way I am."

He gave up and said, "All right, as you like, as you please."

He became aware of his defeatist speech, and took back his words, "I'm sorry, I'm sorry. I'm concerned with your well-being alone. Whenever you want, you can find me here, waiting for you. Any time, in any circumstance and all circumstances, I am at your service."

We both fell silent. I did not even thank him or apologize or accuse him of being a charlatan and a magician. All the accusations I had prepared this morning had evaporated and lost their meaning. I became nothing, just nothing, I was moving in a circle, I was confused and concerned, unaware of the difference between right and wrong, the reasonable and the unreasonable. I was certain of his fake nature first, and now I wondered if he were a charlatan or a magician. He didn't lie, he didn't deny, he didn't pretend to have supernatural powers. He didn't attribute to himself any role except accumulation. He did not mention stories of jinn and walis. He did not even mention God. He talked about energy, human beings, and faith. He talked about abilities stored in the depth of the individual. Is this charlatanism? Is this trickery? Or this is what the archbishop alluded to? I wish I knew.

I was about to tell the priest frankly what I thought of him, despite my state of bewilderment, struggling with my mind and emotions, trying to extract right from wrong and the possible from the impossible. Something happened at that same moment that changed the situation. We heard the shouting of a group of children and a tremor, followed by an uproar and wailing women. We heard Umm Muhammad's door slam and activity in the other room of the clinic where Aziz was waiting for me. The priest hesitated for a moment, then shot out, and I followed him. The accident had taken place in a narrow street at the edge of a very deep valley. The bus of the Association was hanging on the cliff, held only by a rock and the branches of an old oak tree with a thick trunk. Tawfiq, Sakineh's son, was at the wheel of the truck. His mother was shouting like a crazy woman, striking her cheeks, while her mother-in-law was slapping one palm against the other and shouting in Sakineh's face, "Miserable one, your son is lost," and thus adding to her agony. She pleaded for help from those who stood around her watching without coming to her rescue, only clearing their throats and shaking their heads. The larger the crowd, the louder Umm Muhammad and her daughter-in-law's shouting got. We also heard strange comments from some members of the crowd revealing different reactions to the incident. First there was the dialog between the mother-in-law, who blamed her daughter-in-law for allowing her son to drive the bus, while she denied it categorically, citing one of the children as a witness. She was pulling his hair trying to prove her innocence in the matter, constantly repeating, "Hey Said, did I let him drive? Was I with him?" The boy was trying to get away from her, and kicking her with his feet, but despite the pain she did not let him go and repeated her question, "Did I allow him?"

A woman whispered to another, covering her mouth with her hand, "This night is her night. I swear by God Almighty that he will divorce her."

I was distressed by their comment and scolded them for pronouncing her fate. I said, "Why should he divorce her, what did she do?"

They stared at me malevolently, then ignored me. One said to the other, "This is the man who said that his son is in prison."

The other replied, "Does that give him the right to interfere in other people's affairs? It's none of his business."

"Why is it none of my business?" I objected.

My voice was drowned by people's shouting, by the confusion and the preoccupation of those who were following the action in the branches of the oak tree. I saw the priest hanging on the branches trying to get to the bus. He had pulled his robe up revealing white legs and rubber sandals that helped him climb without slipping. My heart was beating very fast, and heavy sweat covered my forehead. I sat on the nearest rock and followed the action in a state of fear and anxiety. Was it fear, sadness, or anger that I felt in this environment? I saw the priest form a knot with his belt to pull the handle of the door open, then I saw Tawfiq in his arms like a little bird without feathers. When he threw him over to the people from that distance, I fainted.

When I recovered, Michael was sitting beside me, on the floor of the hospitality room. The floor was covered with rugs and cushions, there was a TV, Arabic coffee, and tea as well. When I opened my eyes he advised me to relax to get over my dizzy spell. The walls of the hospitality room were decorated with an enlarged photo of the Aqsa Mosque and a photo of the mayor. The door opened on a terrace, revealing the dark shadow of a climbing plant. I got up and sat beside the priest. Outside, the sky was clear, the day was pleasant, and the breeze that blew through the hospitality room gave me the sense that I was a passenger on a ship.

The smell of the village oven reached us from a distance, filling me with great appetite and touching my heart. It was at that moment that I felt the spirit of the homeland and its people: there was the shadow of the climbing plant, the smell of the evergreen cypress, the silvery blue sky, the almond blossom, and a spring that awakened one's sleepy emotions. This was the homeland we missed and to which we had returned, only to find that the past we knew had changed. Then there was this man, this sorcerer—what did he have to give us?

I turned to him and said, still weak, "Tell me, who are you?"

He smiled and asked, "Do you really want to know?"

I shook my head. Then, in response to my curiosity he said, "I don't know."

I observed him, his head leaning against the wall and his face looking toward the door. Sitting in the shadow of the evergreen cypress with the clear blue sky in the background, he looked like someone I knew, his face was familiar; he looked like my uncle, or so I imagined.

He said informally, "I'm an orphan. I grew up in a convent for priests. I searched long for my roots, but I found only myself, so I believed in that. I tried art, religion, philosophy, and theology, but I found only myself in Reike. I saw the people around me swimming in pools of blood, Arabs and Jews, Armenians, Circassians, various ethnic groups, and different peoples with similar stories. I saw massacres and carnage everywhere undertaken in the name of religion and nationalism. Look what happened to the Armenians, the Circassians, the Arabs, and the Jews. The strange thing is that history reverses itself, and one day the aggressor becomes the victim and the victim becomes the aggressor. It's amazing, it's unbelievable. I'm researching the situation on this planet. I read, I meditate, I examine matters and I feel cold inside, a feeling that kills me. I don't love anyone in this world and no one inquires about me. Once one wears this robe, he forgets himself and people forget him. You become nothing and everything, go figure! When I was a kid, I thought I was nothing because I had no family and no identity, but when I grew up I became the world and the world was in me, because I am the world, do you understand me?"

I fell silent as I listened quietly to him. I wished I had a heart like his, the world in me; I wished I could return to myself; I wished I could believe in Reike! I asked him, saddened, "Have you found any member of your family?"

He turned to me and smiled, desperate, "What does it matter at my age? When I was young, the search for my family was the center of my life and the essence of my world, I needed affection and a warm bosom, a sincere smile, a familiar face, but when I grew older the question of my origin became larger than them."

Surprised, I said to him, "But you are a human being; you have feelings and emotions. Do you deny them?"

He said, without looking at me, "I don't deny them."

"What do you do with them?" I asked.

He turned to me and repeated, mysteriously, "I don't deny them."

"What about the holy garment?" I asked.

"Forget the holy garment" he said.

"What about the people?" I asked.

"Forget the people."

I began to worry. I asked him, "What do you mean by 'forget the people?' You are almost a god for them; you are God's intermediary. They worship what you do."

He explained, "People need that. They create gods and adore them in every century."

"Do you enjoy what they give you?" I asked.

"Not exactly, but I tried, believe me I did."

"Then you gave up," I said.

"What can I do? I continually remind them but they don't listen," he commented.

"They are searching, like you," I said. "Do they believe in your powers?"

"They search, like you."

"What do you mean?"

"You too are looking for something," he replied.

"Do you know what I am looking for?" I asked.

"Of course I do."

"What is it?"

"You are looking for a lost love, as if love were a woman," he said.

"What is it then?"

"You'll find out," he said.

"When?"

He twisted his hands, looked out, and said coldly, "You decide."

I was upset and hurt by his attitude. He made me go in circles and left me there. He spoke in riddles, which meant that he didn't know. He threw out a few signs and counted on me to interpret them, like all fortunetellers, whether they use hypnotism, magic oils, shells, or coffee beans. All depend on interpretation; as for certain events and definite matters, they are a matter of the unknown.

I saw him pour tea from the thermos. He filled two cups, one for me and one for him. He sat on the side, near the terrace door, looking out. His face looked familiar, and his features were fine and delicate like those of a bird. He was fair-skinned and his eyes were honey with a shade of green and a touch of sadness in them. He had the look of my uncle the artist, or so I thought. I went on debating with him, cross-examining him. I asked him, "Does a young man with your mind, emotions, and unusual personality find a woman who accepts him?"

He turned to me, smiled, and said patiently, "What do you mean? My search is for something different. What counts now is the fact that my heart is clean like a rose and pure like Indian jasmine. Do you have any doubt?"

I shook my head and said frankly, "I have no doubt; after the bus incident I don't have any doubt."

"And before the incident?" he asked

"It was mixed."

"Mixed? All right, that's only natural," he commented.

"Then what?" I asked.

"What do you still want to know?" he inquired.

"How do you live, with what, and what is your work?"

"I paint and decorate icons, carve statues of saints, and I treat the sick with Reike."

"You are an artist, then."

"And a spiritual person."

"Do you make money from your work?"

"Is that important?" he asked.

I said quickly, "Of course it is."

He turned to me and smiled silently. He did not comment, and his attitude reminded me of myself at his age when I debated with my father. I remembered Mariam, the hostel, and my youth. I remembered what was lost from my life and my lost love. Had I not left, had I not abandoned her, there would have been something for me to hold on to, something to believe in, someone to love. I wished I still had Mariam's love.

After a dinner where *mansaf* was served, the important men of the wasteland met to discuss ways to recover the bus. It was still hanging on the edge of the ravine, between the oak tree and the rock. The mayor explained that delays in the recovery of the bus would affect the functioning of the TV, which would in turn impact the evenings in the hospitality room: the news bulletin and the sitcom. The sitcom was particularly important, more so than the news bulletin, which announced nothing but depressing news, and they knew something about depressing news: war and destruction in the Sudan, war and destruction in Afghanistan, war and destruction in Somalia, and a sinking ship in Greece. They knew all that, and it upset them. The sitcom, on the other hand, transported them to the world of people living in a huge palace, with a garden and a swimming pool, filled with fair girls and men behaving like women.

Someone asked me whether foreign men were truly effeminate and whether there were such people in Jerusalem. I said that women were a blessing. They shouted, "A blessing!" and, forgetting about the bus, began to discuss women. Somebody with a loud, tremulous voice, as if speaking through a loudspeaker, said, "By God, women are the biggest curse. They are brainless, stupid, and lack faith. If one of us is cursed with a baby girl, he should bury her alive and put an end to his worries."

Another one said, brokenhearted, "Girls bring you nothing but worries. I have five daughters, good people, five! What have I done? I pray and fast and I believe in God and follow the teachings of my religion. I went on the hajj and prayed for long hours; when I returned home, I was greeted with a celebration and the ghastly news of a baby girl. Five girls, good people. Tell me what to do."

Some said without hesitation, "Get married."

The whiner replied, "How can I marry, good people? I spent all the money I had for the pilgrimage!"

I nudged Michael and whispered angrily, "Remind them of the bus."

He didn't budge and continued to listen with great interest as if they were discussing philosophical or cosmic matters with serious implications.

A man sitting close to me whispered, "This poor man's wife gave birth to eight girls before having a boy, do something for him."

He then turned to Michael and whispered in his ear. I saw Michael smile patiently, shaking his head and mumbling words I could not hear. I wondered what he was saying and why he was smiling instead of rebuffing the man? Did he agree with him? What if he says he can do it with energy: create pregnancy with energy? Would he inseminate her with energy?

I was anxious, as I was beginning to like and respect the young man. I felt he had something different about him that I didn't understand, but it was noble and grand with cosmic dimensions. But pregnancy by means of energy—this wasn't possible. I asked Michael what the man had told him, but the only reply I received was a disapproving nod as if he were scolding a misbehaving young boy. I wondered why he was keeping me out of his thinking. I thought we understood one other and shared some secrets.

Hadn't we shared some ideas that revealed our compatibility to some extent? What did he have in common with those men?

I listened to them talking about their problems, sometimes angry and violent, and sometimes naive, stupid, and scared. I felt an indescribable sense of estrangement, as if I were in a world with which I had nothing in common, like being in Senegal, in Bengal, or the Amazon. Was it conceivable that the revolution had come from those men, and from their reality? How had this happened? Here they were unable to solve a problem as small as a bus on the edge of a precipice, a bus that was supposed to be the topic of the evening! They quickly replaced it with stories about baby girls and women. My anger was growing and I felt the steam go up through my nose and my brain. I shouted at them, "Good people, good people, the bus, the bus!"

They turned to me for just a few seconds then resumed their group discussions. Some were talking about the price of oil and others about the value of the dinar and the shekel. The man who was complaining about his numerous female progeny was still going on about the same topic, while his friend was trying to convince Michael to find him a solution through energy to provoke a pregnancy that guaranteed the birth of a baby boy.

I got up to go to the terrace to fight a strong feeling of oppression, but they called me and asked me if I wanted to drink coffee or anise. Their kindness embarrassed me as they were generously hosting me and I was selfish in my attitude. It was the generosity of the stingy, because we were generous only in matters of the stomach, a characteristic of illiterates.

I wanted to escape this atmosphere and my thinking, so I went out to the terrace to breathe. I heard the cries of a woman shouting in the middle of the night, "For God's sake!" I shivered because the cries were accompanied with beating and wailing and in the distance, the barking of a stray dog and a screeching like that of an owl. I immediately thought of Sakineh, her husband, and her son Tawfiq. I returned to the door and fearfully told the gathered men, "Good people, I hear a person crying nearby!"

One of them laughed and said flippantly, "It is certainly Sakineh being beaten. I hope he doesn't divorce her."

I became emotional and shouted at them, "Why the beating and the divorce? Why the beating?"

My reaction surprised them; they didn't expect this attitude and such a high-pitched voice to come from me. The mayor said, in an effort to calm me, "Sit down, uncle, relax. Bring him tea and coffee. Your day mustn't have been so good."

I got close to him and said gently, trying to control my nerves, "Mayor, Sakineh is not responsible for her son's actions, she was in the kitchen when it all happened."

One of the men whispered, "How do we know that Sakineh was in the kitchen and not visiting one of her neighbors?"

Another one said, "She was chatting with a neighbor and let the boy drive the bus. That's how women are, that's what they do. They create holes and we have to patch them."

I said nervously, "Sakineh is a victim and I am a witness; and so is Michael."

I looked at Michael hoping for his support, but he remained silent. Doubts filled me again, and I resented him. I remembered Sakineh receiving us this morning, wearing a large dress, her big behind, her plastic slippers and her belly extending before her. I felt sorry for her and I was sweating profusely. Michael whispered to me, "Come sit down, your heart is tired."

I remained standing at the entrance and repeated desperately, "Sakineh is a victim, I am her witness; she was in the kitchen."

Some whispered in a low voice, "This man is from Jerusalem and doesn't know a thing! The Jerusalem women are like Turkish delight while we live here with the likes of Sakineh and Mahfuzeh!"

They all laughed at the joke while I stared at them, shocked. I was paying close attention to what was happening in the dark and to the voice of a woman shouting in the night, "For God's sake."

Feeling sorry for me, the mayor said, "Hey sir, your health is much more important. Why are you standing? Come and sit and don't worry. Sakineh is happy with her life. We don't know whether it is Sakineh's voice or that of another woman. That's how women are; they are always loud, and it isn't conceivable that every time we hear one of them cry we intervene and embarrass her. Even Sakineh would have turned against you had you, God forbid, intervened on her behalf. She would have told you that you had no business meddling in a matter that concerned her and her husband alone."

I whispered desperately, "It can't be true."

They all replied together, "It is possible, it is possible, and a thousand times possible!"

I turned to Michael and asked him whether this was possible. He shook his head, looked out, and didn't answer. I banged the door with my fist and went out in the middle of the night, surrounded by the shadows of the evergreen cypress, the barking of a dog, the screeching of an owl, and the imploring voice of a woman in the dark, shouting, "For God's sake."

I heard them leave one after the other. They discussed everything except the matter for which they had gotten together, retrieving the bus.

There was no light in this desolate place, no water, no money, and even those who could afford to build were not building here. How could we build a nation, then? I was very depressed by my own situation and that of the nation. The two conditions, the personal and the general were confused, and I was not able to tell which had priority, the personal or the national. Which one was more important, which one had more depth? Was it the education or the environment? Was it the emotional or the social? Was it better to begin with the individual or the collective? In the past we believed that changing the public would lead to a change in the private. It was our motto, our conviction, and even our faith. Where did it lead us? We reached neither the public nor the private, and we are suffering. We then said, let's use awareness and culture; in other words, we turned our backs on the armed revolution and adopted a policy of awareness and education for years. Where did it get us, what did we achieve? What an unlucky country!

I felt his steps and heard the sound of his sandals. I did not turn to look at him because my heart was desperate, it was filled with doubt and challenge. He touched my shoulder and whispered gently, "Are you still thinking of Sakineh?"

I listened but heard nothing except silence and the buzzing of the crickets, then the broken complaint of a barking dog. I said, sad and reproachful, "Poor Sakineh has no one to save her. You were talking to me about energy within us; would Sakineh reach the savior and the energy without a guide? When would you act—after a hundred years, a thousand years? Or after death? This is procrastination, postponement, and suicide. It is an escape from reality and people's lives."

He asked apologetically, "What can we do?"

I didn't have an answer and didn't reply. I didn't say: religion, legality; I didn't say power and law; I didn't say revolution and change, because we had tried them all and failed. Here we were, starting all over again, in the heart of the night and in the darkness. The words of the mayor were digging a hole in my head: if you intervene she would turn against you and would tell you to mind your own business.

He asked again, in a tender voice, "What can we do, force her? If Sakineh does not want, can we force her?"

I said, perplexed, guided by my heart rather than my mind, "I don't know. do you know? I do not."

The shops were still empty of customers and visitors, and the asphalt street with the potholes we had crossed yesterday was still empty of pedestrians. The village was almost deserted this morning, as if abandoned. My shoes on the ground and the gravel in the street emitted a double squeaking like broken glass. I could hear it, and so could the sellers in the stores. The sound attracted the attention of some curious pedestrians. I felt doubly estranged and decided to walk in the direction of the valley to get away and be alone. As I turned I saw before me the bellies of the mountains, smooth and blue in the morning fog, and the shining of the light over the edges and the rocks.

The color of the country was not cheerful; it conveyed a sad drought—even the olives lacked greenery. Their leaves and branches were dull; their color was a pale dusty blue-gray. How could plants be green in summer with a shortage of water? People had a miserly subsistence in a country suffering from drought and destroyed by wars. It was not a traditional war or a traditional occupation; it was a settlement process and a fight over a space deprived of natural resources. Here was that settlement spreading like an epidemic in the heart of the mountain, establishing prefabricated homes that resembled dollhouses and stretched out like snails. Despite the pain and because of their poverty, the villagers worked in the settlement as day laborers and construction workers. The village remained empty of its youth from morning till evening, and the women remained without help except for the domestic animals, looking after hordes of children and old men who were difficult to serve. How could we rebuild a wasteland?

I felt my anxiety grow; I was lost in a land that was carrying me without affection. I was walking aimlessly without hope and without love, without family and without faith. When I returned to Jerusalem I tried to look for something I could believe in, but I found only estrangement and past sorrows. I was visited by Mariam's memories and the sorrows of Jerusalem. I felt a stranger in a place where I was not able to find myself, as if it had happened yesterday. Isn't this how I had felt in the past? I was young then, and I had dreamed of books and the spirit of art. Literature was the light of my life, and through it I saw the world. I loved, I hated, I revolted, and I rebelled. I refused my life and my limits. I grew wings for my soul to conquer the veil of the unknown. I saw beauty and I worshiped it. I felt my pulse increase and I threw myself into the heart of a destructive light like a butterfly that dances in the light. I was burned, but what put out my fire: time, exile, loneliness, repeated defeats; or was it age and my failure to reap the fruits of a summer past for a future spring?

If only I had a warm home, a son or a daughter, or something that could stir my emotions and my thinking, a new book, a new idea, a new vision, anything capable of extracting me from myself and pulling me toward the outside. But I have nothing, I have no one, I have no love and no faith. The path I follow is in a land that is growing narrower and more menacing, the promised land! Is the emptiness inside me and my lost life the result of old age or materialism and an empty soul?

I had a strong urge to sleep in my own bed and to hide from the world among my pillows and covers. My bedroom appeared to me as a joyful place that could protect me, a warm cocoon like a womb that would cover me in this cold. Sleep is beautiful; it is the most beautiful thing left in this world.

I reached the clinic, slowly dragging my feet. It was still early in the morning, but I felt overcome with sleep, as if a huge bird were hovering over me and sheltering my senses with its wings. I could see only ashes and weak lines disappear, and the ghosts of trees. As I pushed the door I heard deep crying from behind the wall of the other room. It was the voice of a sobbing woman, and Michael was asking her to concentrate with him. But the woman was crying violently, saying that she wanted to die, asking for a poison or a medication to end her life. Then I heard a sharp cry that shook the glass of the windows, it awakened all my senses, dissipated my sleepiness, and I felt as light as a courageous dog. The voice moved inside me, provoked a deep pain that tore my heart strings and made me feel dizzy. I sat on the nearest chair to avoid collapsing on the floor. The woman continued to cry and wail for a few more minutes, then she calmed down under the influence of Michael's words and his voice that stirred gently like a pendulum. I wondered whether he had hypnotized her. But she soon resumed shouting, "I swear by God that I was not there and I did not see him. Damn this life, I have to deal with his mother and with him and now the children, the cows, the goats, make cheese, soap, oven bread, take care of the olives, and transport water and manure on my head. When my husband returns, his mother says, 'Sakineh did this and that, Sakineh visits the neighbors to chat.' She goes on blaming me for everything, repeating Sakineh this and Sakineh that until he gets up holds me by my hair and beats me with his leather belt. He kicks me everywhere until I am about to die. Do you see my head, my eye, my hands! My children try to intervene and pull him away from me, beg him to stop in God's name, but his mother, this head of a cabbage, does not budge. I swear I'll kill her and then kill myself. Give me a poison, or a medicine, I beg you, save me."

I almost jumped to save her, but I was afraid. What if she reacts as they said and tells me to mind my own business, that I had no business interfering between her and her husband?

I heard Michael repeat with insistence, "Concentrate with me, concentrate, let me help you relax," but she went on asking him to give her a poison to put an end to her life. Under the influence of his words and his tone she finally calmed down. I heard him tell her, "You are now in the middle of deep sleep. You are calm and without problems, you are happy." When I heard the word 'happy' I lost my mind. I rushed to his office, pushed the door and held him from the back, shouting at him, "You must be crazy, what are you doing? You tell her that she is happy to make her put up with more beating! You are a sadist, you are a Nazi, you are a charlatan."

He was surprised and shaken by the force of my grasp and my words. He was shocked and stared at me without blinking. He quickly took hold of himself and asked, "Why did you come? What are you doing?"

I had started pulling Sakineh's stiff arm, telling her to wake up. He scolded me and warned against doing that for fear of hurting her. I paid no attention to him and bent toward her to pull her up, but she was as stiff as a piece of wood. My anger grew, and, crazed by the situation, I asked her once more to get up and come with me.

I felt his strong arms pull me and throw me across the room. I hit a curtain and the examination table and fell on the floor. He bent to help me up, but I slapped his outstretched arm and shouted at him, "Get away from me, you're crazy, you're a sadist, you're a sorcerer. Is this how you cure your patients, with lies, with make-believe and treachery?"

He shouted at me as he never had before, obviously losing control. "What business is it of yours?" he asked.

"What business is it of mine? I see you torture this poor woman and cheat her, hypnotize her, and you want me to remain silent? I will not."

He shouted again, turning red to the roots of his hair, "What business is it of yours? Why do you interfere in my work, and why did you enter the clinic without permission? You have no right to be here. Leave immediately; this is not your place."

I lost my mind when I heard him challenge me. Wasn't he embarrassed and ashamed of himself? How dare he throw me out? Was it because I revealed the truth about him? Does he want to keep everything to himself to put his hold on the people? I will not let this happen, I will not keep quiet, I will do what I have to do no matter how much it costs me. I stood up slowly, pointed my index finger in his face, and said firmly, "I will not keep quiet. You will not stop me whatever happens. I will save Sakineh despite you."

He shouted angrily, "What do you want with Sakineh, I do not understand, why Sakineh?"

I shouted sharply, "Because she is a victim and she is unhappy, don't you understand? She is the victim of this environment. Didn't you hear them last night? But you don't hear, even if you hear, you won't understand. You take advantage of the ignorance of the people, of this wasteland and the villagers in order to implant yourself. I will not allow it, I will not let ignorance rule. I will take Sakineh away and save her."

"Don't wake her up; this is not allowed. You will destroy her," he shouted.

I insisted, pushing him back, "I will wake her up despite you."

He held my hand and pleaded with me, "Don't wake her; it's dangerous. You would destroy her."

I pushed his hands away, "Do you want me to let you fill her mind with delusions? Get out of my way immediately."

His face was close to mine and he looked me straight in the eyes; anger was reflected in his features and a certain radiation came out of his eyes. He said, "You won't take her."

"I will," I said.

He smiled in a strange way, a bitter, resentful smile, and said, "What would you do with the poor woman? Have fun with her to prove something? What do you want to prove, that you are a revolutionary and a freedom fighter, that you are a human being?"

I objected, "Have fun with her? Is that all you think about? Your thinking cannot go to another dimension."

He stared at me, still smiling his mean smile. He looked different from before; he was a different man. He whispered grudgingly, "Another dimension? What exactly is this dimension?"

I took out one of my business cards and threw it in his face, saying firmly, "Come visit my Association if you want to know."

He put his face close to mine and whispered like a devil, "What would I find in your Association, an orphanage? A welcome center for widows and divorced women? Or a home for illegitimate children from the street and sinful women who made a mistake and found nothing but the convents and a death sentence?"

I stared at him, and asked, "What do you mean?"

He was pale and stiff like a white mask of wax. He said in a strangled voice, "Mariam did not find your Association; what would Sakineh find then?"

My heart stopped beating, and I whispered, fearfully, "What do you mean?"

He resumed dryly, "And the illegitimate child was homeless and found nowhere to go except a convent."

I gasped deeply, and said rattled, "You are then . . . ?"

"Yes, I mean Mariam; and I am Mariam's son."

I felt the room move, and I lost consciousness.

He denied totally what he had told me and explained things by my eagerness to have an heir. He pretended that I was clinging to imaginary matters, delusions! He said they were the product of my imagination and resulted from a need to fill an emotional, material, or moral gap. He believed that, in my case, the three factors were combined. I talked at length with him, gently, affectionately, but to no avail. He believed that each one of us should go his own way. I explained that he was my son, my only heir, and the only one left while the others were all gone. He reminded me that no one had left but me, and upon my return I had tried to return to the past, but the past does not come back, and I should now move forward toward the future.

I tried to convince him, to win him over, but in vain. I talked for almost an hour, but he paid no attention to me and stared through the window. When I was done and saw his look I asked him angrily what he was staring at, and he said, "Infinity."

He told me that my words would not sway him, and nothing would convince him, even if I put all the wealth of the world in his hands, he would not change his mind. I said I was willing to change his mind, but he believed that a person changes according to his circumstances, like a liquid that takes the shape of its container. He refused to change and would not change. He would keep his robe, his name, his knowledge, his art, his love for people and icons. I told him that he was very much like my uncle with the beautiful handwriting, a trait he had inherited from him. He was truly a member of the family, his look and his smile; he could not deny the genes he had inherited. But he attributed everything to my imagination and wondered why I hadn't seen all this in him before he had revealed my secret. He had penetrated my inner thoughts and uncovered my story with Mariam and her son as part of his work. He insisted that he was not my son.

I began looking for his mother, and on the way back I learned from Aziz that the priest went regularly to visit an old woman in the village, the place where Mariam used to live with her mother, the place that held my memories with Mariam. He described the old woman as a lady in her eighties, almost totally blind, wearing thick glasses, as thick as the bottom of a coffee cup. The young man was then denying me, either because I had denied him or because I existed outside the circle of his interests and a world I did not understand, the way he did not understand my world.

Aziz dropped me at the entrance of the house. I stood to observe it from a distance. Its stones had turned slightly black; they were not shining as in the past. The trees had grown taller than the roof and covered the house almost completely, making it difficult to see the balcony that overlooked the valley and the mountains of Jerusalem in the distance. The scent of the evergreen cypress, the pine trees, and the ringing of the love bell, as we used to call it, blew with the breeze and changed the silence into nostalgia and visions of ghosts.

I knocked at the door and waited, but there was no reply. The house was soundless, and everything indicated that it was abandoned—the grass that grew on the stairs and the way the vine fell on its branches and on the side of the road. Have they returned to the land of exile? Have they sold the house? Where did the old woman go? Did she die, or did they place her in a hospital? I didn't wait long for an answer. Jamileh told me the whole story.

Jamileh was a widow, a distant relative of the family; she took care of the house and the old woman until they placed her in an old people's home. The house was for sale now. She was in the village shopping, and when I saw her get off the bus I felt relieved. I waited until she appeared between the vine leaves and saw me standing at the entrance. She didn't seem surprised by my presence. I doubted that she could make it to the entrance with her bag of provisions. She was dressed in black from head to toe, a woman in her sixties or even seventies. She was breathing heavily, and when I offered to help carry her bag she did not object and gave it to me without hesitation, as if she had been waiting for this moment of relief.

She said that the house was open and that she had gone for only an hour to buy a few things she needed. She said that if I wanted to visit the house and the garden I would have to do it alone because she was tired of running around, going up and down with every buyer and visitor. The house was mine to inspect, and once done I could join her in the kitchen for a cup of tea or coffee.

The house was mine to search as I pleased, without supervision or control, the mother was in an old people's home, and her sons were overseas. The house, as Jamileh explained, was abandoned; no one cleaned it. She apologized in advance for the dust, the cobwebs, and the rats. Moreover, the window in the ceiling was broken, and rain got in and caused a great deal of damage. The furniture was not important and could be removed or kept for free if I liked the house and wanted to buy it. Jamileh went into the kitchen, leaving me alone in the middle of the hall.

I remembered the day I had come inquiring about Mariam. I was overcome with an overwhelming feeling of estrangement and strong yearning to see her and hear her undulating voice, her hesitant, beautiful look. This hesitant look was her most beautiful feature. It was a look that both warned you and ignored you, a look that attracted and pulled you close, then unexpectedly left you. You then began to run to catch up with her, not to lose sight of her. What had happened then? Why had I pulled back? I remembered when I came to see her and pretended to be her Arabic teacher. She had not learned and I had not learned either and now Michael was rejecting me and denying me, or maybe denying her.

I walked through the rooms and the halls looking for a trace of her but found only dirt and the dust of time, flowerpots filled with dry plants and thorns. I went up the stairs leading to the bedrooms and found photos of her brothers, one with a mustache and the other driving a Chevrolet, a third with his bride in a church. There was a photo of a man wearing the Arab headgear and dress hanging in the most prominent place in the house. It was her father before he emigrated. In another photo taken a few years later, he was a different man, wearing a shirt and without a mustache, standing in front of his shop like a guard, displaying rugs and oriental trinkets. There was an enlarged photo of the mother, wearing black, with gray hair pulled to the back in a bun and without eyeglasses that she had probably removed for the picture. Her eyes appeared to be floating in a fog. There was no photo of Mariam, the only one without a photo, either in the rooms or the halls or on the dresser where dozens of photos of boys and girls were displayed: children on swings, girls with braids and ribbons, inflatable toys in the shape of fish floating over a swimming pool and on the beach. Mariam was the only one without a photo and so was Michael. All the children had their photo except my son. I felt a lump in my throat because I was responsible for his suffering and hers too. Michael had turned his back on the world the way it had turned its back on him. This must be his reaction, but how did Mariam react? What did she do? How did she live? Where did she go? Where did she hide? How did she face events and the real world?

I continued to search frantically for her room. All rooms contained beds and closets, curtains and frames, and all frames contained photos of the brothers and their children playing, photos of gardens and cars, but none showed Mariam and Mariam's son, and I was responsible for that.

I was very upset and defiant, like anyone defending his family, like a victim, like someone deprived of well-being while the others enjoyed everything and didn't care. Mariam was forgotten; she was without a history, my Mariam was without a history. I opened cupboards, drawers; I looked behind curtains and doors. Nothing recalled her past except the sound of the bell we had bought in Bab al-Khalil. We were walking on the stairs above the arches, through the icons, the smell of incense, the thousands of scarves, candles, pictures, and statues, when she saw it. It was hanging among the beads as she stood under it, took hold of its clapper, and began to ring it. She then moved a short distance away from it, still mesmerized. She blew at it and made it ring while the metal pipes moved like the fins of a fish. The effect amused her and she kept saying, much to my embarrassment, "See how beautiful it is; it's made in China."

The salesman was laughing and repeated, "See how beautiful it is; there's nothing more beautiful." I felt angry and defiant, took all the money I had and said rudely, "Take those two dinars and give me the bell." That was a time when the dinar meant something. The salesman asked for an additional dinar, which I did not have. Mariam gave him five dinars and I kept my two dinars. Here was the love bell, priceless, swaying with the breeze, pushed by the wind, taking me back in time. Oh, Mariam, look where we are now!

I heard a noise and the sound of falling copper and something broken like smashed glass. It came from the room above me. I went up the stairs to the source of the noise and found a room full of clutter, boxes, and broken frames. There I finally found her photo thrown on the floor, behind a dresser. I removed the photo from the frame and put it in my inside pocket to take back with me and frame, to protect it from moths. Oh, Mariam, look where we are now!

I joined Jamileh in the kitchen and smelled the coffee and cooking. She asked me to sit in front of her around the kitchen table, and then she poured my coffee and continued to peel the potatoes and eggplants. She asked me where I came from and why I was visiting the village, how I knew about the house, had I known it before? I said I had known it years ago, that I was a returnee and I needed a house. She was surprised that a Jerusalem inhabitant would look for a house in the wilderness. She wondered why a Jerusalemite would choose to live in Ramallah and not buy a house in Jerusalem when there were plenty of houses there? The Jews had not stopped buying, she said, and I was more deserving of one. She asked me whether I had an ID and a permit, and since I did, she said that it would be a good deed to buy a house in Jerusalem; I would be rewarded by God for doing so, and I would be living in the center of the world

instead of the wilderness and Ramallah. I reprimanded her gently for referring to the village as a
wilderness.

"All right, a village, but is the village better than
Jerusalem?" she asked. I was surprised by her attitude
and asked whether she was in charge of selling the
house. She shook her hands and said, "Never," then
explained that she once had been but had learned her
lesson. I was curious to know the lesson she had
learned, but she raised her head and observed me for a
few seconds, then asked, coldly, "How is the coffee?" It
was a sign for me to put an end to my questions, and
I did.

I tried to approach the subject directly to gain time.
I expressed my regret about the condition of the house.
She looked at me and asked for the second time if I had
known the place before. I did not reply and made
another comment about the most beautiful aspect of
the house, its potted green plants, the fern, and the
creeping plants, that they had been the most beautiful
things I had ever seen in my life, but they looked so
pitiful now! She asked me again if I knew the house,
but I didn't reply and spoke about the beauty of the
village in the past—it was greener, had more trees, even
olive trees. It now has streets, buildings, and shops,
emulating the city and ending up being neither a village
nor a city. She asked me wryly if I had seen the
peripheral road and the nearby settlement, before
talking about greenery and olive trees! I did not want
the conversation to lead us to the subject of the settlement, the settlers, the occupiers, the way conversations

begin and end with all people since my return. I tried another bait. I mentioned the priest, his wife, Yvonne, and my work at a public school. Curious, she asked when all that had happened, before the '67 war? I said it was exactly then, and after that date I emigrated. "Where to?" she asked. I did not want to specify the place and said that I went everywhere. I returned to the offensive and mentioned my visit to the house to give Miss Mariam Arabic lessons. "Miss Mariam? You? You . . . ," she said looking at me suspiciously, then asked, "Are you Christian or . . . ."

I felt that she was beginning to have suspicions and even knew about our story, or rather our scandal. I said, joking, completing her question, "Or Jewish, a settler?"

She did not reply and pretended to be busy drinking her coffee. I threw her another bait, saying, "Mariam was like a rose—very beautiful."

She shook her head several times and I said to myself that she must know her. She was the beginning of the thread, and I kept quiet.

She said indifferently, "Did you visit the house? Did you like it? The price is very good, would you like to buy it?"

I tried to go on pulling the thread, well aware that a woman her age would not open up and give me the information I wanted, painlessly. It was going to take some time, and I had better keep hold of the thread until I got close to the heart of the matter. I said to her that it was not a matter of price, its distance from the city or its proximity to the settlement, but that I was put off by the sad condition of the house. It was desolate, gloomy, and in urgent need of repair. She said tersely that the owners had abandoned the house years ago and it had experienced difficulties, as it had been inhabited on and off, this being the third time the poor house was up for sale.

I asked suddenly, "And Mariam?"

She looked at me and then turned away, asking frostily if I had known her.

"I gave her one Arabic lesson and then I emigrated," I explained.

She did not comment. I explained, joking about Mariam's difficulties learning Arabic, but Jamileh shook her head several times without saying a word. I commented further on Mariam's lack of predisposition for the language, but she replied suddenly, "She did, she did. She could speak it and read and write it better than I."

I pretended to be surprised and pleased, and said, "Is it true?"

"True," she said, very tersely and quickly and tried in a roundabout malicious way to learn more about me. "Are you Protestant or Catholic or Greek Orthodox?"

I smiled and said, "We're going back to religion?"

She avoided my look and busied herself with peeling the vegetables, then said distantly, "I'm asking because you mentioned the priest."

She then kept quiet and I did too. After a while she said slowly, "There was a Muslim man, I mean a teacher in the village who taught Mariam, then disappeared and never came back. Do you know him?"

She shook her head and added, "This happened years and years ago; time flies! Mariam used to be a young woman, and she is now like you and me: we're old wood."

Her last words hit me like a slap on the face. We have become old wood, and Mariam too is an old woman. How could Mariam grow old like me and look like me! How could Mariam become exhausted, broken, and suffer from diabetes, high blood pressure, and Alzheimer's? This cannot be. Mariam is beautiful and cute, Mariam dances and plays with fire, Mariam is the one in the photo in my pocket near my heart and another one in my memory and I am searching between the two.

She asked, "What about the house—would you like to buy it?"

I thought at length about it. If I said yes, I would have to buy it and thus lose the thread, and if I said no and then left, I would also lose the thread. I'd better maintain the link. She saw my hesitation and said, feeling sorry for me, "Well, well, you don't know? Or you want to look at houses in Jerusalem?"

I looked at her and said enthusiastically, "That is an idea, by God, and a practical one at that, but I don't know anyone there to help me. Do you? Do you know of houses for sale?"

She shook her head and said sadly, "Once upon a time I had a house and I lost it. The Israelis took it. But they did not take the house at the end of the street, you'd better rush; its owners have been in Kuwait since before the war. It is a beautiful and cheerful house and has a garden. Would you like to visit it? If you buy it, you would do your country a service. Would you like to visit it?"

"What about this house? I'm afraid someone else will buy it!" I said.

She said slowly, "Think about it. Think about this house and the one in Jerusalem, think."

She gave me permission to check the house a second time at my own pace, and she promised to take me to the house in Jerusalem located at the end of the street. "You'd better buy it," she said, "because the Israelis are buying left and right."

I returned to the house in the afternoon of the following day. It was a gloomy day, windy and cloudy and rainy despite its being June. I found the key under the entrance rug, as she had told me. I entered carefully and apprehensively, as if I were pilfering a museum of past memories and visions of ghosts. The house was empty, and the kitchen was as Jamileh had left it, clean, swept, and sprayed, and the covers of pots were washed and left to dry. The smell of cooking, mixed with that of insecticide, gave the place a touch of life. The wind moaned, shaking glass objects in the hallway and making metal objects bang against each other. A small window on the western side of the house was open, and when I went to close it I found something I had not expected—books: a library, shelves of books, and a marble fireplace. In one corner of the room, hidden behind the door, there was a small desk, a rotating chair, and a camera. It was a strange room I hadn't known existed. It was filled with the smell of dust and books. I switched on the light, and a large chandelier spread a blinding golden color, forcing me to turn it off immediately. A photo hanging in the middle of one of the walls had filled my eyes, and I remembered it well. It was that of a young man not yet twenty, thin, weak, with eyes that looked like Mariam's eyes and those of Michael. But it was not Michael, it was Micho, her brother, the sick boy who died. This was Micho's room, then! I was over-whelmed by the memory the room evoked; her memory surrounded me, took hold of me, and an invisible fragrance in the room recalled the smell of pine trees and grass when I ran away and hid in the cave of the valley. It was a spring day and Mariam was walking with her two-horned goat, with a blue stone hanging around its neck to protect it from the evil eye and make it provide milk. It was a white goat like a gazelle that Mariam treated like a cat or a pet dog. The goat was very beautiful, and Mariam and the goat formed an unusual and amazing sight that never failed to make an impact. It was like a magic vision, a young woman dressed in black and carrying a tree branch and a white goat the color of snow.

I had walked side by side with her, and she was telling me stories about the priest whom she had loved passionately. I had cried because I loved her passionately. We sat on the edge of a rock while the goat mewed like a cat or a ghost. It looked at me, and I laughed nervously. Mariam asked if I were afraid; I told her that the goat was like an ogress, that she could hear and stare like a human being. "A human being or an ogress?" said Mariam, and accused me of being crazy, an artist, a writer, a crazy writer with a rich imagination. I told her to watch how the goat stared like someone who understood; if she had had a tongue she would have talked like an ogress. Mariam dried her tears and calmed down and asked jokingly what the ogress was telling me. I did not reply and continued to stare at the goat, and the goat was staring at the plants. She insisted on knowing what the ogress was telling me. I was filled with the jinn in the air, the eyes of the goat, Mariam's story, and my passionate love for her, hiding behind books, my writings and pretensions. I was an artist in her eyes, and I wanted to remain as such to her, a writer, an artist with a rich imagination. I told her, "The ogress says, the ogre says . . . ," then I threw a bunch of branches to the goat and turned toward Mariam staring at her and pretending to look like an ogre, using my nails to eat her up, saying, "I am the ogre and I will eat you."

I then jumped from the rock and began to walk like the hunchback of Notre Dame. She started laughing and saying, "Crazy, by God you are crazy!" I got close to her, my fingers stretched out and my face wrinkled. She ran away and I ran after her, limping and twisting to her amusement. She walked, laughed, and ran and I ran after her and the goat followed us, mewing and ringing its bell until we reached the cave. There I smelled love, the grass and the thorns of the pinyon.

Oh, Mariam! I closed the west window and remained there breathing her memories and sighing, while Micho was in front of me, watching me like the goat, like a ghost.

I sat in the room as if I were bewitched, recalling Mariam's memories and my own, my past, the memory of my madness, my imagination, and my passion for art. Where have all my passions gone? How have those feelings disappeared? Where have I buried them? Is there anything in the world that equals the touch of velvet, the wings of feather, mousseline, the high clouds, the breeze, the sun's rays, the color of the world at dusk, the fog of dawn, the smell of mud and watered grass, the taste of apricots, uncorking almonds, and a sad melody for Abd al-Wahhab that I used to sing—all are looking at me sarcastically, and wondering. He used to sing and I with him, while she stared, saying, "He told me a few words like the breeze on a summer night." Then the bell of love would ring, and that of the goat, inducing her to send me away, concerned for my safety and for fear of being seen by her mother. She would then laugh, feeling sorry for her weakening eyesight, while her hearing was strong. She would ask me to stop singing, but I would go on in a low voice, almost whispering, "He left me, and I still love him. He makes fun of me and there is a vision in my imagination."

She would ask me repeatedly to stop, but nothing stopped me except my feelings and her sighing. Here I was, now aware of her presence and she of mine, mewing like the goat and hearing the wind blowing. Oh, Mariam!

I saw a photocopy of a handwritten paper under the camera. It looked like a letter or a memoir or even a novel. It read, "He said to her and she told him, she felt this way and he felt that way, then they went toward the hostel and the Armenian convent." What was this text, and who had written it? Where was the rest and the original? Those were Mariam's words, but what about the language and the handwriting? Jamileh told me yesterday that Mariam could speak, read, and write Arabic better than she. Did this mean that Mariam was writing novels? Why not—wasn't she mesmerized by my writing? Hadn't she often told me that if she knew Arabic she would write the most extraordinary story to the world, her story! Was this women's literature? A woman writing her story, which she considered to be the most extraordinary story, at least in her opinion. As for the rest of the world, it sees women's stories as effusive writings, not novels. In other words, they are seen as memoirs, confessions, scraps, a woman's way of unburdening herself and telling the world: This is all I've got; this is my pain; this is who I am, a victim. She admitted having made a mistake, but she blamed it on her weakness, her love, and her truthfulness. She explained how she believed what she was told and thus fell into the trap; it was up to the world to decide and judge her. Was this what she did to me? Did she paint me as the aggressor in her story, and herself the victim? Had she mentioned my name at all? Had she mentioned anything about that son—was it a son or a daughter? If he were a son, then he must certainly be Michael, and if she were a daughter where was she? Where was the copy and the original manuscript, the complete manuscript?

I looked for it like a madman, in the desk drawers, on the shelves, between the books, in the cupboard. In my confusion I sat on the revolving chair behind the desk and began going in circles, looking here and there, going through what I had read: he said to her and she said to him, and the hostel, the Armenian convent and the daybreak, then what? What did she say? What did she write about me and her? Did she portray me as a devil and a coward, a womanizer? Did she truly love me as she pretended, or was I a replacement for the priest? And her son Michael, if the baby was a boy or a girl, was it mine as she pretended, or was it his? For the thousandth time I wished Mariam's son to be mine, my own flesh and blood, without doubt. What if Mariam's son were not mine, what would I do? How could I live? Ever since I began looking for Mariam I've had a purpose in my life, one that has pushed me forward, toward the future. I began looking for the past and here I am looking for the future. Mariam was the thread of the past, and her son will be that of the future.

I turned around on the chair and stared at the picture, at Michael's eyes, and whispered like a madman looking for a cure in a mental hospital, "O spirit of death, ghost of death, you who have the energy, if there is life in death or after death and if you are roaming in the air, send me a sign, send me those lost in the open space, you who control energy!"

I turned back suddenly, and behind me was a watercolor painting of the Mount of Olives, of

Gethsemane and the copper domes. The window opened, and I saw my face in the windowpane, reflected over the picture, above the domes and the Mount of Olives, and suddenly I thought that she might be there with the nuns; or was it simply my imagination and Michael's eyes? I looked at him and saw him looking at me, staring at me, warning me against the past and against digging up the dead. But now that I had reached this stage, at this age, in this condition, nothing frightened me or dissuaded me.

My foot hit the wastebasket under the desk. It contained wrinkled scraps of paper—electricity bills, water bills, and a paper like a ball. I opened it and found it to be a birth certificate without a name. The date however, was that date, the date of the defeat and my departure, the date of her delivery. The photocopy was bent and useless, it was photocopied upside down, a copy without a history or names, but the birth was his, his history, the beginning of the thread, but without a name or a surname.

I turned in circles like a madman, and left the room to be met by darkness. The evening had fallen around me while I was searching for her, for a photo and a birth certificate. I wanted something that would prove to me that the date was his and that what was lost was my name beside his. The search started with one name and became two and even three. I had a thousand questions about me, about her, and about the beginning of the thread.

I went back to the attic where I had found the clutter, the boxes, and the suitcases. Most of them were empty except for a dusty one pushed under a pile of wood and metal corners. It was a small suitcase containing baby clothes and diapers. Those were the effects of the baby, a boy or a girl, but what about you, Mariam, where were traces of you? I opened the boxes. The first one contained nothing but old curtains, rings, screws, and a pile of nails. The second box contained books and old notebooks from the fifties, the third box contained the treasure or the beginning of the thread. There were photos of her as a young girl, then a young woman, and an adult, with the goat on the rock, in front of the church with the priest and his wife, Yvonne, with her mother in various poses, under the vine trellis, in the kitchen, under the wall of Jerusalem, below the arches, riding a camel with the tourists on the highest point of the Mount of Olives, with the Dome of the Rock in the background, then the copper domes of the garden of Gethsemane with her mother and a group of scouts. There were photos of her in front of the old people's home, the photo of a nun waving her hand standing near an old woman in a wheelchair, with Mariam beside her. The idea hit me like a rocket: the mother was there and so was the daughter, the nun was the aunt. This was where I must search, and in the boxes looking for the photos, the birth certificate, the novel, and all the events that had taken place. Where was the copy and where was the original?

Finally I found a pile of papers hidden in a leather bag under the magazines. I opened it and found the treasure, lots of large papers, all handwritten, and many photocopies. They were not the original documents but copies; it was better than nothing, they were the beginning of the thread.

I took the bag and, going down to one of the rooms, lay on a large bed, beside an old night table and a lamp. I switched on the light and started reading slowly. I immersed myself in the past and the heat of events, haphazardly, without numbers or dates. The words were those we had exchanged, and the bits of events, the scenes, and the images of the past, were as Mariam's eyes had seen them.

She told him how much she had endured and he cried with her. He was gentle, emotional, and timid. He was a gifted artist who wrote stories. She dreamed of books and wished to write something that people would read, but language was an obstacle. How could she write without a language? There was also experience and knowledge. What would she write about without experience or expertise? Would she write about herself and her brothers, the convent? It was like a prison, but it was a happy place because it allowed her to hide from her brothers and people's eyes. All the Arab girls in Sao Paolo entered the convent to safeguard their traditions, when they grew older they were sent to the old country to continue their lives in a pure, untainted environment. So it was for her—her family had sent her back home, taking her away from everything she knew, from her brothers and her friends. She felt imprisoned and nostalgic, she longed for the school and the nuns, she missed playing with her classmates, she missed a special friend who was her only friend and more than a sister to her. She missed her brothers, the family home, and even her friend in exile. Her sweet widowed mother had turned angry and sad, she was suspicious, hard, and used swearwords. She too felt the injustice of having to return and leave her sons and her home because of the illness of one of her sons.

What would she write about then? Exile and longing? Would she write about exile in her own country, about missing the nuns, about things she didn't know in a language she barely knew? He, on the other hand, was the Arabic-language teacher, he went to Jerusalem, he had parents there while she knew nothing about Jerusalem except what was in pictures, and that country remained a picture and a shadow play.

The page was over, and it was followed by multiple photocopies of the same page and the same words. When I resumed my reading, I noticed that the date on the papers preceded the war, our acquaintance, and my escape.

She felt a deep sense of estrangement and home-sickness. She could not understand people's words, the way they lived, and the way they died. Where was life, where were the lights, the shopping centers? She felt that Sao Paolo was the homeland, although they had told her that the homeland was in the East. She did not know where the East or the West were, where to come and where to go and what to do. She grew up in a convent and lived in a convent, she loved a nun like all girls do, and she did not know any men except her brothers. There was an Italian priest who came to the convent every Sunday. Girls used to gather to watch him because he was very handsome, like a picture. He was young and kind, and spoke French and Italian. He played on the organ and the piano like Chopin. The girls at the convent were at a critical age: in other words, they were young women. They would sit in the back row of the church and whisper, dreaming of him like they would of a Hollywood star. She too dreamed, not as much, but she did. She was the youngest, the most innocent, and the most gifted. She used to write certain things and hide them. Once a girl read her writings and told her admiringly that she was a gifted writer. She advised her to show her compositions to her teacher. She finally did, and the following day the teacher returned her writings with his comments. It was a long letter of praise and admiration in which he referred to her rare and rich imagination and predicted a great future for her. He warned her, nevertheless, of some dangerous feelings that might explode at that age in such a restrictive environment. He recommended that she receive good guidance at her age because of her imagination, otherwise, otherwise . . . .

She didn't like the letter because it ended in preaching, advice, and a warning. Yet the letter left its mark on her because it addressed what was more eloquent, her unique imagination, her success and a promising future. What happened to her later was neither success nor a promising future, but explosion and extreme escape.

The page was over, and there were many copies of it. The following page had no connection with the previous one. While I was looking for another page and an extension of the thread, I was thinking about the phrase "dangerous feelings and an imagination," how Mariam wrote texts and hid them, about her lack of experience and know-how, her limited knowledge of men except her brothers—but what about the priest and her love for him—where did that story go? Was the story of the priest who played the organ and the piano in the church, whom she saw from a distance like the other girls, the whole story? Was it a made-up story, born of her imagination? It couldn't be; she used to tell me about him and cry. She sounded honest in telling her story and its events. But in reality, what do I know? Did I know her reality, what she had experienced and what really had happened and what hadn't happened? How do I know what was made up? How do I know why she returned to the village and of her brother's death? Was his death the reason for her return? Did they come back because he was ill or did their return cause his death, and who was the cause, he or she? Who was the patient—she or he? The important question was about Mariam and if she were sick and made up the whole story about the priest? It couldn't be. I knew her; she was honest. But did I know her deeply? I was young and innocent and inexperienced. I too lived an imaginary life, in my artist dreams. What I knew about people was the product of my imagination; I didn't discover the truth until later: weeks, months, or even years later, and sometimes never. I used to see in them what I liked or imagined. I always pictured them the way I wanted, but what about their reality, what was it? Even now, despite my sixty years and experience, do I really know what reality is? Does anyone know without interference? I interfered with her image, and Mariam was therefore an image and I a photographer. Here she was drawing my portrait, but how did she see me?

I went back to searching among the pictures, what she saw and how she saw me.

They had entered the hostel to get some information and change the dollars they had left. She wanted to discover the world and to discover Jerusalem. The city was full of tourists, and she herself was an Arab tourist who spoke a foreign language. She had difficulty pronouncing 'ayn, which he found amusing because it sounded like an 'a.' She asked him to teach her the right pronunciation to avoid making a mistake, but he found the mistake charming.

They ended up committing a great mistake, a major sin, a deadly mistake. What did they tell her at the convent and why did she go there? Why did she hide, why did she run away? How did she ever dream of having a major story like his stories! He wrote true stories from real life, while she did not know real life—except from what others had told her. Later she knew real life, but at what price!

Where was the rest of the story? The rest of the page was covered up on all the copies, five copies of the same incomplete page. Let's slow down and look closely at what she wrote, let's see how it all happened. She wrote that she had asked him to teach her in order to avoid making a mistake, and he had replied that he would teach her so that they would make a mistake. But he never said those words, he had said exactly the opposite—something similar to those words, but in a different context. They did not go to the hostel to exchange their dollars, but she wanted to take him there. When I came to my senses and realized what had happened, she had run away. I went seeking my father's help, and meanwhile she had disappeared. She put me in a trap and disappeared. It was her habit to attract a person until he got very close to her, then drop him without the slightest concern for him. One had to run like crazy to catch up with her. I was that crazy person running after her. This had been my condition after the Nakba, the defeat, after the exile, and all the events and the failures. I was like a crazy person. She would loom at the horizon like a mirage, then she would turn her back. Oh, Mariam, where is reality? Where is the way? What have we come to?

He thought that she had experience like the tourists and the foreigners. He saw her from two different angles, as a teacher who knew more than him and as a character in a story in an extraordinary world. That milieu fired his thinking and filled his imagination with images and emotions that brought tears to his eyes. He would cry whenever a story touched his heart and provoked his pity and passion. He had wished to live a big story filled with dangers, escape, victims and earthquakes, a story full of palm trees, ships, invasions, and battles, stories with exile, prisons, and hurricanes. He saw in her the woman of fire; she burned him and he became a prisoner of her imagination. She was overcome by a deep feeling of satisfaction and happiness. Isn't it wonderful that people see us as we want them to? Isn't it wonderful that we fire their imagination? It is the best of feelings. She will one day publish what she writes for the people to read. The only problem was that she too had become obsessed by what she wrote; she lived the story and the events became immersed in that world and she believed what she imagined. Did she love him? Without a doubt. But what about him—did he love the original or the copy, did he love Mariam and her story, or did he love Mariam because of her story? She wished she knew.

I threw the page away feeling as if I had been hit by an earthquake. This is what I had been to her, just a stupid man. She had lied to me all those years and tortured me, and I had believed her feelings and her words. Now she revealed how much she had toyed with me. Was this possible? What about the pregnancy, what about the son or daughter—was this another lie? It couldn't be—look at those clothes and diapers. Could they be for a baby of the family, a nephew or those of her brothers from the fifties, something like the notebooks of the fifties. If this was the case, then I didn't have an heir and Michael was right when he denied being my son. If Mariam were only an image and her supposed love only an image, if all the events, the experiences, and the pregnancy were doubtful occurrences, then Michael was also an image and my search was purposeless and useless. Let's slow down—no one could corroborate what she wrote but Jamileh. Where was Jamileh?

I took the papers, closed down the house, and returned to Jerusalem looking for her, for the original copy of her image.

Before letting Jamileh in on my true intentions, I had to study her psyche and her background, the strengths and weaknesses in her personality. I wanted to know whether she was difficult, conservative, stubborn; or lenient and flexible, easy to work with. This would be important if I were to succeed in convincing her that the whole story had been a simple mistake, a matter of fate in a strange world filled with extraordinary things, with stories that writers and bad mouths could never have invented. Though things were different now from the fifties and the sixties, Jamileh, due to her age and her background, belonged to the past generation and those left from the decade of the Nakba.

Jamileh surprised me and proved the fallacy of preconceived notions and my expectations. She had worked as a nurse in St. Elias' Hospital since her youth. She had seen her share of tragedies, miseries, and contradictions, and as a result was open-minded; nothing surprised her. She was responsible for the food supplies and storage at the hospital, a position that had presented her with endless temptations and difficulties. She couldn't remember the number of promises made and enticements offered in exchange for turning a blind eye to what was happening on all levels, high and low. At the higher levels, things were occurring in the administration, accounting, and documents, regarding the number of sacks, the particularities of grains, foods, and their production and expiration dates. At the lower levels, there were the petty thefts of sheets, soap, plates and spoons, sanitary napkins and children's diapers, sugar and tea. She faced all kinds of thievery, large and small, with great calm and resolve, without scandals and threats, always returning the stolen objects to their place. She was basically religious, and the events of the world and people's natures made her stick to principles derived from religion; principles that had become, with time, her religion. She would light a candle to the Virgin for a good deed accomplished and a candle to the devil for an evil action. To her, good and evil consisted in stealing and truthfulness, and keeping secrets. She was silent, a woman of few words who smiled rarely and did not laugh at the jokes heard around her. This might have had something to do with her unhappy childhood, which permanently etched a gloomy expression into her features. She had been an orphan since her childhood and had lived in a convent with orphans. Then she married a sick man who burdened her with worries and responsibilities that increased her silent gloominess and her eternal dependence on the church. This explained her intransigence in matters of truth and lies and keeping trust and secrets. Her husband died after years of suffering. His death freed her of a heavy burden that had exhausted her morally and physically and deprived her of sleep. She felt an unexplainable sense of guilt as a result of the freedom she enjoyed after his death. She had served the man with all her strength and carried him on her back like Christ carried his cross, without complaint or resentment; she had neither asked for help nor neglected her work at the hospital, but had performed her duties efficiently. She would wake up in the morning and find herself free of the usual schedule of medicines, x-rays, standing in the queues at the pharmacy, blood donations, and so on. She would sleep the whole night without the usual interruptions caused by his coughing, his complaints from the fever, and the bouts of pain.

She considered the feeling of relief following his death to be an apostasy and an act of rebellion against God's will. Her sense of guilt increased her preoccupation with truth and honesty and keeping secrets. She became the savior of employees of both sexes, patients, victims, and those who escaped from arrests, hiding in the storerooms waiting for daybreak or downfall. She herself became a victim of abuse when two young American religious Jews broke into her house and settled on the upper floor, explaining that they were fulfilling a promise made to a chosen people to whom God wanted to give the land of Palestine. Since she was not a member of the chosen people, she lost the rights to her property and became involved in legal procedures that had a beginning but have had no end. Her case remained pending with no solution or end in sight, adding to her anger and taciturnity. Her already gloomy face became gloomier, she would not talk unless asked a question, she would not smile unless she was making sarcastic comments, and she would not seek help unless she was unable personally to execute what she was asked to do.

With such a background it was not easy to persuade Jamileh to talk about Mariam and her son and benefit from the information in her possession. It was imperative to get to the subject indirectly without raising her suspicion and closing a valuable source of information. I therefore used the visit to the house in Jerusalem as an excuse. I began with one house and went on to visit more and more houses until I had checked out ten houses. At first I felt guilty because I was wasting her time with an imaginary project that I used to bait her like a fish. With time, I got used to her company and even enjoyed it; she too found the process enjoyable, since every visit was followed by an invitation to a restaurant where we would eat and drink and spend time observing tourists. We talked very little, and what we said was limited to a comparison of the various houses I visited. With time, she became less formal and came out of her shell, making sarcastic, intelligent remarks and asking shrewd targeted questions. One day we were sitting in the Seven Arches restaurant overlooking a panoramic and eternally beautiful view of Jerusalem, tasting delicious appetizers and drinking wine, and she asked me, relaxed and smiling, "Tell me frankly, what do you really want?"

When she asked me the question she was staring at me with her small, wrinkled eyes, sunk in her plump, kind face, exhibiting a half-sarcastic, half-malicious, but kind smile. I was embarrassed and pretended to be absorbed in the beautiful view, then said to change the subject, "I want Jerusalem."

She smiled sarcastically, and said sadly, "And who does not want Jerusalem! But please tell me, and tell the truth."

She then drank wine, ate a piece of cheese with the tip of the knife, and said with confidence, "Feel free to speak openly." Then she tapped her chest with her hand and added, "This is the well of secrets; you can say whatever you'd like."

I had no choice but to tell her everything, the whole story from beginning to end. I told her how, with God's will, I had been successful in everything I did except marriage and children. I was left without a companion, without a family, and without love. My heart was sad and time was passing, I could not walk the paths of love though love was the object, the meaning of life, and all that counted in the world. I explained that my conscience was heavy and that doubts filled my heart. Things would have been different if I had not returned and had doubts that Michael was my son, if I had not seen this view, this sky, and this dome, and felt the morning breeze, heard the ringing of the bell, smelled incense and carnations. Walking in the dark alleys brought back my childhood, my youth, and memories of Mariam. Walking in the streets, smelling incense, hearing old tunes in the market, seeing familiar faces despite my absence and despite the armed soldiers—all this took me to cherished places, and my heart shook with yearning and the signs of love. I had lost my capacity to feel and interact, my heart was rusty, my feelings had died. I faced dangers and massacres, I got used to a life in exile, but I had become garbage. Here, I felt intimacy; my heart had revived. I cried, I yearned, and I remembered. Did she remember me? Would she recognize me after such a long separation and so many years? Would she respond to my feelings?

Jamileh looked at me under the effect of wine, the beautiful view of Jerusalem, and the joy of this moment of open-hearted conversation and whispered, "This is strange. I thought, or I assumed, that you wanted something from the storage room!"

I stared at her in shock, surprised by her comments, which had nothing to do with compassion and pity, or even accusations and blame. I noticed, sadly, that we were on two different planets, going in different directions. While I was talking about Mariam and the past, with my emotions coming directly from my past memories and the longing of the heart, she was thinking about rice and sugar and diapers. A few moments later, while we were both staring at our wine glasses, trying to assimilate all that was said, she whispered, "You mean Mariam? Everything for Mariam?"

I asked, surprised, "Is there anything more important than Mariam?"

She did not reply, but continued to stare and count the olive seeds. I repeated, with a broken heart, "Is there anything more important than Mariam?"

She said dryly and curtly, to my great surprise, "Of course there is—an escaped prisoner in need of a shelter."

Jamileh told me about Mariam. Jamileh's husband was still alive when Mariam took refuge in their house, running away from her brothers, the village, and people's gossip. She settled in the upper floor of the house and stayed there until she delivered her baby. They did not charge her anything at first, though the upper floor was a good source of income whenever they rented it during holidays and special occasions, when the hotels and the motels were full to capacity with pilgrims and tourists of all kind. Suddenly the mother appeared and began visiting her daughter regularly, giving her a few dollars for her needs. Then Mariam found a job in an Armenian photo shop, and she was able to pay rent regularly. When the baby was born, the mother paid money and Jamileh was able to arrange for a birth certificate through the hospital. She wrote her name and her husband's as the parents of the baby. Everybody knew, however, that the couple was sterile and that the birth certificate was phony and belonged to an illegitimate child of unknown origin. The women's main preoccupation was the future of the child, his rights and his identity. They succeeded in their plans, and the husband died and left the baby his name. The baby lived and carried his name.

"What about my name?" I asked sadly. She gave me that special look and I asked again, "And Mariam's name?"

She did not reply. I asked her, "Where are they both?"

"Two years later I went to Beirut, and when I returned she was gone, as if the earth had swallowed her."

"What about the child?" I asked.

"He disappeared with her."

"Has she left anything behind, any trace?" I asked.

Jamileh described what she found upon her return, "Everything remained as it was, the furniture and the baby clothes. When I lost hope of ever seeing her again, I collected all her things and put them in the attic."

"Did you inform anyone about her disappearance?" I asked.

"Her mother."

"What about the police and the security people?" I asked.

She gave me that special look again and said ironically, "You mean the army?"

I didn't reply. I continued to search, or rather began my search in the occupied upper floor of Jamileh's house. I proceeded very carefully, despite the two young men living there. Jamileh designed a solid plan for the search.

We had to be extremely careful to avoid being discovered or caught while searching, as the two young men had obtained an ownership title to the place. How, why, and based on what law did this happen? Mrs. Jamileh was unable to find an explanation. Nothing could justify the fact that two Jewish young men from New York would force their way into the house of a woman and obtain an order for the ownership of the house despite the ownership title Jamileh had in her possession. It was stamped with Ottoman, British, and Jordanian seals. She had suffered bitterly from that judgment and those neighbors; she had nothing but dirt, problems, and threats from them. When she had tried to discuss matters with them using logic and common sense, they replied with threats and by hurling dirt from the floor above: fruit peels, sardine cans, and stones. She would have emigrated like thousands before her had it not been for her sense of defiance. She could have disappeared in mysterious circumstances and her disappearance would have been registered against an unknown person. Was this the beginning of the thread? I must search in order to know.

The search here was more difficult than in other places. We had to sneak into the upper floor during the absence of the young men lest they find out. We designed a plan: she would sit at the entrance of the house to watch the alley and keep her finger on the bell to warn me.

Things did not go well the first day. I had barely stepped in the house when I heard the warning bell loud and clear. I rushed down the stairs to avoid crossing the two foreigners on my way, and I saw Jamileh come up smiling and apologetic, blaming her weak eyesight and her fear for the mistake. I went back up again to the upper floor of the house.

The place was large and beautiful, with colored glass in the windows. There were also arches and large platforms from where one could see the palm trees of the Aqsa Mosque, the Golden Dome, and stone houses stuck to each other. There were openings for lights, mashrabiyas and hanging trellises on the roofs. Directly facing me was the neighbor's washing and a curtain that protected the inhabitants of the house from strangers' eyes. A woman looked up, saw me, and showed hostility toward me, but when she looked down and saw Jamileh sitting at the entrance of the house she understood and said to her, "Jamileh, have you lost anything?" Jamileh looked up and replied sarcastically, "Everything is lost." The neighbor shook a shirt she wanted to hang and said, cheerfully, "Don't worry, Mrs. Jamileh, you'll soon find it." She then looked at me in a friendly way and smiled approvingly, repeating, "Tomorrow you'll find it."

I began looking. The hall was vast like in the old houses. It was surrounded by rooms for various purposes. One of them contained boxes and a computer. The walls were decorated with black-and-white photos, posters showing frowning men with beards and whiskers and wearing hats. Others revealed drawings of guns, candles, and flames. The furniture was as Jamileh had described it in all its details: beds and cupboards in the bedrooms, a set of sofas in the living room made of olive wood and decorated with mother-of-pearl and Hebron blown glass. As for the computer and the boxes, they were new, and so was the smell, the smell of grease and oils and dirty clothes. It was a strange mix difficult to identify. The smell was neither repugnant enough to cause one to faint, nor pleasant enough to become familiar. It was a strange thing in a strange environment and a strange presence, as if I were in an old café in Herzlia or Dizengoff. The boxes contained books, weapons, and fliers, nothing that would have had anything to do with Mariam. There was nothing in the furniture or the cupboards that would have belonged to her or to the baby. The furniture was truly a reflection of Jamileh, as was the arrangement of the house. It revealed her ancestry, her father and grandfather. It was a vast house, a welcoming house, with southern windows and old glass. I looked through the window and called Jamileh in a low voice, but she didn't hear me. The neighbor who was hanging her washing volunteered to call her. Jamileh looked up and said something I could not figure out. Again the neighbor helped transmit her words and told me, "Look in the boxes in the attic," and smiled.

I went back to my search. I used the ladder I found behind the door to climb to the attic. There I found many boxes. I turned on the weak light and opened the window to air out the place and get more light. The first box contained baby clothes that had been destroyed by termites and mildew. There was a shirt that looked like a sieve, a jacket filled with holes, and a flimsy blanket. Thirty years, or rather, thirty-five years, destroy metal, cars, and the asphalt of the roads, let alone a baby's clothes. The baby is now a man, so what am I looking for? I'm looking for a trace, an entity, a birth certificate, a proof that the young man is my child, that he is mine and my heir, though he carries someone else's name, that he is a branch in my family tree. I am looking for the woman, the one I loved, her memory and who she truly was, not what I thought she was.

I searched non-stop, in this container, in that box, in another box and another. There were no papers. Time was passing quickly and the neighbor hanging her washing on the roof was shouting, "Hey Ismail, be careful going down the stairs."

I was suffocating from the smell and the pressure in the attic, the heat and the spittle of the termites. At last I found some papers in the bottom of another box, a notebook. It was an agenda with a calendar, a different page for each day. On the first page was written: a milk bottle. Nido, Cerelac powder, cream, and a kilo of apples. The following day indicated cashing $200, sponges for the kitchen, eggs, cheese, orange-blossom water for the baby's colic, bread, and olives. Then there was a series of comments here and there in short sentences in the midst of the shopping list:

> I feel dizzy in this world, pressure is making my head explode, I am oppressed, the baby is getting on my nerves, loneliness is killing me, I took a membership in a nearby library, I take Arabic language lessons, the teacher says that I am the brightest of all the students, he also says that whoever writes in one language can write in all the languages of the earth.

I turned the pages and read the comments; then came pages without dates, or rather with the dates erased. The dates were mixed. The spaces were larger than the days and history. What she had written was history, memoirs, words to get matters off her chest, not a novel, and this was better! No one had seen those papers except me, and Mariam of course. The secret was safe, in the world of forgetfulness, no scandals to fear.

On one of the pages and the one that followed I read these comments:

> One day he will look for the child and he won't find him. Do I hate him? They say that motherhood is miraculous, pure love, pure affection, sacrifice, devotion, and gratefulness, but I only feel oppression and revolt, I want to run away from my heart. Why should I be the only one tied down? This feeling and this baby hurt me and overwhelm me. The pressure on my head is increasing, I am oppressed, I am lonely.

There was some empty space, a few lines without a single word written on them, then the start of a new mood:

> I find myself when I am with the Armenians. It was Christmas yesterday, I left the baby with Jamileh and I spent the evening with them. I stayed up late, I drank, danced, and smoked, and when I woke up I was alone. I remembered the baby and I began to

cry. They all surrounded me and asked what was wrong with me. They said I was young and beautiful and I should enjoy my life. They said that all was well and soon my son would grow up and be a man, he would support me, that nothing remains the same except motherhood and blood relations. But what about me, I thought? My needs and my deeds? Should I dance or write or look after the baby? I borrow books and return them, and I look for a job, but what do I want? What shall I do?

There were other shopping and revenue lists and pages full of her comments on the baby:

He laughs, plays, crawls, and walks. I adore him, he is my life. Fertook said, Haig loves you. I laughed and said, I love only myself and the milk of the baby, this beautiful baby. This creature is a source of pain for me. Love is painful, love is suffering. My mother says that no matter how severe we get with the children we forgive them. My mother forgave me, but will God forgive me? My aunt says something else, she says that love is from God and what comes from God is rest. To offer one's soul to God is relaxing. I will visit my aunt on Sunday.

The neighbor shouts to attract my attention, "Hey people, why are you so late!"

I was totally involved in the sentences Mariam had written. There was an empty space on the page, then money received, travels and other short, incomplete sentences:

I visited Nazareth on Sunday. I placed the baby in the convent daycare. I borrowed a book and some references. I bought some items and a ticket.

There was nothing more until the end of the page, and it was the last page. I searched again for something new, a document, his birth certificate, his name. What was his name? She had never once mentioned it. Jamileh did not mention his name either and I forgot to ask her. I'd ask her when I went down; I would remember. I felt so sad, I was depressed. I was surrounded with Mariam's presence, I felt her, my heart returned to its youth, and a sad feeling like a delicate thread penetrated my heart and dug into it. My heart moaned like that of a lover. Was it possible to be in love after sixty? Could the heart return to its youth after sixty?

I went on looking, and the pile of removed items grew. There were the boxes, the heat of the low bulb, and the summer heat when the bell blared, and I heard the neighbor call me as if calling a child playing, "Hey Ismail, come down! Hey, Ismail hurry up! Be careful, don't fall."

The bell was blaring, and I was returning the things to the boxes while the voice of the neighbor repeated the same warning. But I fell from fear while rushing; I fell off the ladder. I managed to get up and I dragged my sprained foot as the bell continued to blare. I closed the door behind me and went down the stairs, limping, and when I reached Jamileh's house, I collapsed.

At dinner, I was totally distraught and told Jamileh that I was responsible for what had happened, that I was lost. But Jamileh challenged this and herself took responsibility for the turn of events. She explained, "I am responsible. If I had not been stubborn and hardheaded Mariam would have stayed and I would have had an heir to inherit the house and give me some peace of mind. Who will inherit the house when I die, the lower and upper floors? Who will pursue the court cases? Who will throw them out?"

The food stuck in my throat as I heard her speak. There were many who were claiming Mariam's son, wishing to have him, looking and waiting for him! I was now competing with Jamileh over her heir! She confessed to me, as I had confessed to her, that she was the cause, but for what was she responsible? Why was she distressed?

"Listen to me," she said, "I am old-fashioned and I cannot accept that a woman stays out at night. She had gone to the Armenian convent and stayed there all night and left her son with me. He was crying for his mother. I had just lost my husband, and I was in mourning. My heart was heavy; I was sad, and my conscience was still nagging me. I felt I hadn't done all I could for the man, but I was happy to be free of the burden. Believe me, Ibrahim, the man was an angel, despite his suffering he never complained but always thanked me, wished me good health, and treated me like a lady. He used to say that I was his life, the best of all women. No one had ever treated me like he did. It scared me to feel so relieved after losing such a kind man, who appreciated me despite my infertility. I didn't give him a son or a daughter, and I'm not a beauty queen, but a broken-hearted orphan with a gloomy face that had forgotten how to smile. I do not smile. Everybody says that the sun rises when I smile. Khalil was happy and made me feel that I was beautiful and a princess. He respected me, cheered me up, filled my life with joy and made me feel safe, until his illness, when I became scared. I became a broken-hearted orphan again. I feared the world, his illness and his suffering, I dreaded the x-rays, blood tests, and chemotherapy. I forgot how to be happy and became gloomy. By the time he died, I had had enough of grief and his long suffering. I took a vacation and slept. I slept day and night, and when I woke up, I opened the kitchen window, I saw the sun, I smelled the scents of the world and the Arabian jasmine. I felt I was breathing for the first time, I felt that the sun was beautiful and happy, and the morning breeze was as sweet as sugar. I felt light; I could fly and breathe. I raised my head and said, 'Thank you God, thank you, thank you.' Then I became aware of what I was saying, thanking God for taking him? He was generous and good-hearted, while I was a wretched dwarf, a worm of the earth." She carried on, "I went to church, confessed, and took communion. The priest said not to worry, that it was normal, that I should live my life and be proud. God had given and God had taken away. It was God's will, and I must live my life. But God wanted otherwise because Mariam got me involved in her life. She would leave the baby and be gone for long periods of time. The child cried for her, and I didn't know what to do for him. He cried when I carried him, and he cried when I gave him his milk. He wanted his mother, and I was his mother only on paper. Believe me, though, this boy was my life. You should have seen how beautiful his eyes and cheeks were. He was plump as a duck, with dimples on the back of his hands. When I held his hands and kissed his beautiful fingers, he would look at me with eyes like narcissi and almond blossom. He was so beautiful, you should have seen him, ya Ibrahim, I have never loved anyone like him, he was more than a son to me, believe me. But I was stubborn. Drink Ibrahim, drink. Bring another bottle and pour some for me. What's wrong? Are you tired? Your foot is fine, a simple sprain. You won't feel anything by tomorrow. What were we saying?"

I whispered, "The boy was plump as a duck, there were dimples on the back of his hands, and his eyes like open narcissi and almond blossom, ya Ibrahim!"

She held her glass and drank like me, then we were lost in our silence. I looked at her a short time later and saw tears in her eyes. When I stretched my arm out to pat her hand, she took hold of my hand and said sadly, "I am responsible; I didn't understand. If it weren't for my stubbornness and my education Mariam would have remained, and I would have had someone with me in the house. Do you see how my house is always empty and gloomy, and if it weren't for the neighbors I would have died of loneliness and melancholy. But Mariam, oh Mariam! I was young, with a nun's education, and depressed. I didn't understand. Now I understand, and I regret it. I mean that after the sadness and what we endured, after the loneliness, I finally understand Mariam. I used to blame her and tell her that such a beautiful baby shouldn't be left alone for a single minute. I couldn't understand how she had the courage to leave him; I wondered if she had a mother's heart. She would cry and hug the baby, and go on crying, and the baby would cry. Later on, I understood the situation and said to myself that if I felt fear and needed warmth, if I felt the burden and despite my stiffness and severe look, I missed him and longed to hold him, why then did I blame her for her feelings? Do you know something? Sometimes we are weary with those we love and we drop the responsibility to breathe, do you understand me?"

I shook my head and sighed, "Of course I understand."

She went on, pensive and reflective, "Then we regret and are bored. Do you understand me?"

"Of course I do."

She went on, "The price we pay is a terrible loneliness, cold and freezing. Do you see my house? It is an empty house, bare and cold. Had it not been for you I would have been deeply asleep by now. Had Khalil remained in the house despite his illness, had she stayed, had the baby stayed, I wouldn't have been alone. I have no one; I'm like you. We're in the same boat. Promise me, swear by God and by all those you hold dear to you, swear, swear."

I asked surprised, "Why should I swear?"

"Swear by God and promise me that if you find the boy, your son and mine, this certificate is his. Don't forget. Take it and keep it with you. My house is not safe. If you find Michael, you know what to do."

I whispered, relaxed, feeling relieved, "Michael, you say? Of course, of course, give me the certificate."

I resumed my search the following morning. The neighbor was up on the roof hanging her washing or pretending to do so, while Jamileh was downstairs watching the alley and the street. I went up despite my sprained foot and began looking.

Before I went up she said fearfully, "I'm scared; what if they catch us and they shoot you!"

I said proudly, "I'm not afraid, I'm up to the responsibility."

But I truly was afraid because they had weapons and I was not armed; they had judges and court-houses; they had an army and a government, whereas I was sixty and Jamileh was seventy, and I had a limp. I felt like a racehorse whose time is past, while the road is still long and the race is not over. Had I been a svelte young man, had my heart been healthy, had I been young and enthusiastic, believing in something or having hope, things would have been different. However, what could I lose? I wouldn't lose anything I didn't gain. I was the only one without a family, without an heir, without a child and a loved one. What did I own? If I didn't succeed, I wouldn't lose. So I went up, and Jamileh went down to the entrance of the house.

What was in this box? Pictures, a cross, icons under magazines, a New Testament still wrapped in its paper, and beside it a greeting card in its envelope. I opened the envelope and saw a white card decorated with foliage and Christ's blood, a cross carried by a young angel on his back. At the bottom of the card there were a few words written in large characters and pale ink, "We find peace in God's spirit. Your loving aunt, Sister Eugenie. Nazareth, 12/26/1969."

She must have gone to her aunt at the old people's home where her mother was living. I remembered the picture of the aunt and the wheelchair with Mariam standing behind it. The mother must be there with the aunt, and the girl was there too, living like her, the life of a nun. I liked the idea that Mariam was living with the nuns, their same pure life. I was upset with the idea of her visits to the Armenian convent, the late evenings, and the Christmas party. She had left the baby crying till the morning under Jamileh's care. She drank and stayed up late, and Jamileh blamed her for neglecting her son. I, too, wondered how she could have left him and me. I knew that this was pure nonsense, but it was how I was brought up. I was as conservative as Jamileh and maybe more; that is why I liked the idea of her presence in the convent, living like a nun, like her aunt. Let's suppose she was there and had gotten used to that life, would she be willing to return to me? I tried to calm myself, to refrain from anticipating matters, to take things one step at a time. I did not know what to expect.

I had hardly started when I heard the sound of the bell and the voice of the neighbor saying, "Hey Ismail, come down, come down, hurry up. Be careful, don't fall."

I was confused, my foot was hurting, and I was very nervous. I was limping, I hit a chair and a hanger. I heard the sound of steps. I closed the door and saw Jamileh in the middle of the stairs close to where I was standing while the neighbor was urging me on to leave and predicting that I would receive a serious beating.

Jamileh came heavily up the stairs, breathing with difficulty and advised me to return and climb up to where the antenna was located. I did as she asked, climbing, limping in pain, trying to save myself and my poor heart, telling myself that I wouldn't go down, not yet. When we got there she stood breathless. I looked down and saw how the house was surrounded, with machine guns, fabric bags, and whiskers. I also saw the neighbor behind the clothes, terrified at what she was seeing. When they entered and the door of their apartment was closed, we sneaked down like thieves.

We entered the house without making any noise and closed the door. Jamileh sat on the sofa but didn't say a word. We remained silent and still, as if we were spying on the inhabitants of the house, as if they were the owners of the house and we were the neighbors!

The Covenant

A beautiful morning reigned over Nazareth in Galilee and a song was humming in my heart. I come to you searching for a love we shared, for the scent of the past and for a green branch of hope. I left behind vast spaces dozing in the shade to seek your light and share in your sun and your tenderness, hoping to be transformed into a youthful mare baptized by the East.

They told me that Mariam was in a convent there and that the convent was next door to the body-building gym and summer camps of a youth association. Her mother was in an old people's home run by the nuns of the convent and the Association. Mariam was seen there, appearing and disappearing frequently, ahead of the preparations for the summer season.

I started looking for Mariam, but where was she? I was told she had left for al-Ludd, then to Ras al-Naqurah. She had then gone with the pilgrims to the Church of the Holy Sepulcher and the Mount of Olives. I looked for her in all of Galilee, on the coast from Ras al-Naqurah to the Negev. Some advised me to wait for her in the evenings, stay close to her mother as she might return to see her at the beginning of summer.

I went to the convent, then visited the hospital and the old people's home. I walked through the area that overlooked the camp and the forest of oak trees.

I saw the elderly people, and the doctors and nuns wearing their white robes and moving in a vast space with shining tiled floors that reflected my shadow like a mirror.

I inquired at the reception desk. The nun asked who I was, and I explained, pleadingly, that I was a relative who had come from Jerusalem. She smiled, welcomed me and invited me to feel at home. She asked how I was. I described the difficulties on the road, the long trip despite the proximity of the place. I told her about the many buses I had had to change to get there. I had stopped at many stations filled with strangers, and had felt as if I were in the West, as if I were in New York. I had been concerned about the search and the new attack in Haifa. I had gotten through, miraculously. I had seen the search operations and the military checkpoints looking for any Arab going through, but maybe because of the way I look and . . . she looked at me inquisitively. Embarrassed, I said, "Because of my age." I looked around me and saw the wheelchairs and the stretchers, a woman walking with crutches, and an old man moving unsteadily, almost crawling, his shadow reflected beneath his feet. He was about to fall, and seeing him in that condition made me repeat, "Because of my age too."

She whispered, "Do not despair, here ages are renewable."

I asked bewildered, "Here, in this place?"

She replied, "Look through the window, under the balcony, what do you see?"

"A camp," I said.

She explained, "That is right, here there are old people, and there, the young people. Do you understand now?"

Of course I did, but suddenly I heard a noise I couldn't identify.

I went out to the balcony to investigate. What I saw made me believe that the end of the world was at hand. There were many young people working in groups, some building fences, others paving the streets and painting the metal; some were digging in the ground, and others carried baskets and buckets of paint. The work was in its early stages, and directions were given through loudspeakers. I was concerned about the noise level, wondering if this didn't disturb the residents, but the nun reassured me that there was complete silence and quiet in the rooms. She took me to the rooms, where I could see for myself the mother in her seat, surrounded by complete silence. I saw the youth camp through the windowpane, and in the room there was a speechless and motionless mother.

The doctor said that she was not deaf but in a coma; in other words, she lived in her own world. Sometimes she woke up and interacted, asking about Mariam and the children. She said things we did not remember, and said all the nonsense that her age entitled her to. The doctor explained, as he examined me, that it was normal at that age. I said, fearfully, "I know, I know." I sat on the edge of the chair observing her. She was in a wheelchair without her glasses, her uncovered head revealed thin gray hair, and the veins of her hands looked like worms. The changes in appearance at that age are frightening. What mattered, however, was not the way we looked but the nap, the coma, the dwindling awareness and the dying brain cells.

I ran away from the odor of death and went out to the balcony. The doctor followed me and asked me about Jerusalem, what we had done about it, how conditions were there. He asked about the road and the operation, whether I was bothered on my way. He asked about my work, whether I was a relative, whether I had someone I could stay with in Galilee. He recommended a small hotel nearby that was not subject to searches or controls. He said he would see me in the evening at the camp, where dancing, music, and singing were the attraction.

Where was the aunt, that aunt who used to come through the Mandelbaum Gate? Her name had once caused a heated discussion between Mariam and myself, I remember well what we had said, the words we had uttered that now seem like a joke. Mariam had said that the place was like paradise, and I agree with her now. I have never seen more beautiful gardens than those of Carmel and the springs of Galilee. I passed through the place, half bent, fearing that I would be stopped by a policeman looking for my pass. Fear didn't stop me from forging ahead and neither did the operation, but where was the aunt?

I knocked at the door, filled with apprehension, but I soon heard a voice inviting me to enter. I went in fearfully, advancing carefully. Standing before me was a nun slightly taller than me, still sturdy despite the signs of aging on her face. There was another nun, wearing big eyeglasses over large eyes and a stern look. She asked my name and the purpose of my visit. I told her about the West Bank, the mountains of Jerusalem and the longing of the heart for the right direction. I told her about my lost dreams, my lost love, and my lost future. I had roamed the world looking for a purpose and a cause. I carried my grandfather's name and my father's traits of character, but I had failed to find a son who would accept me and be my heir. I made a mistake and I regret it, but would Christ accept that I suffer forever, would I remain guilty and never find a fair judge who would overturn my guilty verdict? If Jesus can permit this situation, then how different is he from common mortals? I am in a constant state of searching for a past I lived, a beautiful woman who belonged to me, and a son who doesn't know his father's name. My son is lost and Mariam is his mother, while I am here looking for the beginning of the thread that would show me the way.

She lowered her eyes, thinking of Jesus's decision for me. Would he forgive me or not, would he save a sinner from his sin? Dreading the verdict, I sat on the edge of my seat and looked out across the glass of the balcony door. I heard the young people singing a song I used to hear in Rome, which made me feel homesick and desperate. I had heard it in the car, driving through mountainous roads, looking at the trees, the almond blossoms, the shade of pine trees and a scent that spread in the evening all the way to the coast and the banks of the river. Fairouz would sing for the sea while our boats moved us through the sands of exile and the trajectory of departure. At that time and from that distance, my return to paradise was only a dream, I was hoping for an encounter I once experienced, but it was scattered across the spheres and we were dispersed.

The singing of the young people came loudly through the microphones, making me cry. When the nun saw my tears she took my hand and led me to the balcony. She pointed out the spot where Mariam sometimes may be. She said that she might come today, tomorrow, or any other day, she did not know when, but with patience I could see her because of her mother, and this convent where she usually stayed. She might come today because the volunteers were celebrating the pouring of the cement today. The guests would come from Galilee and the West Bank.

"You might find her with her mother. Have you asked her mother?" she said.

"She is deaf," I said.

"It's a passing thing. One day she's totally oblivious to the world, like a statue, and the next day she can be alert and reasonable, in a state of complete awareness. Try again."

I asked if she had forgiven me. She said, reproachfully, that it was not up to her to forgive. She then stared at me and whispered, "Would you forgive?"

She shook my hand, preparing to take leave of me. I kissed it and said, "Paradise will always be here, with the aunt."

I told her what we had said then about the place where she lived. She pardoned us and said that those were mere words and that paradise is in paradise and nowhere else. I left then.

The hotel was in a back street, only a couple of minutes walk from the convent. Its entrance looked like that of a large family home, while its small garden didn't convey any commercial or tourist use. The façade of the hotel didn't differ from the appearance of any house on a quiet residential street. I crossed the short entry hall and rang the bell. A smiling hotel clerk met me, took my luggage without asking any questions, and walked me to a small counter in the corner of a large living room. There were no formalities. When I told the receptionist that I had no permit, he lowered his glasses on his nose as he wrote down the room number and said in a friendly way, "Have I asked you for anything? I know who you are, I got the news from the doctor who was here a while ago. Would you like coffee or orange juice? Welcome, consider yourself one of us, this is your home."

We sat at the bar drinking beer and talking about the situation and the future. An hour later, I knew him and his relationship with the lodgers. I learned that the hotel belonged to his paternal uncle, who had immigrated in 1948, the year of the Nakba and the establishment of the State of Israel. The State had taken possession of the building, renting it according to the law. He in turn rented it from the Israeli government according to the law, and turned it into a hotel for family members, relatives, and a few pilgrims during special festivals. Its proximity to the convent brought lodgers without a permit such as myself. All those who came from Jerusalem and the West Bank over the years since the Nakba have stayed with him.

I asked eagerly, "Since the Nakba?"

He confirmed that, smiled, straightened his mustaches and said jokingly, "Do I look as old as that?"

I smiled and said sadly, "Of course you look it. We all grew older."

He raised his glass and said loudly, "Why are you afraid? Take heart, we're still young."

Young, young! What was wrong with him, what is wrong with all of them? They're like birds, they love to dance and they adore singing. They never miss an opportunity to celebrate, drink, and sing *mawawil.* Aren't they part of our people, haven't they endured what we endured? Haven't they been hit by the same storms and broken their boats on the rocks of exile?

He smiled and said confidently, twisting his mustaches, "If the heart loses its youth, you're done for. Laugh and be merry and live like a sultan. We're the same age, aren't we? But don't ever address me as an older man, because my heart is young and I feel young and my life is full of experiences. This hotel, if you like to call it that, has seen many young, beautiful women with murderous eyes, and let me tell you a secret: don't believe that time reduces your energy. It is your feelings that count, and you can do whatever you want with them. I have fallen in love with all the girls I've met, regardless of the way they looked. What counts is keeping your heart full and young, true?"

I looked at him sideways and said hesitantly, "It might be true."

He resumed enthusiastically, "Life is beautiful for those who are beautiful. Would you like to drink some more? Yussef, get me another bottle from the freezer, I put it aside for the another lodger, but our compatriots are more deserving. The lodger in question is a Red, I mean a Russian. He is an actor or an artist, God only knows what. The poor man was encouraged to emigrate to the land of honey, but instead of eating honey, guess what he ate?"

I looked up and watched him for a moment, but before I replied he nudged my shoulder, laughed loudly and said, "Onions, onions, believe me, he ate onions."

I didn't react and remained silent, fearing another boring talk about the State, the rules and regulations, and the worries of Galilee. I had enough to worry about while looking for Mariam.

He nudged me again in the shoulder and said, "Do you know what, brother? The Russian Jews are even worse than the European Jews—I don't know why. How can you explain a Communist forgetting his philosophy whenever he sees money? Are all the Soviets like this? Why then have they bothered us about Lenin and his teachings, Stalin and the others? It's all nonsense! To tell you the truth, I only believe what I see; what is written in the books is for dervishes, but those who have traveled the world and delved into people's secrets are not fooled by such talk. Let me tell you something, when I returned from Lebanon where I first immigrated, I was still young. I worked on a farm that was transformed into a kibbutz. Do you know what a kibbutz is?"

I nodded my head affirmatively a few times but he objected, shouting,

"No, you don't know what it is! There are totally white kibbutzim and totally red kibbutzim and there are some white and red. My friend, I worked in a totally red kibbutz, in other words a communist or a socialist kibbutz, call it whatever you want. People there were decent, but don't think that because they treated each other decently they treated us well. I can't deny, however, that they gave me my salary to the last penny; they never took away anything. They used to invite me to their club to educate me. They wanted me to learn how workers lived and to listen to their defense of workers' rights. I accepted their invitations, and every day when I finished my work I went to the club to listen to lectures, explanations of political leaflets and such matters. This lasted a few months and then the snow melted and things became clear. They asked me to leave, they insulted me and told me to drive my car across other people's lands. I told them that I couldn't trespass, that the farmers would retaliate. They whispered, 'We know,' but I heard them. They forced me to drive through the fields despite the thorny fence. I was young then and I had just returned to the country illegally. I was afraid they would deport me to the Lebanese border to stay with my uncle, so I did drive over the land. No sooner had

I done so than a hail of stones rained on me from all directions. It was like a stream of stones thrown from left and right, from above and below. I had nowhere to hide. One of those attacking me from the back had been, two days earlier, reading from a book about workers' rights, distribution of wealth, and the poor! He was shouting, 'Go ahead, donkey, move! Drive! Step on the accelerator!' How could I do it with the farmers around me, men, women, and children? He wouldn't stop, pushing me to move, but I stopped in the middle of the road, got out of the car and said, 'I will not press ahead.' You can't imagine what happened as soon as I pronounced those words. I don't know how and from where I was beaten, shot at, and surrounded by cars. I saw with my own eyes what no one else had seen in the world. Have you ever seen something like that?"

"Of course I have," I said.

"What do you say then?" he asked.

"I say we drink."

He stared at me for a few minutes, his eyes bulging from their sockets and beer foam covering his lips. Meanwhile, I was wondering to myself about the situation I had put myself in, as if I needed that. A minute later he wiped his face and shouted energetically, "Come on Yussef, where is the beer? Give us the Russian's beer, we deserve it more. Well brother, they bring the Russians and ask us to leave. They can do whatever they want, I will not leave, my mind has been made up ever since I experienced life in South Lebanon with my uncle.

I started sweet-talking them, rallying them, taking their liras and returning to Nazareth at the end of the day. I was able to buy back my uncle Jamal's house. It doesn't matter much to me whether I own or rent it, but I'm staying here, eating, drinking, bringing up my children and marrying at will. When my wife died, I took another one, and now I have a pack of children. If you asked me what freedom is, I would tell you that it is the one life we have, if we lose it we can't get it back. They wanted the land, they confiscated the land, they wanted the real estate, they confiscated the real estate, but life and the heartbeat cannot be confiscated. I don't worry, I pretend to be blind and deaf and I ignore them. They don't occupy a space in my mind, in other words, I live according to the law, the law of the present and the absentee landlords. It is an especially tailored law, they tailor it and we wear it. They say we are absentee? My mind tells me that they are absentee, according to the law. I pretend not to see them. Do you understand what I'm saying? Is it necessary for me to attack, kill, and cause trouble? No sir, soon my children and yours will overwhelm the voting booths, get the votes and fill the Knesset, according to the law. It is a specially tailored law, do you understand what I'm saying?"

As he finished talking he looked around him and shouted angrily, "Hey Yussef, where is the beer? May he never taste it, just as well. They tell me, go bray, go away and step on the accelerator, step on people, according to the law! All right, I will step on others, but going in reverse, according to the law. Do you understand me?"

I smiled at him and he smiled at me and went on pouring his heart out, "What counts is the heart, true? What counts is the heart."

I didn't reply. I was reflecting on his words, wondering which of the two of us was right.

He drank his glass, tapped me on the shoulder and said with a great deal of familiarity and affection, "Tell me, why shouldn't I be happy? I'm happy despite all of them. I will continue to be happy no matter what they do. I'm not afraid of their taxes and their laws, and the word 'Arafim' does not scare me. I will remain here, drink beer, receive people, tell stories, and see wonderful women; I am still young."

I asked, jokingly, to cheer him up and lighten the atmosphere, "Are you sure you're young, or is it the Viagra?"

He roared and said, "Everything except Viagra! Do you want me to die?"

He got close to me and whispered, laughing sadly, "At this age, what is left in us? Between you and me, let's keep it a secret, you know better! What counts is the heart."

He got very close to my face, stared at me and said, "All that counts is the heart, a young heart, isn't that true?"

I shook my glass against his, smiling and agreeing with him, then I invited him to go out for the evening.

I went out with Abu Yussef to attend the celebration of the pouring of the cement. We ate lunch, we drank together and we opened our hearts to one another, then I took a nap so that I would be able to stay up for the late night party. Staying up late usually tired me. As I was leaving I saw the Russian at the edge of the hallway. He smiled to me and mumbled words I did not understand, but I picked up the word "Shalom." I ignored him and hurried toward the stairs, and he followed me. I walked faster and so did he, so we arrived at the same time at the counter as Abu Yussef was handing over the room keys to the night shift. He smiled to us while continuing his work. The Russian addressed the same words to him that he had to me along with others I did not understand. Was he speaking Russian, Hebrew, or Yiddish? Then I realized that he was saying Arabic words in a distorted manner that made them sound like stretched shapeless dough, like something between the shape of pita bread and a horseshoe. I picked up on the word *khabibi* and I understood Abu Yussef and his shouting when he had opened up his heart to me over the bottle of beer, and said, "He has never tasted it and may he never do so," which had not been intended to reach the ears of that Russian, either because he was an important customer or because of concerns that Abu Yussef had and that I do not. It might also be—and this is the strangest thing—that Abu Yussef did not mean what he said when he opened up his heart. I signaled to him and whispered in his ear from behind the counter, telling him that the Russian had been following me. He tapped me on the shoulder and announced that the Russian was going out with us. I felt as if a bucket of cold water had been poured on my head. I was unhappy while the Russian was whistling joyfully, watching the pedestrians from behind the glass door. I experienced the same feeling that I had had when I was in Jamileh's house when the two men came up the stairs as I watched them, hiding near the antenna, spying on them and fearing them as if they were the owners of the house and we were the neighbors.

I considered going back to my room and forgetting about the party, but I was attending the party for Mariam, and Mariam would be there. If I didn't go, the whole trip would be useless. I decided to go alone, without Abu Yussef, and leave him alone with the Russian. What a terrible choice—should I let a stranger divide us? This can't be. I will go on condition that he stays away from me. I don't want to see his face, I don't want to talk with him and I don't want him to talk with me, I want to forget that he exists on the face of the earth. And that is what happened. We walked together on either side of Abu Yussef and did not exchange a word. Abu Yussef talked and joked, while I listened and didn't say a word, and so did the Russian, as he shook his head and missed no opportunity to smile, wink at me, or wonder about the meaning of a word. I grumbled to Abu Yussef wondering about the Russian, but he shook my hand and whispered, "Vodka, vodka, do not worry, he will be busy drinking vodka. He will have no time for you."

The truth is that he had a lot on his plate, according to Abu Yussef. Elay—that was his name—had worked in the Chekhov theater before he retired: in other words, before the state retired him by ending its support for artists. The state had gone bankrupt, causing conditions to deteriorate in the theater. Writers, artists, and dancers left the country, and Nina, the love of Elay's life, was among them. He had abandoned his wife and children and lived with her during the prosperous period when playwrights were important and respected. He had had power, prestige, a house, and a good salary, while Nina was too young to be supported by the state in any substantial way. She found great satisfaction in Elay's prestige despite their age difference and the little satisfaction he had given her. When she lived with him his literary production had diminished and he had gradually lost his importance; he found some consolation in alcohol. When the state withdrew its support, his prestige was totally lost and his drinking increased. Elay was in a difficult position, not young enough to satisfy Nina and not wealthy enough to fulfill all her requests. The only choice left for her was to immigrate to Israel like many others in her position. Elay followed her, but he had nothing to offer in this new environment but his pen; she, on the other hand, joined a market eager for young blood, for dancers and for striptease in nightclubs. The playwright couldn't write about a society he didn't know and whose language he had not learned. The new state didn't support writers, and expected each citizen to fight for himself and fulfill the demands of the market. But Elay was no longer a hot commodity and he was too old-fashioned to adapt to the mentality of the new society. He moved to a small, affordable hotel, awaiting his repatriation. But Moscow didn't want him back, leaving him in a situation much like yours and mine, and according to the law, he became both present and absent.

Elay's case bore other similarities to mine. He was looking for Nina, and I was searching for Mariam. As a Jew, however, he was in a better position than I, a Muslim. He had a permit and I didn't, and he was not haunted by the ghost of Shin Bet and the laws of the state that trampled human beings as if they were animals. Elay loved vodka, tabbuleh, and dancing dabkeh. He wanted to dance, have fun, and forget Nina.

The party began with food, drinks, and music, followed by the dabkeh dancers, young people flying through in the air to the sound of the reed flute and the clapping of the audience. Then came a band with a drum, an *'oud*, a *qanun*, and a young singer whose mawwal broke the silence of the night. The audience was elated and shook their heads in approval and appreciation, some shedding tears of nostalgia, and drank *arak* in abundance. I drank like a stork, and the Russian did the same, until he collapsed on the floor. He soon regained control of himself and waved his napkin to show everyone that he was enjoying himself and the company of the Arabs. Abu Yussef asked him to sit down and be quiet. They were both funny and pathetic, one apprehensive and annoyed, and the other bent on uncontrollable enjoyment. I was first intrigued by the latter's attitude, then I found it amusing and was envious of his lack of concern for others' opinion of him. Was it because he was a foreigner, not bound by the traditions of this society, or was this the attitude of an artist unconcerned by right and wrong, decency and indecency? Could it also be his status as a passerby in a culture he neither knew or understood nor even had tried to understand? As he was waving his napkin, swaying left and right, pouring arak on the plates of seeds and nuts, he turned to us, placed his hand on his chest and asked for our forgiveness. He went back to his drinking, loud shouting, waving, swaying, and burping, and then he sat down, closed his eyes, and said, passionately and brokenheartedly, "Oh! Nina!"

People moved onto the dance floor, including Abu Yussef, who left me alone with the Russian. We continued to drink like two sponges, to the point of dizziness. We collapsed on the table, he calling Nina's name, and I Mariam's. I then lost consciousness and awoke to a strange movement in my bowels. I felt nauseated and ran to the closest tree to empty my stomach of its contents, feeling a little better. I suddenly became aware of my behavior and drunkenness and decided to walk between the trees to regain some strength and self-control. I sat on a rock and watched the scene from a distance.

Abu Yussef thought that I was upset because he had gone to dance and left me. He also thought that the Russian was bothering me. To salvage the situation, he climbed on the stage, grabbed the mike, and began saluting the guests of the party, repeating, "Long live the young people and their efforts, we salute them." The audience responded, cheered, and shouted encouragements. Abu Yussef greeted the camp leader, the volunteers, and the drum player and invited them all to join in the dance. Everybody responded to the invitation and filled the dance floor, including Abu Yussef himself, who moved like an elephant. He asked me to join in, but I was still too dizzy and nauseated to move. In a last-ditch effort to involve me, he addressed me directly, saying, "We must salute our guest from the West Bank who has brought us the scent of Jerusalem, our brother Ibrahim; come on Ibrahim, come on."

The audience cheered and looked at me while the music played on and the singer went on singing, "Our loved ones have arrived, let the breeze of the homeland blow." Seeing that I didn't move, Abu Yussef took hold of the mike and repeated his invitation to me to join the dancing crowd, unaware that my immobility was due to my general state of fatigue. The public responded and repeated its invitation to me, shouting, "We want Ibrahim, we want Ibrahim!"

Suddenly I saw the Russian stand up and shout, "Me too, khabibi!"

Someone asked him to sit down and keep quiet but he fought back and tried to join me, angering some members of the audience, who wondered who he was. I heard him bang against a chair and pour arak over the plates of seeds and nuts, then apologize in the midst of his passionate lamentation, and call

Nina's name. I felt inexplicable sadness, which dissipated as I stood on the stage surrounded by the enthusiastic cheers of the audience and their loving eyes; all this made my heart melt. I felt as if my soul could fly, as if I were in paradise in the company of the Prophet's family. But was this truly paradise and were those its inhabitants, young and old people, and I among them, having forgotten Mariam, but getting the impression that she was with the crowds sitting on a chair at a table in the middle, telling me what she used to repeat to me in the past, "Go ahead, show me your imagination! You're crazy!" I used to tell her that I saw a goat that looked like an ogress, but that she was more beautiful than the ogress. All the while Abu Yussef was egging me on to say something to the crowd, but as I opened my mouth to greet those present and express my joy at being with them, I heard the Russian shouting, "Oh, Nina!" He was quickly asked to keep quiet and sit down.

I felt that Mariam's specter was excited and I was trembling with emotion, intimidated by the mike and the people around me. Embarrassed, I stammered, said meaningless words, and, with tears flowing down my cheeks, opened my mouth to address the audience, to tell them, people of the house, beloved of the heart, our imagination. As I was preparing to say those words, I heard the Russian shout, "Oh, Nina!" Somebody scolded him and asked him to keep quiet. Mariam's shadow moved before me. My head, the people, and my intestines were bothering me, and I trembled, emotional and intimidated by the mike. I said, with tears flowing down my cheeks, "I can't talk, I'm sorry."

The words stuck in my throat, my voice was hoarse and my eyes filled with tears. Abu Yussef urged me to speak, to address the young people and their captain as the audience fell silent. I looked at the young people sitting in the front row, this bright group of people, fresh as basil and the heart of lettuce, and I said, enthusiastically, "Long live the youth and their captain Ishaq, we are all with you."

I don't know what moved me to speak, their smiles, their tears, or a certain nostalgia for the past. They responded, shouting, as if waking up from a profound emotional experience and a great surprise, "Long live, long live."

Abu Yussef whispered in my ear a sentence he asked me to repeat. My shyness disappeared and I shouted, "Young hearts, go on, move ahead!"

They responded, "Move on!"

The party took on a new life, and the sound of music and ululations reached a higher pitch that could be heard from the tops of the mountains, the tips of the trees, and Nazareth.

A woman entered and Elay shouted, "Oh, Nina!" and then looked at me as I shouted, "Mariam!" and collapsed next to him. But Nina paid no attention to him or me and started dancing. She was accompanied by an inspector from the port of Haifa who was known for smuggling whiskey and chocolate. She looked like Mariam in her twenties, but she could not be Mariam because Mariam was my age, she was in her sixties. Nina was blonde and about thirty years old, as tall as Mariam with the same small waist, the same shape of the face, and the chestnut-green eyes. She wore a transparent chiffon skirt with nothing under it to cover her naked body except threads that didn't hide much. Elay was snoring and I was staring at her, bewildered.

Captain Ishaq walked by and was concerned to see me so pale. I reassured him and told him not to worry. Elay was delirious and repeated, "Nina, Nina, Nina," then mumbled Russian, Hebrew, and Arabic words, laughing hysterically.

Dancing resumed first to the rhythm of *dal'uneh* and *mejaneh* songs, and then it changed, and the language of the DJ followed suit, using a mixture of Arabic, Hebrew, and Russian with some Ethiopian. The drumbeats changed from Arabic to Western and African. Nina/Mariam was twisting before my eyes, dancing with a shawl and sometimes without it, using Spanish and Egyptian castanets. Abu Yussef joined her on the stage, dancing in a sexually suggestive manner, stepping heavily as he tried to perform the dabkeh. He was as heavy as a bear, and his dancing amused the audience and the commissioner from Haifa, who left the stage and clapped for Abu Yussef. I was mesmerized by her and watched totally captivated. Elay continued to drink, looking at Nina and shaking his head.

Abu Yussef collapsed beside me, breathless, and whispered laughing, "That accursed woman never tires of dancing."

Abu Yussef was expecting a reaction from me but I didn't respond. He took hold of my glass, drank from it, wiped his sweat, breathing heavily and laughing at himself. When he saw me still mesmerized by her, he nudged me and asked, enigmatically, "Do you like her?"

Still getting no response from me, he added, warning, "Be careful, stay away from her if you don't want to drown."

I looked at him in an effort to understand his words, but he went on winking in the direction of the Russian, "Do you see the condition he is in? He has melted like a lit candle."

He nudged me for a reaction, but still getting no response, he went on, "What's with you? Are you dizzy, or drunk, or remembering your youth and your adventures?"

I smiled sadly, but didn't say a word. He nudged me again and said, surprised, "This accursed woman looks so much like her, like Mariam before her story, before her pregnancy when her appearance changed."

I turned to him, opened my eyes and asked anxiously, "Mariam? Mariam? Which Mariam?"

He shook one hand and took my glass in the other, took a sip, and waited a moment before swallowing it, as I awaited his answer to my question. I watched his eyes fixed on Nina dancing under the lights of the stage. He looked at me and whispered, haughtily, "Mariam, Mariam Ayyub, don't you know her?"

I didn't reply, but I was breathless and my weak heart was shaking violently, while a cold sweat ran down my back like grains of rice. The Galilee breeze penetrated my skin and changed the sweat into layers of ice. I remembered the day she took me to the big hotel in Ramallah where the upper-class families and the immigrants met. There was the spirit of the West and the breeze of the East and the sunset light was visible through the golden needles and the high pine trees rising above the summer clouds. The shade of the pinyon formed dark clouds that oscillated over the passageway, and cinnamon- and mint-colored heavy cotton cushions were placed over wooden chairs. Pleated straw and Hebron glass shone under the light. There was chilling sweat on the beer bottles, and the songs of Enrico Massias swayed with the shade as the westerly breeze blew through the trees across shoulders of people engrossed in their own world before that September. It was dusk when we entered a magical fenced square containing stone kiosks, a small band, a young singer, and eyes that shone in the dark. We were dancing the tango and swaying slowly with the music while she hummed the words of the song with the singer as the small band played for love. I too began to hum the words of the familiar song to prove to her that I was with her and that I was hers, forever. She wept as she repeated the words of the song, "When the flower withers and dies because hands fight over it, destroy it and make it lose its beauty, killing the charm in the most beautiful eyelids."

I looked at her, examined the scene before me, and drew a comparison. I pulled out what was left of the memory and the compassion of the heart and found only a woman who looked like her, belly dancing under the light, but the dance was not authentic. Where was her likeness to Mariam, her beauty, her eyes? Where was the magical ambience created by the westerly breeze, caressing us and calling us? Where were the stories born of past memories, the love for forgotten priests in the caves buried under the ruins? God have mercy, even if I am innocent in this love, I will not be exempt from the son's blood, and the suffering of the soul immolated in the promised land.

On the way back to the hotel I told Abu Yussef my story and revealed the reason for my sadness. He looked at me and said, surprised, "It was you? What a story, what a piece of history!"

He then remembered something, stood before me, took hold of my shoulder and said eagerly, "Do you remember when Nina was dancing, do you remember seeing a nun on the balcony of the top floor of the hospital? There was a nun standing at the door."

"I don't remember"

"A nun at the door."

"I don't remember."

He insisted, "On the top floor of the hospital, there was a nun in black standing there."

I didn't remember seeing anybody, but he wouldn't give in: "At the hospital, under the floodlight while Nina was dancing," he added.

"She danced while I was drunk," I explained.

"Good man, it was Mariam!"

I tried to remember that moment, at night, at that distance, the location of the building high among the forest of pine trees, the noise of the place, the broken rhyme, the drums beaten for the dancers, Egyptian castanets, and the bad belly dancing of a blonde woman who mesmerized me, a woman who had come from Moscow and riveted me. My eyes were on her; she had revived the dormant feelings connected with that dream. Out of this encrusted drought Mariam had appeared, but my eyes had been busy watching the young body covered with a chiffon skirt move under the light. Mariam appeared through the memories and the bleeding heart. She came and went, and closed the door behind her.

Two days later we traveled to Jerusalem together. I was looking for Mariam, Elay wanted to visit the city, and Abu Yussef was seeking its blessings. We contacted the convent but were told that Mariam had come to visit her mother, then returned to the Muscovite convent, where she entered a retreat. Both decided to join me, Elay to visit the place known as Gethsemane and Abu Yussef to pray at the Dome of the Rock for the first time since June. I, on the other hand, wanted to look for the mother of my son. It was not love that I was seeking, that was over, but simply the memories and the nostalgia of the heart. What mattered was the son, the future and the essence of my life, my sorrows, and the loss of my soul. What would I do without an heir?

How could I go forward along this twisting road without a companion? I was tired of being alone. Should I seek consolation in power, money, or books? Everything that had seemed meaningful to me lost its significance and proved to be phony and useless. It was as if all we believed in and sought had been reduced to a mirage. What an unlucky time. Here was my son dedicating his soul to a new mirage, wasting his time on empty roads and believing in illusions. Wasn't what my generation and the generation that preceded it, and the future generations offered, enough? Land of misfortune!

I felt sorry for Elay. Like me, he could not find a woman who would accept him. He had abandoned his wife, his children, and the Chekhov theater to follow Nina, but Nina left him for the man with money who smuggles whiskey and chocolate. At this age Elay was a prisoner of loneliness, with no family, no acquaintances, and no country to adopt him. For whom would he write and in what language, in this jungle? He had experienced Moscow's glorious times, when writers dreamed of the revolution, the liberation of the people, and the discovery of the moon. Before the moon there had been other achievements, and literature was the most sincere history of humanity, from Tolstoy to Gorky. Then the pole of poles shook, and the bear collapsed. Searching for a refuge for his dreams, he discovered the Negev, Dimona, the massacres of Sabra and Shatila, and the scandal of Hebron. He could not believe that those midgets were the descendents of Karl Marx and Emma Goldman. Could he, such a goodhearted man, take what did not belong to him? The refined intellectual, the distinguished dreamer had fallen low because of an insignificant woman who had nothing to offer but the ability to dance and a naive dream of being a movie star and performing in a casino in Las Vegas where women bare all except feathers, she playing the role of a queen descending from the roof lit with floodlights and small stars spread out like diamond pearls around a silk swing. There would be a lit screen in the background, revealing forests of palm trees, African monkeys, snakes, Arabs with turbans, and offerings for the queen of Sheba. She imagined herself that queen and he Solomon singing as she danced while the camera would be shooting the way it did for Barbra Streisand and Tootsie. She would be like the giants of the golden screen, with tons of makeup, CNN, the cinematic tricks when the lion changes into a frog and the frog into a human being. This is her dream, a dream of glory, the dream of dreams from California to New York. While the Californian dream was not guaranteed, things were easier here because the Arabs were like the monkeys in Africa, and the dances of the blacks and the shouting of the American Indians in a battle where the white man wins over the black and the red, and she was white like wax, like Snow White, and like Streisand.

As we walked back we saw a peasant with a rake thrashing a rocky ground while a modern yellow rake stood shining under the sun, on the hill. It was managed by a settler wearing a hat moving in the vineyards. Elay shook his head and said, saddened, "Do you see this? Who would believe it!"

He asked me about the name of the woman, and I whispered, "Mariam Ayyub."

He smiled and shook his head as if to say we were in the same boat. Abu Yussef shouted in a heavy voice, "Mariam Ayyub was more beautiful, she was a thousand times more beautiful than Nina."

Elay asked whether Mariam was truly more beautiful than Nina. Abu Yussef was quick to confirm it, "Oh ho, there is no comparison, she was a thousand times more beautiful, wasn't she?" he asked me as I was lost in my thoughts.

I mumbled, "True," and looked into the distance to remove myself from this useless conversation. Words didn't help at this point and what would complaining about the injustice of the beloved do for me?

They left me at the entrance of Bab al-Amoud and went to visit the Aqsa Mosque. I was still too tired, broken-hearted, exhausted, and crushed without hope. I was neither with my son nor with his mother and not in the heart of Jerusalem. It was a different Jerusalem, a city in ruin, a dying dream in the present and the future, depressing me all the way to the Strait of Bab al-Mandab and Gibraltar. O you who traveled across the wilderness and then scattered, do you have anything to revive the dead? All around me I see a forest of human shoulders pushing me, throwing me from one to the other, walking and faltering, and spreading over my headache and the throbbing of my blood as I wander in the square like the beggars of Granada.

The bells toll, chasing the birds away and making the ravens croak. The statue of the Virgin opens its arms to those who approach it while I still wander in the square, surrounded by the bougainvillea and the hubbub of the tourists.

I searched for her all over Jerusalem, in the markets, going up the stairs that took me to alleys that shaded me from the heat of the sun. In the heart of Jerusalem, under the stony arches and the bridges, under the domed ceilings, there are plants and birds. As children, we used to walk and throw the marbles and see them roll from the gate of the Greek convent to the Aqsa Mosque. The Imam of the mosque would scold us, saying, "Behave yourself children, you little devils, this is a place of worship not a playground." We used to hide behind the wall and watch the marbles roll and jump like house sparrows, scratching the floor of Omar's square like birds. The Imam used to threaten us with his stick, shouting, "Damn you children, go to your homes. If God sees what you are doing he will punish you," then he would close the gate. Here I was, walking endlessly, fearing God's wrath and the door being shut.

I heard a children's chorale at the edge of the marketplace. I stopped to make way standing as close to the wall as I could. The children wore white, flowing clothes and carried palm branches, rose baskets, and long candles decorated with pink ribbons and whistles.

The children were led by a nervous nun moving her arms like a maestro, opening her mouth without singing. The children's singing filled the place, attracting the attention of the merchants and the Italian tourists, the women selling dill and mint, and the man selling carob drink. He stopped tapping his container and searched for a tourist to take his picture or buy a drink from him. I watched them all until the children, the priests, and the nuns passed by, followed by the merchants and the carob seller.

Suddenly, a woman in black appeared from behind the wall of Bab al-Asbat and caught up with the chorale, walking with some difficulty toward the church of Notre Dame. I was watching her when I heard her call me, "Ibrahim, come quickly, come." I saw Jamileh across the street, I waved to her and she waved back, urging me to hurry, but the traffic light, the hubbub of the pedestrians, and the clamor of the traffic prevented me from crossing the street, I had to wait until the red light changed. When I arrived, the group had already entered the church.

Jamileh asked me sadly, "Why were you late? Catch up with them quickly." As I stood motionless, she indicated the building where the chorale entered and said breathlessly, "She might be Mariam!"

I held her hand and asked if she were certain, "No, I'm not certain, it might be her. The bishop said . . . ."

I didn't wait for the end of the sentence, but rushed to catch up with the chorale, I went up the stairs and entered the hall where the tourists were standing with all their luggage. The clerk told me that that place was the hotel not the church. I entered one alleyway, then another, climbed stairs, then went through more alleys lit with Hebron glass and decorated with pots of fern. When I arrived, the priest was giving his sermon. I walked furtively along the wall, examining people sitting in the various rows, among the nuns and between the children and near the altar, but there was no one, no trace of her.

When I left I saw Jamileh sitting in the last row praying and listening to the sermon. I whispered to her, "It wasn't Mariam."

She looked down and hushed me to avoid spoiling the atmosphere. When I didn't move she whispered, rebuking me to silence me, "You were late!"

She then went back to reading the words of God in the New Testament.

The little window in the gate opened revealing a young nun. I asked, carefully, "Mariam Ayyub?" She was surprised, then turned her back to me and I heard her talk in a language I did not understand. She left her place for another older nun who asked while examining my face, "Mariam Ayyub? That was her name in the past, now she is Mary. Come in."

I sat on the edge of a seat in the garden waiting for Sister Mary. The needles of the pinyon covered the passage and the basins of grass. An old nun was watering the plants and trimming them. She looked at me, smiled, and resumed her work in total silence interrupted only by the sound of the water.

I looked at Jerusalem from this high point. I saw the Aqsa Mosque, the walls and the bell towers, thousands of houses connected to each other at the horizon, all the way to the twilight and the western borders. It was the beginning of a slow dusk that left behind it golden threads and shining metal sheets on the roofs of the houses. Jerusalem was more beautiful seen from here, it projected the scent of the Mount of Olives, the piety of the convent, and the saintliness of the priests. At the tanneries there were tinted pieces of leather ready for tourists and for travel luggage. There were huge quantities of rugs, embroidered clothes, and slippers. Mariam had stopped at that shop, checked a dress and a fiery belt, and asked in her broken Arabic, "How much for the dress?" The salesman had said, staring at her, "Whatever you'd like, you are more beautiful than the belt, pretty woman." When she had tried it on he had slapped his forehead and exclaimed admiringly, "Oh, Virgin Mary!" She had smiled at me, then at him, and looked in the mirror.

O Virgin Mary, where has my time gone? Where is my place in life? Where is history? Where is the mirror? Thirty years? Fifty years have gone by? Who would have thought that time would pass so quickly and leave us behind, deprived of our youth and mirrors? What would this nun see if she looked in a mirror—a time gone by? Years that had passed, a youth lost behind walls. I had lived my life outside the walls; what have I seen? If only Mariam knew that life was the same within the walls or behind the walls when one stands before a mirror.

When I raised my head I saw her watching me, dressed in black and white, a large cross around her neck. Her face had not changed, the same eyes, the same lips, her teeth slightly protruding, the oval face, with some wrinkles in her cheeks and around the eyes. She had the same delicate complexion, her face seemed calmer, the rested face of a life without passion.

Slowly I stood up, my heart beating like a mortar and my tears clouding my vision. I was struck dumb with a captivating passion, perplexity, defiance, and surrender. I didn't know what to say, should I ask for her compassion, should I offer my life to save her, would I tell her about my love, my passion, and my fears, would I tell her that I had looked for her everywhere? She would tell me that I ran away without warning her. If I talk about my loss beyond the walls, she will tell me about her lost youth. If I tell her that I'm looking for a family, an abode and a child, she will reply, a family is for those who keep the promise of love; if I tell her about my youth and hers, she will tell me that her youth is in her soul and the peace of the heart; if I ask about her son, she will tell me that her son is represented by all humanity and Jesus's suffering. I knew all this, I knew. This is what he said in his sermon and in the New Testament.

She offered her hand, smiling emotionlessly, as if I were a relative who had paid her a surprise visit after an absence of an hour or two. I extended both my hands to her, my heart was melting like a lover's and my tears flowed obscuring my vision, clouding my sight. She took my hand, guided me to a seat under the pinyon, and said, smiling kindly, "Oh, Ibrahim! Oh, Ibrahim!"

She sat quietly and invited me to do the same while examining my hair, my eyes, and the liver spots around my jaws, signs of chronic heart disease. She shook her head as if to say, "You have aged!" But I didn't think the same about her because her only signs of aging were some slight touches like those made by a light brush. I was envious of her peace and painless life. Like a fool I had thought I was the guilty party and she was the victim. For years I had endured a feeling of guilt, stuck like a knife in my memory and the essence of my conscience, believing that she had lived the worst of lives. Here she was peaceful, so who was the guilty party?

She shook her head and whispered again, "Oh, Ibrahim!"

I withdrew into myself, trying to hide from her look, while a feeling of inferiority was eating me up. I put my hands around my chest, then in my pockets.

She asked, "Are you back?"

I was overcome with a powerful feeling of anger. It was as if she were wondering why I had returned, as if she were making fun of me. So what if I had returned, isn't it the right of every exile to return to his homeland after an absence? Isn't it normal and natural for an absentee to return from exile and search for his people and his identity? Isn't it logical and natural for a lost person to look for his past love, his memories, and his future? Should I tell her about her photo in my pocket? Should I tell her how I had looked for her and her image all over the world and when I found it in the attic between the piles and the dusty furniture, I had taken it, hidden it in my chest to save it from moths and the effects of the cold?

I took her photo out of my pocket and said, whispering, "I found this in the attic."

She didn't touch it, looked at it smiling, and said quietly, "A photograph?"

I got the impression from the tone of her voice that a photo was a stupid thing, nothing, a photo was only a piece of paper without words and without a history.

I pleaded with her in a broken voice until I got her attention to explain what I endured in my search, "It is an old photograph that was lying under the dust in the attic, look at it."

She stretched her arm and pushed my hand away from her, then whispered reproachfully, "It's an old photo, I have no need for it now."

I felt as if she had stabbed me in the heart. What did she mean by an old photo? Did she mean that love lasted only during our youth and was now over; did she mean that the promise in those times was old and therefore meaningless? What then would remain of her and me, what was the use of my search? I said quickly, trying to hold on to the remnants of that old promise, "I found the birth certificate in Michael's room and a camera. He is my son, isn't he?"

She didn't reply; her smile told a story of regret and disdain. I said, sharply, "The birth certificate is with Jamileh. I know her; she told me the story from the beginning. Where did you go? Why did you sacrifice the child? What is his fault?"

She paid no attention to me and continued to smile and shake her head. I squeezed her hand to communicate my feelings to her. Her hand was warmer than mine, it was delicate and more relaxed than mine. I was overcome with desperation and angered by her calm to the point of wanting to commit a desperate act. Should I beat her? Should I cry? Should I insult her? I stood up and kneeled at her feet, pulling at her habit, pleading with her, "My son Michael, yours and mine, how could you leave him? This face, this body, and your love for the world and your feelings, how could you run away? Was it because I ran away, because I was ungrateful, because the selfish man I was did not act? Is that why you punished the child? What is his fault?"

She didn't look at me, but fixed her eyes on the horizon and the clouds of the south. The red horizon was burning with a blood-colored red. A breeze blowing through the pine trees and faint noises annoyed me, they seemed to defy me, they filled my ears with chaos and a terrible race to take advantage of the last ray of light in the south. I said hurriedly, as if in a race with the light of day,

"The bishop said things I didn't understand; I don't understand your son either. He talks about Reike, the spirit, and the hidden forces of the human being. He talks about frightening and stupid things. The peasants are like goats; your son is crazy—go and see him. He wears a habit like that of a priest and lives a wild, selfless life, like a dervish. I told him he is my heir. Why won't he enjoy his life, why doesn't he accept his inheritance? Do you know all this, or has life in the convent made you forget people, your affection and kindness, and your blood ties?"

She whispered, and said slowly, her hand on my head, caressing it, "You have come back then?"

"What do you mean, Mariam, what do you mean?" I shouted bitterly, because I felt that she didn't care about my feelings and she was unconcerned by my words.

She didn't seem to care about my son and his life spent between Reike and spirits, neglecting to live his life, while I was struggling with the world, with my feelings and with finding an heir. I shouted again to her, "Who will be my heir?"

She took a long look at me for the first time, a distant look as if from behind a curtain. She said words that she didn't utter but ones that I understood. I understood all the hatred she was hiding and I screamed at her, "You hold grudges, is that what Christ preaches? If I made a mistake, call me a sinner, a coward, a traitor, say whatever you want, but the child, what fault is it of his?"

"What is my fault?" she whispered.

"It is true then that you hold grudges and that revenge gives you satisfaction. I deserve what I get, but not the child," I replied.

She whispered calmly, "He isn't a child anymore."

I screamed in agony, "But he is a child because he plays with spirit and Reike—he forgets himself and the human being in him."

"Forgets the human being!" she replied, smiling, kindly.

I didn't know what to say. I stood up and moved further away from her to get hold of myself and give her an answer that would silence her and hurt her, to make her feel what I felt and show concern for her son. I said, "You should know that your son has never known a woman all his life. Your son is sick, he is crazy and suffers from a complex. He does not know where his head and his feet are. Your son has not known love and its wonders."

She smiled and looked away. I felt as if she were making fun of me and my words, as if I were saying stupid, meaningless words, as if I were stupid, superficial, and naive. What does love mean to me, and what does it mean to her? Am I the only one who was in love? I remembered him when he told me, "You search for love as if love were only a woman."

I screamed at her, "Tell me what love is, tell me, tell me."

She didn't reply, but smiled maliciously, a bewitched smile visible through the mask of her face. I shouted at her in despair, "Don't smile, tell me what love is. If love is not a woman, the touch of a hand, the body of a woman sighing from passion, the love of a child, motherhood, and the affection of the family, tell me what love is then."

She didn't reply. I looked at the cell of the convent and felt a grudge against it. I saw it as a prison that put distance between me and her. What kind of prison was it? I saw it as a fortress that dated back to a distant past, a past that tripped and slowed down before it returned to me. It appeared huge, larger than me. I felt like a dwarf beside it. I continued to mumble hopelessly, "What is love, then?"

The question remained hanging in the sky above the convent, at the edge of the place, in the southern section. I took a few steps toward the alley in order to leave. I was still holding her photo in my hand, I waved to her with it, then turned back to tell her that the photo was hers and had a history, that photos with history are valuable, they are a treasure, a memory, a nostalgia, they are what is left, they are the fingerprints of life. She was looking in a different direction and didn't care for me or hear me. I whispered sadly to myself as I was leaving, "An old photo!"

I looked into the distance to forget, I saw the horizon and the shadow of the pine tree turning black as night was approaching. Then the colors followed, bright red, dark blue, then a powerful light, the floodlights around the citadel looking like lined pillows and God's lanterns.

It was a fortress of pure silver light that pulled me toward the *qibla* and the thresholds of the heart. God have mercy on me, if I am guilty enlighten me, punish me, reward me with the return of love.

I left the convent and took a taxi to Bab al-Asbat. I went through the gate, walked down the stairs to the markets but all the shops were closed. When I got near the Church of the Holy Sepulcher I heard a children's chorale and distant organ music, pure and transparent like a breeze and the call of the soul. I sat on the stairs of the church listening to my soul and God's call, asking for reward for my lost love and for the return of love itself.

I walked silently, listening to the sounds of the organ, but the silence was quickly shattered by the noise of a group of soldiers and the engine of a jeep. Someone shouted, "Be careful Tahseen, an army patrol. Turn to the Via Dolorosa, near the Aqsa Mosque—there is an army patrol."

I walked quietly, but the soldiers filled the place.

We spent the night at the hostel run by priests in Casanova because it was cheaper. Abu Yussef said that Elay would pay very little because he was penniless but that he would pay a reasonable amount. I had the choice of either staying with them or going to a five-star hotel nearby where tourists go and eat western food. In the hotel I would eat, drink, and have fun like Italians do because the priests and the residents were Italian. The wine was from Cremona and the food consisted of lasagne and pasta.

Abu Yussef's expectations proved wrong as we discovered that many of the hotel guests that evening were not Italians or foreigners but pure Arabs from the West Bank and Israel. I was told that they usually filled the place on Thursday evening so they could pray at the Aqsa Mosque on Friday. This was a guaranteed pass to paradise on the Day of Judgment.

It was strange to have this combination of events taking place in Jerusalem on Friday, prayer at the Aqsa

Mosque, priests, and Cremona wine. This was Jerusalem for those who knew it or those who did not know it. We were close to God in our moments of awakening, and they were close to God in their drunkenness, but God's forgiveness was as vast as the esplanade of the mosque, vast enough for us and for them. This was the case with the priests in Casanova as well.

Then came a new group of villagers and among them the priest Michael, my son. He brought a large group because the road was blocked with mud checkpoints and military controls, because Friday was a day of prayer and demonstrations, a day of disarray and stone throwing at the security forces and the army. There was in the Casanova hostel that night a mixed crowd of Italians wearing shorts and T-shirts and with guitars, and a type of westernized Arab without headgear and without the traditional qunbaz. In their thinking, being in Jerusalem, a city, meant wearing what one liked and drinking and having fun without control.

They all sat in a vast hall that had served in the past as a library for the convent or a church, and had been transformed into a hostel when things changed in Jerusalem. The dinner consisted of lasagne with tomato sauce and ravioli with wine, followed by apple pie. After the first serving of wine came more wine and then guitar playing and beautiful songs. Abu Yussef, Elay, and Michael drank, then Mahmoud, Sakineh's husband, and the mayor were audacious enough to drink as well. Sakineh did not drink because she is a woman, but she disapprovingly watched Mahmoud drinking and did not dare tell him to be moderate. He was having fun and stealing daring looks at the Italian women, at their naked thighs and their tight T-shirts revealing their braless breasts.

Michael's table and his group were close to ours. Michael, Mahmoud, the mayor, and Sakineh greeted me. She looked taller in a new embroidered dress that her husband had given her to make up for his beatings. She was not used to this kind of society and remained stuck between the wall and Mahmoud's seat. Every now and then she pointed timidly to his glass in a disapproving manner. Her husband, however, under the influence of the Cremona wine was laughing loudly, clapping and looking boldly at the Italian women. Sakineh was very upset at seeing her husband lose his self-control under the influence of wine and the sight of the naked thighs. Under the pretext of a visit to the restroom and the need to check on her son Tawfiq, she left her husband to his noisy pleasure, trying to prove that he was used to being with westerners because he worked in a kibbutz. Wine was like water to him, and the half-naked chests were normal; as for the guitars, they were like 'ouds without a feather, almost a rababa: it was all very normal.

An Italian resident began to dance under the influence of wine. His companions made room for him and the music became louder accompanied by words of encouragement and the shouting of the drunks. Elay said his usual, "Ya khabibi!" and Abu Yussef joined in and drank to the Italians' health. A priest from Rome raised his glass and drank to the health of the Arabs.

Michael smiled politely and took a sip with the tip of his lips. I was saddened by his gesture as I saw him, a stupid young man turning his back on the world and on his feelings. Was this my son, al-Hajjar's son, or the convent's son? Why did the priest from Rome drink, clap, and sing while my son remained stiff?

Elay took a napkin and began waving it, and Abu Yussef was encouraged to do a dance before the inhabitants of the village. They clapped enthusiastically and the mayor shouted words of approval to show the others "what we were capable of." It became a competition between the two groups, each trying to show off his skills. The mayor considered it a patriotic situation where they would reveal their manliness and the character of Arab Jerusalem. He pushed Mahmoud to join Abu Yussef who was alone on the dance floor. He was too drunk to feel inhibited or shy, and his feeling of inferiority abandoned him. He stood in front of me and began shaking his shoulders violently like professional dabkeh dancers. When Abu Yussef saw Mahmoud dancing he panicked, knowing the superiority of a village dweller over a city dweller in dabkeh dancing. The inhabitant of the famous city of Nazareth that tourists considered the center of the world and the place where Christ walked was no match for him.

A competition was under way between the Nazarene and the villager, and the Italians were forgotten. One was shaking his hips and the other was stepping hard, oblivious to the sounds of the guitar and making noises that felt like confrontation and the Jerusalem hubbub after the Friday prayer. But the Friday prayers hadn't started yet and the Italians hadn't joined in the dance in full force. Soon three young women, one in shorts, another in jeans, and a third wearing an Indian skirt, joined the dancers, waving and shaking their bodies with their blond hair swaying, to the amazement of the two Arab dancers. They thought that their battle was with the Italians and they had beaten them but now the situation had turned in favor of the westerners thanks to the women. Abu Yussef and Mahmoud called on their people to save the situation, but there was no response because I had a heart problem and my son suffered from coldness, while the mayor was not a gifted dancer. It was Sakineh's bad luck that she appeared at that specific moment on her way back from the restroom; she was shocked by what she saw. She looked at the dancers, the naked thighs of the Italians, and said words that we could not hear in this chaos and the fever of the dance that proved to be an uneven competition thanks to the western women. They excelled over the Arab women, who were veiled and could only participate with their ululation. Mahmoud called to his wife for one of her famous ululations but Sakineh was in a state of shock and concern. He repeated his request to her, but the shocked woman didn't respond and continued to watch the scene in a state of disbelief. At this moment one of the Italian women made some provocative movements which electrified the atmosphere and drew whistles from the crowd. Abu Yussef reacted by pulling Sakineh onto the dance floor to join in. Mahmoud was shocked to see a strange man invade his kingdom and touch his wife for no reason. No excuse was good enough to bring a respectable woman onto the dance floor, even a competition with the Italians. Mahmoud tapped his partner on the back, but he didn't feel anything in the heat of the action; he tried a second and a third time but to no avail. He then pulled him, slapped him on the back of his neck, causing him finally to turn his back, and the two men faced each other like two roosters, their eyes bulging and sweat running down their faces, while Sakineh shouted, "Oh, wretched me!" Mahmoud reprimanded her for this mild reaction and wondered why she didn't spit in Abu Yussef's face. Insulted, Abu Yussef swore at Mahmoud and raised the exchange of swearing to another level. Mahmoud claimed to be superior to Abu Yussef, and better than his father and grandfather. Abu Yussef answered in more insulting terms, saying, "You're better than me, son of the Khirbeh! You are an illiterate peasant, not worth even a piaster!"

This turn of events widened the scope of the confrontation as the mayor of the Khirbeh stood up, pushed his chair with his foot, pulled his e'gal from his front pocket, shook it above his head and roared like a buffalo, saying, "You'd better watch what you're saying, you stupid, and worthless man. What's wrong with being peasant? A peasant is better than you and those who gave you birth, friend of the Jews!"

Abu Yussef was taken off guard; he began shouting like a crazy man, saying, "I'm a friend of the Jews? I'm a friend of the Jews, you bastards? I am a friend of the Jews, you damned, illiterate, and worthless peasants!"

Elay stood up and waved his napkin saying, "No, khabibi." The mayor pulled his sleeve and forced him to sit down, damned the man who had brought him to this place, and asked Mahmoud to break his head and show him who the peasants were. Mahmoud wasted no time responding and began beating this and that one in the face, bloodying their noses. These were signs of a battle being enjoined, to the surprise of the Italians, who couldn't understand the words but understood the significance of the beating and the bleeding. They also understood some of the words exchanged, since one of them knew Arabic. The Italians were talking among themselves and watching from a distance with interest but without interfering. Suddenly a child's cries were heard, calling, "Baba, baba!" Tawfiq had awakened and, finding himself in a strange room without his parents, was looking for them. Seeing his father's face covered in blood, he called to him and stood in the midst of the fighters, raised his hands, and threw himself at Abu Yussef, hitting him and saying, "No uncle, please, for God's sake." The Italians were concerned for the child and Elay shouted, "Oh! Khabibi!" The mayor asked him to sit down, swearing at the man who had brought him to this place.

I said angrily, "He came with me."

But the mayor paid no attention to me, dismissing my intrusion as a polite but futile effort to calm things down. He continued to mumble insults and repeat angrily, "Peasant? A peasant? What's wrong with the peasant? What's wrong with the Khirbeh?"

Seeing the battle cool down thanks to Tawfiq's interference, yet still angry, the mayor shouted, "Hey, Mahmoud, break his head, damn his father, and teach him who a peasant is."

I pleaded with him again, calming him, saying, "No mayor, it isn't fitting to behave like this, blame it on me, mayor."

But the mayor didn't respond and went on swearing, spitting, and warning Elay who was shouting, "No, khabibi!"

I turned to Michael, pleading with him to intervene and put an end to the fight to spare us from more trouble. He was pale and in shock, looking as if the blood had left his face. I said, imploring him, "Please do something, say something, a good word."

He mumbled in shock and turned his face, saying, "What would words do with stone-drunk people!"

I was angry at him for his indifference and I said, sarcastic and mocking, "Where are the spirits?"

He looked at me and mumbled, "We lost them."

Then he left the place and went away.

That evening I blamed Michael for the turn of events. He didn't reply but kept walking quickly, his habit hitting his heels and the rope tied around his waist moving incessantly. I ran after him, grabbed him around the waist and forced him to slow down. He looked at me, calmed down, and walked more slowly, his face turned forward. We crossed the marketplace and the gate, left the wall and went out to the street and its lights. We stood facing Notre Dame waiting for the traffic light to change. I asked him, "Where to?" but he didn't reply and kept looking forward, his face a taut mask.

When we arrived at the Bab al-Khalil in front of the square that resembled a stage, I remembered my encounter with the bishop after my return from exile and my inquiry about Mariam. That evening when I had asked about her I hadn't expected matters to become what they were now. I had thought Mariam would give me back my innocence, but the past will not return even if this son were to come back to me. What use is the son if he denies his family? What use is blood if it freezes in people's veins, leaving behind pale ghosts? What use are the soul, the church, the Dome of the Rock, and the Holy Sepulcher if they fail to prevent people from doing evil?

Mahmoud and Abu Yussef came here, the former to pray and the latter to seek blessings for the first time since the June war, but both fell into the trap of a musical party and the Cremona wine. This young man who pretends to have power over the soul and the forces of Reike runs away from the first sight of blood at the party, leaving people to their stupidities, refuses to give in and say the truth. Did he consider himself superior to the others, better than them, nobler? If this were the case why did he bring them from the Khirbeh to the Aqsa? Why did he join them in their Khirbeh and live there like a shepherd? Why did he pretend to be able to uncover the unknown, reveal the future, and heal the sick? Is this Reike, is this the work of spirits, or is it an escape from his blood like his mother's retreat to the convent?

I looked at him as the lights of the street and the cars lit his face. His features seemed deeper and the arching of his brows appeared, from my side, sharper. I found myself looking at a stranger's face, a man I didn't know and one who didn't know me, a man who was, regardless of his name, my own son, Ibrahim's son.

I said to him, "Say something, say what you think, say something to justify your silence this evening. You should have intervened."

He mumbled, reticent, "Why didn't you intervene?"

I replied angrily, "Because I'm ill, and I'm old and too weak to intervene between two men who were fighting like billy goats."

He said stiffly, "You just gave the answer; you explained it."

I retreated carefully, "I didn't mean it that way. I said 'billy goats' only to describe the way they were fighting. How could a man like me face their confrontation? Could my weak heart have taken it? You're in your thirties, strong and educated with powers that you and I know. I saw how you jumped from a rock to a tree at the Khirbeh, you saved a child in a bus hanging on the edge of a precipice. Had it not been for your quick reaction and help, the bus would have toppled down and the child would have died. But you risked your own life and soul for his sake. Why, then, didn't you intervene?"

He shook his head and said coldly, "For the sake of the child, the way you intervened."

I turned to him and said, "Well, I understand and know what you are alluding to. We're going back to the beginning of the story. I'm aware of my guilt, I know it by heart and here I am coming back to redeem myself, but tell me how do you want me to do it? Shall I kiss your hands and wipe your feet? Shall I kneel at your feet as I kneeled at hers? I came back empty-handed, humiliated and alone, with nothing left for me except the hope of meeting you, and here we are, what do I see?"

He mumbled, "And what do you see?"

"I see a man like any other man, with nothing going for him except words and this habit. You are no different from the others, you are like them all, a lost man with a complex and bitter soul, a defeated man who hasn't known love. Open your heart, open yourself, get rid of your complex and your habit, and live in this world. You are a handsome man at the height of your youth and any woman would fall in love with you. Your mother understandably left us and ran away to the convent, but you have it all, you are a strong man, an educated man, a gifted man like my uncle, the artist. You are my son, me the writer or the would-be writer. Had I not been lost in exile and in politics I would have been the greatest writer. Did you think that your love for souls, for Reike, and your madness have no connection to your roots? No, not all, you inherited them from me, my uncle, and your grandfather in al-Asitana. You are the descendent of respectable people with beautiful things to offer, but you are ashamed of them and of me. Why are you embarrassed? We are respectable people, poor people who dreamed of love and wished for it like other human beings—and like you, do you deny that? You are one of us, you are from me, you are my son and I want you to return to me, to help me and unburden me. I am getting old and tired of the world and the loss of love. Take anything you want and return love to me, take everything."

He mumbled absent-mindedly, "What would you give me except grudges?"

"Grudges? Grudges? Is that all I would give you? I would rather give you all the love, the feelings, and the wealth of the world. Take all I have, even my life, take all the world and replace it with the hope of an encounter in the world, a new world."

"A new world, where would I find it?" he asked.

"In a child's smile, in a child's world: is there anything more beautiful in the world than a child? A paradise full of children is the joy of the world, the feast of feasts. Is there anything more beautiful in the world than a child playing on his father's lap? A waking child whose eyes look like narcissus, a young child, oh, my son!"

I had remembered Jamileh's description of the baby, she had said that he was plump like a duck with dimples on the back of his hands, which she used to kiss nonstop as he looked at her with eyes like narcissus and almond blossom!

My voice shook and broke, and I had tears in my eyes, but he was not moved and remained still, looking ahead at the western lights. What did he see, what did he dream of, what was he thinking about? Souls, surely!

I regretted my old age; what souls would bring back this stiff man?

I said, trying to get close to him and his world, "You said that souls do not forget us and come back if we need them, isn't that true?"

He didn't respond, and I resumed, "I heard you say so as I lay unconscious. I heard you at the Khirbeh the morning we fought about Sakineh, do you remember?"

He said, indifferent, "That situation!"

"I was lying on the ground, but I heard you say that the souls come to us and death is not the end. The souls come back if we call them with an open heart, isn't that so?"

"Yes, I did say that," he affirmed.

"Why do you deny today what you said?" I asked.

He replied, annoyed, "I don't deny it."

"But I see you are a different man this evening, like a dead person, a body without a soul; you don't feel anything, you don't interact. Tell me, why have you changed?"

He replied angrily beginning to lose his composure, "Because I'm angry."

"You were angry, angry at a bunch of drunks, a bunch of drunk men! What would you have done if you had faced battles and seen blood around you drowning people's corpses? What would you have done if you had seen the massacres, if you had been with us in the middle of the ruins, people running away in all directions like stray dogs in the streets, escaping the bombardments? You are angry because of a bunch of drunks, a bunch of drunk men?"

"I was angry with you," he said.

"With me? Why would you be angry with me, son? What have I done? What have I said? I didn't budge, why then be angry with me?"

"Because you interfered in my business and spied on me," he explained.

"Spied on you?" I asked, surprised.

"You looked for me everywhere. You looked for my mother in the village, in the Khirbeh, among the ruins in Jamileh's house, at my aunt Eugenie's; you searched for my mother's picture in the attic where it had been for years. You looked for my mother in Galilee and now you're looking for her in Jerusalem. What do you want? Do you want my mother? She doesn't want you. You want me back—I won't return. You want me to accept you—I won't do so. I told you when we first met that I have my own path, my own soul, my own life. Leave me alone. Why do you want to take me back to a past I'm trying to forget? My mother has died; she joined the convent. When I see her, I see an older sister. When I see you, I see a defeated stranger who means nothing to me, holding on to a straw, and I am that straw. But I'm a human being, body and soul. I have feelings and depth. Do you believe that one can forget the past in the present, do you think that people's wounds heal and disappear with the passage of time? Do you think that people's worries and their suffering are lessened and diminished when you apologize?"

I shouted in shock, "You're holding a grudge then!"

He replied sharply, "Why wouldn't I hold a grudge? I don't feel any grudge now, but I beseech you to forget my mother and me and leave us each to our world. We have forgotten you. Get away from us, leave us in peace."

I mumbled, frightened, "No, it's not possible, you are my son, my only hope, you are my life. If you go away, who would be left for me?"

"You would have Abu Yussef and Nina's lover, the drunk and the cranes."

What did he mean by the cranes? Wouldn't he stop punishing me?

He insisted again in a strong voice, "I have my own life! Get away from me, let me have some peace."

I said, amazed, "I don't understand."

He said, emotional, "I feel sorry for you, I pity you, and sometimes I have a certain feeling that comes in glimmers, but I try to extinguish it because if I return to the past it will come back to me."

"What if we do go back to the past?" I asked.

He put his hand on his upper chest and smiling sadly, said, "You want me to go back to the past? Me go back to the past?"

He looked far away from me, mumbling, shaking his head and lamenting, repeating to himself, "Me go back to the past and the suffering of my childhood?"

I remembered then Jamileh's words and what she said about his incessant crying: he cried when she carried him, he cried when she gave him milk, he cried when she gave him chamomile to drink, and he continued to cry because he wanted his mother. But his mother ran away to the convent, leaving behind the world and all it contained. Now the son is doing the same and seeks refuge in the convent. This son of mine is neither in the convent nor in the world, however. He is lost like me; where is his abode?

I tried to talk to him using common sense, not emotion, because emotion pushed him miles back, reminding him of a past he couldn't forget, but was trying hard to forget. I said, "Your mother is in the convent and has found peace there, but you are neither in the convent nor in the world. What do you do between two worlds?"

He smiled, saying, "Between two worlds!"

Then he turned to me, smiled for the first time, and said, "Between two worlds, a beautiful expression—where did you come up with it?"

I said enthusiastically, to win him over to my side and get him interested in me, listening to me, "Because I'm a writer. Haven't I told you that I am a writer? But the world of politics, exile, and worldly matters took me away from it. If I hadn't lost myself in politics and wandered the world, I would have been the greatest writer in the world."

He smiled, repeating, "The greatest writer!"

"Why not?" I said, "What qualities does a writer have that I do not? I'm artistic, I have imagination and beautiful expressions. Why can't I be a writer? I'm a writer and you are an artist, we have common traits."

He shook his head saying, "In between."

"I understand your feelings because I am a writer."

He repeated again, "In between."

"That is why I feel what you feel," I explained.

He asked, mocking, "Because you are a writer?" I didn't know what to say. He asked again, "Because you're a writer?"

I replied affectionately, but brokenhearted, "Because I am you and you are me."

He shook his head and said calmly, "You are not me."

"Who are you then?"

He turned to me and asked, "Do you truly want to know?"

"Of course I do."

He went on, "What do you want to know, tell me frankly and simply. What do you want to know?"

I fell silent and was lost in my thoughts. I wanted to ask him why he had a grudge against me, he the man lost in a world of the soul. I wanted to know why he didn't want to forget the sad past if he could. I wanted to say that life is meaningless without love, and that love was not a woman as I used to think. It was rather the love of a mother, a father, a brother, a sister, and all humanity. He knew all this and we agreed on it. I did not understand, however, why he made fun of drunks and didn't intervene to end the fight, embarrassing us in front of the Italians. Were love and matters of the soul available only in the clinic and did he forget his teachings when he went out in the world? If love were not a truth practiced in life, it was reduced to a picture that we handed out to tourists in Notre Dame and Casanova. Was this love? If it wasn't, why did he ignore Sakineh that evening? Why didn't he intervene to put an end to the fight in Casanova? Why didn't he feel sorry for my weakness and show mercy despite my regret? Why did he risk his life for the sake of a child and stop there? I didn't understand this confusion!

I spoke quietly, as the sound of cars had died down in the middle of the night, and the Jerusalem breeze carried the September dew and a cold that penetrated my bones and those of Jerusalem. It was almost the end of September, the last days of a hot summer and the pain of searching. I said to him, "I don't understand and neither do I want to understand, because understanding blocks love."

He asked stiffly, "Is that your final decision?"

I said, determined, "I don't promise. I won't leave you, you are my son, you are love."

We returned to the hostel without exchanging a single word.

They refused reconciliation over breakfast and then, like children, they made peace, much to the astonishment of the Italians, who watched the hugging, the greetings, and the laughter in amazement. We were not surprised. Abu Yussef had said grudgingly, "Who is this illiterate man who says that I am on the side of the Israelis?" His opponent asked who was this lowly man who said I was "a peasant not worth a penny." Then, in the blink of an eye they made peace. Meanwhile, breakfast got cold, but people ate it, and the tourists went off in various directions—to the Church of the Nativity, to the Mount of Olives—and missed the reconciliation party. They left in groups, carrying their cameras, their dollars, and accompanied by the young beautiful women. I said joking to Mahmoud to remind him of the Cremona wine he had drunk last evening, "Go quickly, catch up with them, there are sweet girls in their group."

But he replied sternly, "I'm not free today, I'm sober and I plan to pray in the mosque."

They all left to perform ablutions and pray the Friday noon prayer at the Aqsa Mosque. Jerusalem looked like a wedding day, crowds of people coming to pray, carrying candles and incense burners, with birds under a blue sky. The sun was shining brightly on this September day despite the proverb that says September is wet.

That September proved to be burning hot because it began with the throwing of stones, then shoes flying like ravens, it was a bad omen. Then the bullets began to fall like raindrops and grains of rice. The tourists scattered like chickens, the priests hid in convents and I looked for my son in the crowd like someone searching for a needle in a haystack. People seemed crazy, running in all directions, fighting and shouting and calling for help. I ran into the midst of the tourists, the journalists and their cameras, looking for my son, for Abu Yussef and his group. Then I saw the mayor alone, without Mahmoud and Sakineh. I asked him about the others, but he didn't hear me and kept running, then he tripped and fell on the ground. But Sakineh pulled him from the shoulder and looked around her shouting warnings to her son Tawfiq. But Tawfiq had quickly disappeared among the people, the confrontations, the tear gas bombs, the Molotov cocktails, and police that hit people with bats while seated on their horses. She kept asking people around her about Abu Tawfiq and her son Tawfiq.

I saw Jamileh at the window calling me in a strangled voice, asking me to go up to her house. I took Sakineh by the hand and started in the direction of Jamileh's house. She ran with me for a few steps, then stopped and shouted angrily, "What about my son Tawfiq?"

She looked around her and called his name while Jamileh told us which way to take to avoid the police. But Sakineh didn't follow. She slapped my hand, staring like a crazy woman, and said, "What about my son Tawfiq and my son's father? I won't go."

She resumed her search for Tawfiq while threatening him verbally with hell's fire for disappearing.

I joined Jamileh in her house and viewed the scene from above. There were huge moving crowds, tear gas bombs, people shouting, and masked young men throwing stones. Tawfiq was at the edge of the wall among the stone throwers and the bullets of the army. I called him but he didn't hear me; he was giving small stones to a young man who put them in his slingshot and aimed them at a horse's head. He hit the horse, making it jump suddenly and spin around crazily, throwing the policeman riding it to the ground. The horse lost its muzzle and went on stepping on people, kicking and neighing, enraged. The same young man aimed his stone at a group of soldiers and hit one making him bleed. The officer identified him, and another shot him in cold blood. The young man fell and Tawfiq threw himself on top of him crying, but a masked young man pulled Tawfiq away and told him something I could not hear. He tapped him on the head, removed the kufiyyeh of the dead young man and tied it around Tawfiq's head. Sakineh saw Tawfiq wearing the kufiyyeh like the grown-ups and began beating her cheeks and lamenting her fate. I pointed her out to Jamileh, saying that she was losing her mind. Jamileh pulled me away and said, "Let's go down."

I turned to her swiftly, pointed out the street, the square, and the crowds running away, the horns of the ambulances, the military on their horses, and the police, then said frightened, "Go down there?"

She replied firmly, without hesitation, "Let's go down."

She was holding a bag containing medications, and rushed down the stairs. I carried the bag for her and reflected on my cowardice, similar to that of Mariam and her son. I didn't see him among the others; he had disappeared like the priests in one of the convents or inside a church. But it was early in the day, and from where I stood I could not see Abu Yussef, the mayor, or Sakineh's husband—how could I find Michael from this distance? My son Michael was not a coward; he had pulled up his habit and tied his belt to save a child. He had risked his life to save him, and I had no doubt that he would see Sakineh and her son and do something we would all admire. I couldn't understand my son, however, when he showed courage and when he got angry, when he didn't run away. My son was moody, complicated, and frustrated. I didn't know what to say about him—was he my son or the convent's son?

We joined the crowds and were lost among them but Jamileh knew her way. She turned to me and said, "From here it's closer."

I shouted to her, asking where we were going. She shouted back, beginning to lose her temper, "Move, people are dying!"

We crossed a stone alley and I was breathless. After a few steps we found ourselves under the Aqsa Mosque, the columns of the wall, while the stones and heavy smoke, the slings, people's cries, cameras, journalists, machine guns, and the smoke of the tear gas reached us from above and below the wall. Jamileh pushed me to the side and ordered me to open the bag. She pulled out gauze and alcohol, then gave me a piece and said, "Breathe it."

I asked what it was, but she placed a similar one on her mouth and didn't reply. Then we both started running in the midst of a human flood, pushing and running away while Sakineh was shouting threats at her son Tawfiq.

Mahmoud appeared in the crowd and pulled Sakineh asking, "Why did you let him go?"

She explained, scared, "I didn't let him go, by God Almighty I did not, he ran away."

He raised his hand and made a fist to hit her, mumbling, "By God, woman . . . ," but didn't finish his sentence.

He went back to climb the wall where his son was standing. Immediately, the memory of the Khirbeh and Michael rushing to save the child came back to me. But Michael hadn't yet appeared. I didn't see him here or among the journalists and the cars, near the stretcher and the rescuers. I didn't see him between the wounded or the attackers, the nurses and the running crowds. Where had he gone? All the members of our group were around me even the Italians, except my son. I even heard Elay call Abu Yussef in a hoarse voice. But Abu Yussef didn't show up and neither did the mayor or Mahmoud. Sakineh was pointing at the spot where Tawfiq and the young men were standing.

She was shouting, "The boy is lost, wretched Sakineh." She then turned to me seeking help, she shook my shoulder and, wailing, said, "Please do something."

I felt helpless. What could I do in this atmosphere? I couldn't handle it; I was not up to the task.

Jamileh pulled me from my sleeve and said, "Open."

I opened the bag, trembling at the sight of the wounded, the blood, and the smell of iodine, bandages, and alcohol. She went on and I walked behind her; at every step she would say, "Open," and I would open the bag without thinking. I gradually got used to the situation and fear left me; blood didn't shock me anymore. I would stare at deep wounds and find them normal. Even the guns became a familiar sight and so were the cries of the people. The dead, the wounded, the victims of stoning, and the soldiers' bullets became a normal sight. What was happening to me, why was I numb? Why had I become devoid of feelings, hearing the firing without being startled? Why didn't I smell the iodine anymore, the tear gas, or the dust of the earth? Why had I become used to the sight of the wounded and the shadow of death? The shadow of death didn't appear black anymore; it had become one of us, moved among us, we had become fearless. How have you, wretched country, gotten used to all this?

I remembered September, that September, it was a different September, spent among brothers and family. Then came Beirut and the war of brothers and the country of relatives, and later the Gulf War, the war among brothers and the country of relatives. Whose side was I on? I had lost faith in them all and returned to my father and his saw.

A wave of people rushed before the mounted police. Jamileh pulled me from my sleeve and drew me against the wall. Elay continued to call Abu Yussef, but the policeman hit him on the head with his bat, throwing him to the ground, under the feet of the horses. People were shouting and bats fell on heads while horses stepped on those who fell. I cried sadly, "Elay, Elay!" and rushed to pull him up but Jamileh held me back and shouted angrily, "Are you crazy?" I pointed to Elay but she didn't understand, she scolded me and ordered me to stay put. I stood saddened by the sight of the poor man lying on the ground, trampled underfoot while Abu Yussef, breathless asked me if I had seen Elay. I pointed to the ground, and he shouted angrily at me, "He fell before your eyes and you did nothing to help him?"

Sakineh slapped her face and said, "I swear by God Almighty I did not allow him to go, he ran away."

A few minutes later the situation cleared up on my side and I saw Elay swimming in his own blood. Abu Yussef sat beside him and shook him, saying, "Elay, Elay, stand up, let's go home." But Elay was like dough, a body without a soul or features. The sight of him scared Abu Yussef when he saw the remains of a human being. He was wailing, calling Elay and reprimanding him for having gone too far. I took hold of him and told him that Elay was dead. He turned to me and said sharply, "You're from Jerusalem and you don't understand the situation. What will I say when they ask me about Elay? Shall I say he was trampled underfoot? How can I go back to Nazareth without a companion? Tell me what to do, what to say?"

I said, "Tell them the deceased passed in Jerusalem."

He objected to my sentence and said, "No, he is not deceased. Come on Elay, let's go, Elay, Elay!"

I was pulling him away and he was pulling the dead man and Jamileh was pulling me and ordering me to open the box, saying, "People are dying."

I turned to her and pointed at Elay, but she took the bag from me and said firmly, "The living have priority over the dead."

The iodine was poured over the bandages, blood was spilled, and the tear gas bombs were heard, while Sakineh was calling her son, "Hey Tawfiq, come down, come down, damn you."

I was looking around me, searching for my son among the people, but I saw Mahmoud on the edge of the wall running and calling his son. The bullets of the army and the stones were flying in all directions, surrounded by the sound of the ambulances, the cars, and the planes flying in the sky. I raised my head and saw a group of planes approaching, planes that had once fought in the Vietnam War. We had become another Vietnam!

A plane flew over the wall in a circular movement, hovering like a bird, as if it were a kite. I felt as if I were in a movie theater watching an American film filled with action and suspense. But I wondered why the journalist was taking pictures and another was making a recording, while a third one was asking for rolls of film. I was running after Sakineh fearlessly, as if the scene wasn't real, as if it were a film or a TV program. We had become a show!

Mahmoud looked above his head and was frightened by the sound. He took a few steps back and lost his balance, then fell like a feather, a big black feather floating in the midst of tear gas. His hatta flew like a sail in the wind and he fell on the ground. Sakineh shouted and ran to him like a crazy woman, kneeled beside him and said, "Mahmoud, father of my children, go on, move."

But he pronounced her name and stayed motionless. Jamileh asked for the bag, the iodine, and the alcohol, and administered them to him. He sneezed, coughed, and we relaxed, but it was a short-term relief, like those of all the Fridays, a false relief, a mirage. We believe that the rain will stop, but it does not; we expect the drought to have mercy on us, but it does not; we expect the seasons of the year to show their true face, but they do not; and the seasons change like a stage set while the scene remains the same, revealing the game of death. We wait for rain, but it does not fall; we pray for the end of a drought that burns us, we pray to God but he damns us and we close the door. But the door is like hell, like a long-necked bottle.

O God, I am not denying your existence, but I have lost faith because I am weak and I depend on you. Why play with the lives of people, with their tears and their blood? Why do you take from us and not give back? Why Sakineh, of all people? Sakineh began to wail as Mahmoud breathed his last breath. When he was carried on a stretcher and she saw his deep wound she forgot Tawfiq and began to beat her cheeks, saying to him, "Hey Mahmoud, father of my children, how can you leave me like this? Get up, man, and do not make me a widow, get up!" She looked around, searching for the mayor who was close to her. She stretched her arm and pointed at him, but he said kindly, "Get up woman, that was his fate."

She started shouting, pulling her hair, and removed her veil. She threw it away, wailing and repeating, "Mahmoud, father of my children, stand up, son of a bitch. Do not make me a widow."

The mayor scolded her saying, "Shame on you woman, have faith in God. He is a martyr for Palestine, have faith in God."

She looked at him crazed, "For Palestine's sake? Would Palestine have pity on me? Who will feed me? Who will protect me and protect my honor? Hey Mahmoud, you are the crown of my head."

I whispered to myself, "Your crown? What about the leather belt?" But Sakineh was only a woman weeping for a man and a loaf of bread.

I moved close to her to console her and told her that the world would not forget her, that people of goodwill would not forget her, neither would the mayor, Abu Yussef, Jamileh, or I. She shouted stridently, "People of goodwill? What a black calamity has fallen on you, Sakineh, people of goodwill? What a misery has afflicted you, Sakineh, people of goodwill? I wish I had died and I had not prayed."

The mayor scolded her, "Shame on you woman, you say that in the Aqsa Mosque! Behave yourself."

She cried and lamented saying, "Let me shout and get it off my chest, let me shout."

The mayor raised his voice, talking to her in a commanding tone, "Enough woman! This is a sin. Mahmoud is a martyr for the Aqsa; another person would have uttered ululations of joy."

Jamileh pushed him with her bag and told him to get out of the way. She sat beside Sakineh on the ground and said sadly, "Yes, my daughter, cry and shout, say whatever you have on your heart and don't be scared like all the others." Then she hugged her until Mahmoud was taken away.

I looked for my son among the human remains, in the ruins, and behind the wall, but I saw only headgear, human remains, and dark blood coagulating under the sun. I looked up at the sky as the sunset stretched its wings and the silence of the tombs covered the square and the market. All the shops were closed, and the cars moved slowly, in silence—or so it seemed to me after the noise and the chaos that had come before.

The square was empty of people except for me and Jamileh. Abu Yussef had left for Galilee without Elay, the mayor had taken Sakineh and Tawfiq to the Khirbeh, and Jamileh and I had stayed in the square. We sat on the edge of the old stairs looking at the square and seeing nothing but ghosts and the events of the day.

She said, "Let's go back."

"Where to?" I asked.

"To my house, to eat something."

"How can I eat while Sakineh is hungry?" I asked.

"Come wash your hands and your face."

"Will my hands become clean if I wash them?"

She said hopefully, "Be optimistic and don't lose hope."

How could I be optimistic, and why would I be? The Friday prayer had turned into a bloodbath, Mahmoud had died, and Elay had disappeared like a bullet in a wedding party. Sakineh wailed and had no tears left to cry, and, on top of all that, my son was lost and I am lost. I have to start the search all over again, although I thought I had found him. He is nowhere to be found. Is it conceivable that I could go on living without seeing him or getting his news? Could he be in

Jerusalem? Maybe he hadn't run away like the others? I hadn't seen him here; he wasn't among the victims, the journalists, or the rescuers.

When Elay had died and they had taken Mahmoud away on a stretcher I hadn't seen him among the young porters. He hadn't carried a wounded person on his shoulders, he hadn't jumped to a tree or a rock to rescue a child—where then had he gone? Was he wounded? Was he arrested? Is he a martyr? After having searched so long for him, would he be killed? I couldn't believe that if he were alive he wouldn't show up; why would he hide? Where was he hiding, in a convent or a church? What good would a church be for his doubting mind, a mind that knows nothing other than Reike and the power of spirits and the religion of spirits? Nonsense! To be concerned with Reike and treating the villagers while he, a young artist in his thirties, had not experienced love. Was this the reason for his disgruntled attitude and his rebellion? Was this why he held grudges and asked for accounts like the others? Was this why he said he was angry, why he got angry at me? Why would he be angry with the others when he was angry at me? What had they done to him? Was it Sakineh's fault? Elay and Abu Yussef's fault? The children's fault? Love's fault?

If love is nothing but cheap goods, why, then, the Friday prayer and the bells of Jerusalem? Why the thousands of mosques and bell towers, and masses that begin and others that end while I sit on the stairs of the Church of the Holy Sepulcher at dusk, listening to the children's chorale and saying to myself that God will not forget me, that I will meet her and him, and when I do I will not ask what he does or does not do, what he knows and I do not, and what I do not want to know, because knowledge blocks love?

I told him that night, in all sincerity, that I wouldn't leave him because he was my son, he was love. Now I wonder, what is the use of the son? Is that love? What use is the son if he denies the family ties? What use is blood if it coagulates and leaves behind pale ghosts? Has he run away from us and returned to her? Has he taken refuge in the convent as she did, while I search everywhere for them both and dream of a meeting that would bring us together? Will it be here, will it be there, or did I bury him the way Elay and Mahmoud will be buried in the ground and Sakineh's youth will be buried in the Khirbeh awaiting charity from the people of goodwill?

If I have lost faith, if I am doubtful, if I digress, it is because the search has exhausted me. My hair has turned gray and my heart has melted away. My writer's imagination has called me and told me that heaven was awakening in the middle of fall, that the leaves of mint and narcissus were turning green and blue rays twinkled in a winter cloud.

I wonder if they have arrested him, or if his retreating mother has pulled him up to her? If she has done that and he has forgotten the world, why then did he go to the people in their Khirbeh and bring them to Jerusalem? Why did he then deny me, his father? And did he deny them, his people, despite what they had endured—not a crime, but hell and the suffering of the tomb? Is this the son? What use is the son, my own son, your son, Mariam, and the cross of love?

I looked up toward the top of the Mount of Olives and saw the night advancing from there, from the east, while the lights of the municipality and the floodlights around the Aqsa Mosque lit my way. I turned to Jamileh to console her, but I saw a worried face that reflected the lights of Jerusalem. I said quietly, "Let's go."

She turned to me and asked what I had said. I repeated my words, slowly, "Let's go get a bite to eat."

We walked together toward the alley.

Translator's Note

I t is needless to talk about the usual challenges that a translator faces in any work, moving between two languages. Each text presents its own difficulties and every translator handles them in his or her own way. The translation process is often an exercise in confrontation, with abstract ideas, hidden meanings, and idiomatic expressions searching for their counterpart in the target language. In the case of *The Image, the Icon, and the Covenant*, it was a seemingly innocent word, sura, that sent meaning spinning in various directions. It played a game of hide and seek as it moved from Arabic into English, changing its meaning as a chameleon changes its color.

While the significance of the word *sura* in Arabic depends greatly on context and lends itself easily to both concrete and abstract meanings, the situation is quite different in English. Translated, the word has three distinct meanings—photograph, picture, and image—and all three meanings are at work in the text. It was thus a rare struggle for me, a particularly taxing exercise in alertness as I considered this three-winged word.

Furthermore, a translation project is not always a detached exercise in transmission of meaning and selection of words. Some topics carry an emotional

dimension that vibrates through the heart and soul, forbidding intellectual detachment. The events of the novel lead the reader to the city of Jerusalem, its old cobbled streets, its traditional foods, and its diverse visitors, some seeking spiritual comfort and others struggling to survive in a polarizing conflict. It takes a huge effort on the part of a Jerusalemite to remain indifferent to the city and the torments of its inhabitants. Mourid Barghouti translates the special attachment of the Jerusalemites to their city—so different from that of a tourist, a casual visitor or a political analyst—when he writes, "This is the city of our senses, our bodies and our childhood. The Jerusalem that we walk in without much noticing its 'sacredness,' because we are in it, because it is in us."*
Extracting myself from memories and emotions to chase the *Image* was a constant exercise in stoic determination to bring the work to fruition with the utmost fidelity, which is every translator's goal.

*Mourid Barghouti, *I Saw Ramallah*, trans. Ahdaf Soueif (Cairo: The American University in Cairo Press, 2003).

Glossary

al-Asitanah: old name for Istanbul.

arak: a strong alcoholic drink made of distilled grape juice flavored with anis.

dabkeh: Arab folk dance.

Dal'uneh: popular Palestinian song.

'egal ('iqal in standard Arabic): part of the headgear used to hold the hatta or kufiyyeh (or ghutra) in place.

fida'i: freedom or guerilla fighter.

ghutra: also known as kufiyyeh, it is a term used in some countries of the Arabian Gulf to refer to a long scarf worn under the 'egal.

hatta: name used for the headcloth worn under the 'egal in Arab countries.

khabibi: distorted pronunciation of the Arabic term *habibi*, "my beloved."

knafeh: dough shaped like shredded wheat, stuffed with walnuts or sweet cheese and baked in syrup and melted butter.

kufiyyeh: long scarf worn under the 'egal as a headdress or around the neck.

kumbaz: long robe open in the front that is worn by men in Arab countries.

mahaleb: type of goat's milk cheese.

Mahfuzeh: female proper name.

mashrabiya: latticed wooden window screen that allows one to see outside without being seen; it also filters out sunlight to keep the inside of a house cool.

mawawil (pl. of mawwal): sung colloquial Arabic poems.

Mejaneh: popular Arabic folk song.

oud: fretless lute.

qanun: a zither-like musical instrument.

rababa: Arab stringed musical instrument, with one to three strings.

serwal: traditional pants worn by men, wide around the hips and ending with a narrow bracelet near the ankle.

tabbuleh: salad consisting of bulgur, parsley, tomatoes, and onions.

ustadh: literally 'professor,' but is often used as a title denoting respect.

wali: a holy man.

ya: informal vocative, equivalent to 'hey' in English; it is also an exclamatory particle.